The
Timepiece

Books by Beverly Lewis

The Tinderbox • *The Timepiece*

The First Love • *The Road Home*
The Proving • *The Ebb Tide*
The Wish • *The Atonement*
The Photograph
The Love Letters • *The River*

HOME TO HICKORY HOLLOW
The Fiddler
The Bridesmaid • *The Guardian*
The Secret Keeper
The Last Bride

THE ROSE TRILOGY
The Thorn
The Judgment • *The Mercy*

ABRAM'S DAUGHTERS
The Covenant
The Betrayal • *The Sacrifice*
The Prodigal • *The Revelation*

THE HERITAGE OF
LANCASTER COUNTY
The Shunning • *The Confession*
The Reckoning

ANNIE'S PEOPLE
The Preacher's Daughter
The Englisher • *The Brethren*

THE COURTSHIP OF
NELLIE FISHER
The Parting
The Forbidden
The Longing

SEASONS OF GRACE
The Secret • *The Missing*
The Telling

The Postcard • *The Crossroad*

The Redemption of Sarah Cain
Sanctuary (with David Lewis)
Child of Mine (with David Lewis)
The Sunroom • *October Song*

Amish Prayers
*The Beverly Lewis Amish
Heritage Cookbook*

www.beverlylewis.com

The Timepiece

BEVERLY LEWIS

BETHANYHOUSE
a division of Baker Publishing Group
Minneapolis, Minnesota

© 2019 by Beverly M. Lewis, Inc.

Published by Bethany House Publishers
11400 Hampshire Avenue South
Bloomington, Minnesota 55438
www.bethanyhouse.com

Bethany House Publishers is a division of
Baker Publishing Group, Grand Rapids, Michigan

Printed in the United States of America

ISBN 978-0-7642-3307-4 (trade paper)
ISBN 978-0-7642-3325-8 (cloth)

Library of Congress Control Number: 2019942020

Scripture quotations are from the King James Version of the Bible.

This story is a work of fiction. Names, characters, incidents, and dialogues are products of the author's imagination and are not to be construed as real. Any resemblance to any person, living or dead, is purely coincidental.

Cover design by Dan Thornberg, Design Source Creative Services
Art direction by Paul Higdon

19 20 21 22 23 24 25   7 6 5 4 3 2 1

To
Jeanette Buckner,
encouraging reader-friend and prayer partner.

And
in fond memory of
Louis Hagel,
"Uncle Louie,"
watchmaker and longtime family friend.

Time ripens the substance of a life as the seasons mellow and perfect its fruits. The best apples fall latest and keep longest.

—Amos Bronson Alcott, *Table Talk*

Prologue

It was the last day of July, a sweltering Friday evening, and I took my sweet time heading back from the meadow where I had been walking, trying to make sense of the day. A day like no other.

Out of nowhere, a young blue-eyed woman had shown up in her sleek red car at our farmhouse, declaring to be *Dat's* daughter. The shock of it still had my head spinning, but my heart was with dearest *Mamma*, wondering how she was holding up back at the house with my father and the *Englischer* named Adeline Pelham.

The neighbors' watchdog to the west of us had been barking so long and so loudly, the poor thing sounded nearly hoarse. What with that and a multitude of crickets chirruping in the background and birds calling high in the trees, I could scarcely make out what my younger brothers were saying as I approached the stable door. Inside, the four of them were freshening bedding straw for the mules and horses. Stepping closer, I leaned into the doorway and heard the voice of my youngest brother, eight-year-old Tommy.

"We've got us another sister, then?" he asked.

Thirteen-year-old Adam shook his head. "*Puh!* That fancy woman ain't *my* sister!"

Calvin, eleven, shot back, "But she has a birth certificate and pictures to prove it."

"You don't have to remind us—I heard what Dat said," Adam replied, sounding peeved.

"Boys." I stepped inside, making myself clearly visible, the strong, sweet smell of fresh hay hitting my nose. "*Was is letz do?*"

"I'll tell ya what's wrong." Fifteen-year-old Ernie, next oldest after me, leaned on his hay fork. "This whole sister thing's a little farfetched, ain't it?"

Tommy was nodding, wide-eyed, his broadfall trousers grubby with dust from the straw bedding. "And Mamma seemed real *ferhoodled*, to tell the truth," he said.

"Well, if ya stop and think 'bout it," I told them, "Adeline herself looked *ferhoodled*. I doubt such a fancy woman expected to discover she has an Amish father." I paused and looked at my younger brothers, wishing to ease their confused astonishment, my heart full of love for them.

Ernie adjusted his straw hat. "Then I guess we're all *ferhoodled*."

My bare feet grimy from the unswept cement floor, I glanced out the stable window, toward the house. "Are Dat and Mamma still in the kitchen with her?" I asked.

"*Nee*," Adam said as he scattered the new straw around the stall. "They're over at Dat's clock shop, prob'ly showing her round. A customer brought in a specialty clock to be repaired. It's really somethin'—it has a miniature clock shop inside the working clock. There's even a tiny clockmaker, holding a pocket watch."

Calvin nodded. "You should go an' see it, Sylvie."

So many emotions were washing over me that I shivered. The last thing I wanted to do was look at clocks right now.

"Did ya come out to help, Sylvie?" Tommy asked, his eyes hopeful.

"I really oughta finish up some mending," I said, though I knew it was a poor excuse.

"What're ya doin' here, then?" Adam asked, his black suspenders dusty. "Eavesdroppin'?"

"S'pose so," I admitted, still worried about them. "Actually, I was wondering how you boys felt 'bout Adeline spending the night. Yous were all so quiet during supper with her . . . wasn't like ya."

"Honestly, I wouldn't have been as welcoming as Mamma." Calvin fluffed up the straw in the stall of our older driving horse, Lily.

"Mamma is awful nice," Ernie said, carrying water, then dumping it into the watering trough. "She didn't have to invite her."

"*Nee*, but Mamma's always kind," I replied. *By her very nature . . .*

"Adeline's stayin' just one night," Ernie said with a glance at Adam, who still wore a deep frown.

"I sure hope so!" Adam wiped his sweaty brow with his forearm.

"Me too," Calvin replied, saying out loud just what I was thinking.

I looked toward the clock showroom, where I sometimes enjoyed helping my clockmaker father with his many customers—Amish and English alike. Mamma was standing in the doorway now, and by her stance, it looked as if she was about to turn and leave Dat and Adeline alone to talk.

"How do ya think poor Mamma feels?" young Tommy asked quietly.

I shook my head. "*Ach*, can't imagine."

Then, walking out of the stable, I made a beeline for the house, running through the backyard, the grass still warm on my bare feet from the heat of the day. I half hoped I wouldn't have to talk further to Adeline this evening. Her sudden arrival was overwhelming when I was still coming to grips with my father's first marriage—until recently, something he'd kept secret for all the years since he'd come to Hickory Hollow as a seeker and met Mamma.

Oddly, it seemed Adeline's mother had kept a secret of her own.

One

*A*deline Pelham was impressed by the row after row of beautiful clocks in Earnest Miller's showroom—a sight to behold. Clocks old and new and of all styles and woods were each set to chime a few seconds apart, according to Earnest. Despite his strange haircut and simple way of dress, the man was well-spoken. It was a mystery to her why he had ever decided to become Amish. She was also surprised at how talkative he was now—much more so than upon their first meeting that afternoon, when she had parked at the end of the driveway, near the family's roadside vegetable stand.

At present, Earnest was describing his woodworking equipment, a wide range of tools that included saws and lathes run by air compressors powered by a diesel engine.

No need for electricity? she thought, marveling at the variety of tools—from large to miniature—some of which she had never known existed. "Did you always want to do this?" she asked in the stillness of the narrow woodworking shop.

"Make clocks?" Earnest tugged on his wavy brown beard

and motioned for her to have a seat on the comfortable swivel chair near his workbench, which held a long, neat stack of tiger maple planks. Quickly, he pulled up another chair for himself. "I've always been curious about what made clocks tick." He chuckled a little at his pun. "But no, making clocks wasn't my plan. It was something I was fortunate enough to stumble onto . . . after I came here."

She flinched. The significance of his words wasn't lost on her. *After things ended with Mom, he means.*

"It's been a *wunnerbaar-gut* profession," he added.

She noticed again the way he spoke sometimes, slipping foreign words in here and there—half English, half something else she somewhat recognized. *Possibly a German dialect,* she thought, having taken two years of German in high school.

Earnest's gaze was steady and penetrating as he inhaled sharply. "I guess even the birth certificate you brought hasn't fully convinced you that we're related," he said.

Adeline gave a little shrug and looked away. "It's just that Mom never even hinted you were Amish."

"Well, she couldn't have known." He paused a moment. "Actually, no one knew where I disappeared to." He went on to explain his desire to turn over a new leaf once the divorce was final, and that the opportunity to acquire the previous clockmaker's business had fallen into his lap around that time. "I was already staying in the home of some Old Order friends I'd met, and I decided to seek counsel from the bishop here. He suggested I begin a Proving time to show I was serious about becoming a part of this community. A year later, I officially joined the Hickory Hollow Amish church."

Sought counsel from a bishop? Adeline puzzled over this, having never considered turning to a religious figure for advice of any kind. *A bishop must certainly be high up in the church hierarchy.*

"Eventually I fell in love with Rhoda." Earnest quickly added that he had originally planned to remain single for the rest of his life.

So was it Mom's idea to end the marriage? Adeline wondered.

Sighing, she wished her mother were alive to fill in the unexpected blanks, because many more questions were coming to mind. Her mom had told her so little, yet Adeline wouldn't press Earnest Miller for these answers when she had known him only a few hours.

"I understand wanting to turn over a new leaf," she said, then bit her lip. "But I'm still trying to wrap my brain around this. Forgive me for saying so." She hesitated, unsure how to ask her next question without offending him.

Earnest's face broke into an encouraging smile.

"Sorry." Her cheeks warmed. "We're basically strangers."

"I don't blame you for having questions." He paused and ran his callused hands through his dark brown hair, cut as bluntly as if a large bowl had been set on his head as a guide.

Adeline held her breath, genuinely baffled that her sophisticated, occasionally elitist mother would have taken a second glance at such a man. *He must have been completely different back when they met in college.* She tried to imagine his youthful appearance all those years ago, dressed in normal clothes. Yet Adeline could not keep from stealing glances at his gray shirt and black suspenders . . . or the baggy trousers minus a belt. Sawdust stuck to Earnest's black work shoes following the short stroll through the woodworking area.

Suddenly ill at ease, Adeline wished she had not agreed

to stay the night. It was impossible to reconcile the natural father she had imagined with this man. Her long search had ended in a part of the globe where things were still done the old-fashioned way, as they had been done for generations.

Can this man really be my father?

Earnest steepled long, slender fingers beneath his lips. He broke the silence. "You seem distressed."

More so now than when she had first entered the shop, she was aware of the rhythmic ticking of the many clocks—a veritable symphony took place every hour on the hour. "Why Amish?" she blurted out.

Earnest shifted in his chair, nodding his head as if he'd anticipated this. "It's simple, really," he said. "My mother's parents were Old Order Mennonite—horse-and-buggy people. Guess I must have acquired an attraction to the Plain life while spending time with them at Christmas and during the summer . . . a fondness that came back to me when I was doing an internship near here after my sophomore year of college."

Adeline tried to process this. "So you're saying your family heritage convinced you to make a life here?"

Earnest nodded thoughtfully. "It's *your* heritage, too."

She was taken aback. *Mine?*

"Otherwise, it's unlikely that I would've ended up Amish." Earnest pushed a sigh through his tight lips. "It takes a lot— well, it *took* a lot to release my grasp on the modern world I'd grown up in. But I felt like I needed that sort of drastic change in my life."

This was all still so hard to believe. "Did my mother know about your Mennonite roots?"

Earnest shook his head somewhat apologetically. "I mentioned it in passing, but we scarcely knew each other, I'm afraid. Ours was an impulsive marriage, and that's an understatement." He told her how he and Rosalind had gone to the justice of the peace and shocked her parents at Christmas by announcing they had eloped. "We rushed headlong into it."

"Grandpa and Grandy Ellison couldn't have wanted that for my mother. . . . I understand why they were shocked," Adeline said, then quickly realized how rude that must have sounded. "I mean, they're very traditional."

"No need to explain." Earnest gave her an understanding smile.

Adeline was interested to know if her grandparents had eventually accepted the marriage, but she had already stuck her foot in her mouth.

"Would you like to see some photos of my younger sister?" Earnest asked, going on to explain that Charlene had died at age thirteen of a rare form of cancer.

"How very sad," she said, then acknowledged her interest in seeing his photos.

"Actually, you remind me of Charlie," Earnest said as he pulled a small brass box the size of a cigar box out of a cupboard. He opened it and fumbled through it, then held up several pictures. "Here are a few of her school photos." He handed them to Adeline. "What do you think?"

Looking at the pretty young girl, Adeline felt a jolt of surprise. "I do see a resemblance. Almost like a sister." She didn't reveal it, but she had always wished for a sister. "Thanks for showing me," she said, handing them back.

Earnest looked over at her. "You even wear your hair similarly."

Smiling at that, Adeline wondered if her aunt Charlie would have approved of her big brother's becoming Amish.

Daylight was fading quickly, and Adeline noticed there were

no lights inside the shop, other than a large lantern on the floor near the open door. "I'm afraid I'm keeping you from your family."

"It is nearly time for our evening prayers," Earnest said, rising just then. "Would you like to join us?"

Evening prayers? She had little experience with praying but decided to accept since she was his guest. "Sure," she said, getting up from her chair, too. "I know I said it earlier . . . but I don't want to be a nuisance."

"Oh, don't fret about that," Earnest replied obligingly.

Is he really comfortable with my staying? She walked with him across to the back porch of the main house, where several rocking chairs sat empty. Gazing at the rustic red barn and connecting stable, the tall white silo and picturesque wood-shed and windmill to the east, as well as the two horses and four mules grazing in the misty green meadow, she felt as if she had been transported to a different era. *Like a character in a novel plucked from one book and pasted into another*, she thought.

If not for Mom's urging all those months ago, I would never have come here, she acknowledged, still wondering if she wouldn't have been better off not knowing the truth.

Sylvia took a clean bath towel and washcloth into the spare room and placed them on the blanket chest at the foot of the double bed. She glanced around the room, making sure everything was in order, even though Adeline had already taken over the place somewhat—her overnight case lay open on the floor near the windows, and a light bathrobe was flung haphazardly across the bed.

Checking the small closet for extra hangers, Sylvia saw only two and hurried upstairs to her own room to find another hanger in her closet. Spotting her best blue dress and white organdy apron—her church clothes—she thought of her fiancé, Titus Kauffman. She had worn that very dress and apron the last time she'd seen him, at the baptismal instruction class before Preaching service nearly a week ago. And even though they hadn't spoken in a while, having agreed to take some time apart, she wondered every day how he was doing.

Downstairs again, once she had touched up the spare room sufficiently, Sylvia went to the kitchen to see how much home-made ice cream was left in the freezer. In so doing, she recalled Titus's favorite flavor, chocolate almond, and remembered how they had ordered the exact same kind at Lapp Valley Farm the last time they were there. She caught herself smiling at the memory.

How soon will he want to talk things over? she wondered, missing him.

Adeline gathered with Earnest and Rhoda and their children in what they referred to as "the front room," an insufferably warm space without air conditioning or even a fan. Adeline sat near an open window in a straight-backed wooden chair with a needlepoint seat. The occasional breeze blew even more hot, humid air into the room, and perspiring profusely, she wished she'd had the nerve to change into shorts and a tank top. But everyone else in the room was so covered up. The hems of Rhoda's and Sylvia's dresses fell nearly to their ankles when they stood, and each wore a full black apron, as well. *They must be roasting!*

She observed the boys—precise images of their father,

except for Earnest's untrimmed beard. There was something fascinating about their uniformity, and Adeline realized that she never wanted to blend in with a group any more than she wanted to go along with the crowd. No, she, like her mom before her, wanted to make her individual mark on the world and be unique, not look or dress like everyone else.

One of the younger boys had carried a black leather Bible into the room and placed it gently, even reverently, on Earnest's lap, in the glow of the nearby gas lamp.

Adeline had been raised with minimal religious instruction: Christmas Eve candlelight services, an occasional Easter Sunday at church, but little else. Until the months prior to her stepdad's death, when he'd sometimes asked her mother to read to him from the Bible, neither of her parents had ever even mentioned it. Adeline had no other recollection of "the Lord God," as Earnest described Him now when introducing the passage he was about to read.

Her stomach clenched, she was so ill at ease. She eyed her presumed half siblings as if all of this were a surreal dream.

I'll be on my way first thing tomorrow, she thought as she wiped her moist forehead with her hand, *and everything will be normal again.* She tried to envision what her fiancé would say about this backwoodsy setting.

Adeline smiled thinly. *Yes, that's exactly how Brendon would describe it!*

Sylvia sat in a cane-backed chair near her mother, eyes trained on her brothers so as not to gawk at Adeline. Ernie's and Adam's hair was damp with sweat as they sat near the black heat stove, which would not be in use for another three months. Her two youngest brothers, Calvin and Tommy, perched themselves on the wide windowsill near Ernie and Adam, all of them feigning disinterest and casting only furtive glances toward Adeline.

Shadows from the setting sun skimmed across the far wall, and Sylvia couldn't help noticing how strained and uncomfortable Adeline appeared. She crossed her long legs at the knees, then a few moments later, quickly recrossed them at the ankles, her white jeans looking utterly out of place there in the large room, where the People gathered for worship once a year.

Sylvia glanced at Dat and hoped he wouldn't pass the Good Book around to each of them, as he sometimes did to make sure they were all paying attention. *Surely not tonight,* she thought, relieved when he looked at Mamma and smiled thoughtfully before turning to chapter fifteen in the Gospel of John. "'I am the vine, ye are the branches: He that abideth in me, and I in him,'" he began to read, "'the same bringeth forth much fruit: for without me ye can do nothing.'"

Her father continued, and Sylvia's gaze drifted back to Adeline, who stared at Dat skeptically, her frown still evident, although now there was an inquisitive look in her striking blue eyes. She seemed to be studying him, and Sylvia wished she knew what the young woman was thinking.

She probably can't wait to return home. . . .

CHAPTER
Two

*E*arnest felt out of breath as he read from God's Word. The annoying sensation so unsettled him that he paused for a moment. *I have* two *daughters*, he thought, turning the page. *One I might never have met. . . .*

Looking at Adeline now, he could clearly see Rosalind's features, but Adeline bore an even stronger resemblance to his younger sister, Charlie. For a moment, he felt like a teenager, living at home with her again. Nearly everything about Adeline reminded him of the little sister he'd missed every day since her premature passing decades ago.

Like Charlie, Adeline was also thoroughly modern as she sat there fidgeting as he read. Perhaps she was too warm in her jeans, her shoulder-length hair like a curtain around her neck.

Has she had any kind of religious upbringing? he wondered later as they knelt for silent prayer at their seats. He happened to catch Adeline's confused look as she got down on her knees along with the rest of the family.

When Earnest bowed for the prayer, he asked God for an

extra measure of wisdom during Adeline's short visit. He struggled to be as openhearted as Rhoda had been in inviting the young woman to remain as an overnight guest.

Almighty God, he prayed, *bless my wife for her great kindness, portraying Thy constant grace and goodness to our family.*

Following the Miller family gathering, Adeline politely excused herself and headed into the room where she was to sleep. She looked about at the meagerly furnished space, where a tall oak chest of drawers and double bed with its plain-looking headboard and footboard filled up most of the room. A lone chair sat near two open windows. Someone had brought a bath towel and washcloth and placed them on the chest at the foot of the bed. She was aware of the dark green shades, rolled high, as she moved closer to the windows and looked out at the Millers' barn and windmill, quaint and picturesque in the falling dusk.

Sighing, Adeline shook her head. *Mom never would have believed this,* she thought, a lump in her throat.

She turned to sit on the bed and immediately noted the firmness of the mattress. At least it wasn't a rope bed like she had once read about in a historical novel.

The words from the Bible reading rolled around in her head: *"For without me ye can do nothing."* And although she tried to brush it off, the phrase continued its echo.

It seemed pretty pointless to someone who had been raised to believe that she could accomplish whatever she chose to do in life, if she worked hard enough. She could be as successful as her well-to-do grandfather Ellison and her mother and stepfather, William Pelham, too. They'd all achieved their goals without any help from God.

Getting up, Adeline went to her overnight bag and removed her sleep shorts and cami, wondering how long she might have to wait her turn for the only bathroom in the house. *Is there a particular order for a family of seven?* The idea of sharing with that many on a daily basis was incomprehensible. *How do Rhoda and Sylvia survive?* She smiled at that. It had to help that neither wore even a dash of makeup.

Poking her head out the bedroom door, she noticed Sylvia coming down the stairs wearing a long white cotton robe, a pale yellow nightgown draped over her arm. "Pss-t," she called, motioning to Sylvia. "Should I take a number for my turn—"

"*Nee*, you're next after Mamma," Sylvia said immediately. "As soon as she's out."

"Are you sure?"

Sylvia gave her a quick smile. "Positive."

"But weren't you—"

"Honestly, I'm in no hurry." Sylvia stood there, tilting her head as though trying to look into the spare room. "Are ya comfortable enough?"

Nodding, Adeline assured her she had everything she needed for the night.

"Well, just ask if you're missin' anything." Sylvia paused as though she had more to say. Then she frowned. "This must be quite a day for ya," she observed softly. "Finding out your father's Amish an' all."

Adeline was surprised the other young woman was thinking that way. "Your family has been so generous to me, considering everything."

"Well, I hope ya sleep soundly. I'm sure it was a long drive here." With that, Sylvia hurried toward the kitchen and out of sight around the corner, where Adeline could hear her knocking on the bathroom door, saying something muffled to her mother.

She didn't have to do that, Adeline thought, realizing that Sylvia had given up her spot next. All the same, Adeline yearned for the comforts of her former home with her parents. Even Adeline's current apartment near Georgia Tech was luxurious compared to this old place.

Glancing at her watch, Adeline felt antsy but would never let on to Sylvia. *My Amish half sister,* she thought, dumbfounded again. This afternoon, when she'd pulled in past the Millers' vegetable stand and parked her red Camaro convertible in their drive, she'd certainly had no idea what she would find.

Though she was still eager to return to her life in Georgia, she knew it was unlikely she would ever return here.

They're all so nice, she thought. *So welcoming.*

It was very strange. She hadn't even made her exit, and a part of her already felt a tinge of regret, as if missing out on a family she'd never known she had.

But they're so . . . unusual, she reminded herself.

No matter, she thought. *It's not like they're falling over themselves to get to know me, either.*

She moved away from the doorway, not wanting to be seen looking out and checking for Rhoda to head to the stairs. While she waited, Adeline realized she had forgotten to bring along her phone charger.

Sighing, she noticed the Double Wedding Ring bed quilt, with its familiar-looking pattern and attractive blend of rich brown, cherry red, and bright purple juxtaposed with sunlight yellow, sapphire, then gray. *Mom had one like this. Perfectly symmetrical,* she mused and turned the quilt over to peer at the back, where a stitched pattern of hearts came into focus.

"Gorgeous," she murmured, recalling the quilt her mother said she had received as a wedding gift, made by a relative Adeline did not know. She wished she had been more attentive when Mom first showed it to her, years ago. Adeline had come across the quilt again recently while sorting through her mother's things with her younger brother, fourteen-year-old Liam, who'd naturally shown zero interest in the heirloom quilt.

Who has time to do such painstaking work? she wondered as she reexamined the beautiful quilt before her. Turning it over, she smoothed the quilt against the mattress, then stepped back to look at it on the neatly made bed. Tears sprang to her eyes—a familiar sight was the last thing Adeline had expected to find here.

When the knock came at the bedroom door, Adeline slipped into her lightweight robe and opened the door.

Rhoda Miller stood there in a long bathrobe, her hair wrapped in a towel. "The washroom's all yours," the woman said, then turned to leave.

"Wait," Adeline said quickly. "May I ask you something?"

Rhoda faced her again. "Of course. What is it, dear?"

Dear? thought Adeline, surprised. She pointed. "This bed quilt is lovely. Did you make it?"

"Oh *jah.* Sylvia and I did several years ago, with help from my mother and her sisters."

Adeline caught herself shaking her head as she admired it. "It's—"

"Somethin' wrong?" Rhoda asked.

"It's a work of art. I mean . . . you're gifted artists."

Rhoda frowned. "It would be prideful to think of ourselves thataway." She paused and pulled her robe tighter around her waist. "Our quilts are made with loving hands and intended to be used in a practical manner. With strong stitchin' that lasts a long, long time."

Adeline considered that. "What would it take to learn to stitch like this? To make a quilt, I mean."

"Well, plenty-a practice." Rhoda explained that tiny stitches didn't just happen on the first try. Or the second or third. "It's like anything, really," she said. "Practice makes perfect."

Adeline remained quiet, wondering if learning this art really was as simple as that.

"Would ya like to learn?" Rhoda's smile spread across her pretty face.

Adeline was amazed at the offer. Surely such a process would take days, if not weeks. *And I'm leaving tomorrow,* she reminded herself. "I'm afraid I wouldn't have time."

"How long can ya stay?"

Adeline paused, feeling conflicted again. *Does she mean it?* "Really, I don't want to impose."

Rhoda looked as if she could barely contain her laugh. "Oh my. But ya just got here."

Adeline thought ahead to the reality of her situation and surprised herself by thinking out loud, "Well, I do have some time before classes start."

The woman's golden brown eyes lit up. "*Gut.* I was hopin' ya might wanna stay awhile."

She hoped? Adeline had not a clue what to say. Not when she had basically burst into her biological father's life. She felt nervous suddenly, as if she had gotten in over her head.

Rhoda seemed to read her expression. "Just think it over, *jah?*" She smiled, then excused herself to go upstairs.

Gathering up her toiletry bag, Adeline walked toward the kitchen, where a gas lamp high over the table hissed and hummed. She shook her head at her impulsive questions and Rhoda's swift invitation, then realized this might be an opportunity to get to know Earnest better.

And Rhoda and Sylvia, as well.

CHAPTER

Three

Next morning at breakfast, Sylvia was flabbergasted to hear Mamma saying something to Adeline about maybe squeezing in some time later to practice making stitches on fabric scraps. Her interest piqued, Sylvia wondered how this had come about. *I thought Adeline was leaving today. . . .*

Dat walked into the sunny kitchen, his hair mashed down from his straw hat. He went to stand behind his chair at the head of the table and pushed his hands into his gray trouser pockets. Typically, he would be heading out to Saturday market, but she assumed he'd stayed home to visit with Adeline.

Silently, Sylvia observed him while she set Mamma's pretty new plates carefully on the table, a recent gift from Dat to mark their engagement twenty years ago. Adeline, too, seemed interested in helping, and she asked Mamma just now about putting napkins at each place setting.

"Oh, we don't use cloth napkins, if that's what ya mean," Mamma told her politely. "Not even at big celebrations like weddings."

Adeline's eyelids fluttered. "Oh," she said, apparently surprised.

"Sometimes, if we have finger food, like fried chicken, we use paper towels," Mamma added.

Dat motioned for Adeline to take the seat at the foot of the table, where the guest of honor always sat. "We do plenty of things different around here," he told her, smiling as he pulled out his chair. "I'm sure you're discovering that, *jah?*"

Dat's going out of his way to make her feel at ease, thought Sylvia, untying her work apron and placing it on the counter. She walked around Dat's chair to sit at her usual spot, to the right of Mamma. And once Ernie and the boys hurried inside from washing up at the well pump, they quietly settled themselves at the table, too. Dat bowed his head to ask the silent blessing, everyone following his lead.

After the prayer, Dat asked Adeline, "Would you mind telling us something about your life? I remember your grandparents used to live on the beach."

Adeline's head bobbed. "Yes, and they still do. Actually, the ocean is my go-to place to wind down after exams or whenever I can get to Hilton Head," she said. "My brother, Liam, lives there full-time now."

"Does he swim in the ocean?" young Tommy asked.

"Sure," Adeline replied, appearing a bit baffled. "And Liam and I enjoy paddleboarding, snorkeling, and sailing together when I visit."

Tommy shook his head in apparent awe. "I wanna see the ocean someday."

Dat chuckled under his breath. "We'll have to think about that, son."

"What else do ya like to do?" Tommy asked her, reaching for his glass of milk.

Sylvia wondered what had gotten into her littlest brother. He was falling all over himself!

"I like to play tennis, especially doubles with Liam and his friends, or with my fiancé and another couple," Adeline replied. "But most of the year I'm in Georgia at college, pursuing the same course of study as Mom planned, though she never finished her degree."

Sylvia thought it was interesting the way Adeline looked at Dat all the while she was supposedly answering Tommy's question.

"Is that right?" Dat asked suddenly. "You're going for a degree in biomedical engineering at Georgia Tech?"

"Graduating with honors next May, if I can keep up my GPA."

Dat shook his head. "What do you know. I suppose your mom mentioned that I went there, too."

Adeline nodded, and Ernie asked, "What's a GPA?"

Sylvia paid attention as Dat explained what a grade point average was; she'd never heard of such a thing in the one-room schoolhouse she had attended for eight grades.

"If you don't mind sticking around a little longer, Adeline, I'd be happy to show you our farming community," Dat said, giving her a quick smile. "If that would interest you."

Mamma jerked her head toward Dat, her eyes registering a concern Sylvia hadn't expected to see.

"I don't want to take time away from your work," Adeline said.

Dat ran his hand through his beard. "I wouldn't offer if I didn't want to," he said. "Besides, there's no place like Hickory Hollow."

Glancing at her wristwatch, Adeline replied, "Sure, but if

I stay longer than another day or two, I'll have to purchase a few extra items of clothing. I didn't exactly come prepared."

"*Ach*, Sylvia can sew up some skirts or whatever ya need," Mamma volunteered, nudging Sylvia under the table.

Too taken aback to say anything, Sylvia simply nodded her head and reached for her water glass.

"Some skirts?" Adeline asked, looking surprised.

Dat grinned. "Don't worry, we won't have you dressing Amish. Not anytime soon, that is." He chuckled.

"*Ach*, Earnest," Mamma said.

Adeline looked at Mamma and Sylvia in turn. "Thanks for the offer, but it's really no trouble to pick up a few things." Then she asked the location of the nearest shopping center.

Sylvia remained quiet during the rest of the meal as Dat talked with Adeline about his adjustment to Plain life—the differences he had encountered and the difficulties. It was like he was replaying his entry into his required Proving so long ago. Sylvia had never heard him talk so much about that time and wondered at his willingness to do so now.

Ernie and the younger boys were busy eating across the table, eyes fixed on their surprisingly talkative father, who continued conversing with Adeline. Adam was staring at Adeline, his mouth pressed firmly closed, not eating for long segments of time. Calvin was nearly scowling as he took a bite of sausage and then observed the young woman who claimed to be their eldest sister.

Sylvia found a small measure of comfort in her brothers' reactions. Apparently, she wasn't the only one feeling uneasy about Adeline's presence. And to think that Dat and Mamma were encouraging her to stay on with them! But witnessing Dat's seeming interest in his other daughter and his attempts to make her feel comfortable, Sylvia assumed that her parents had discussed this privately before breakfast.

Why then did Mamma look so surprised when Dat volunteered to show Adeline around the area?

Rhoda offered Adeline a second helping of scrambled eggs and sausage, but Adeline declined as graciously as she could. She did find it amazing how heartily Earnest, his wife, and his children could eat at this early hour. Granola, a piece of fruit, and green tea with raw honey had been her preferred breakfast fare since her move to an apartment near campus the fall of her sophomore year. Although she never had been one for much of a breakfast. *Mom was the one who insisted on having several types of fresh fruit, oatmeal, and green tea,* she thought fondly. *Not so much Dad, who loved his poached eggs and bacon.*

Thinking ahead to her senior year starting in a couple of weeks, Adeline realized that her appetite had diminished in the months since her mother's passing. A light breakfast was also easier to put together, and she was quite satisfied to eat less. Besides, the last thing she needed was a sluggish brain.

Reaching for her glass of water, Adeline noticed Calvin—the boy with the most expressive mannerisms. His perpetual frown seemed to indicate his negative feelings toward her. From the way Adam stole sly glances at her, one hand tucked under a black suspender, he also seemed to have reservations about her. *He acted much the same at the family gathering last night,* she recalled.

Adeline thought of Liam, nearly a high-school freshman, and wondered what her brother would think if he knew. It crossed her mind that if Liam could drive and had discovered *his* biological father were Amish, he would have turned the car right around and floored it!

I'm invading these people's lives, Adeline thought. *Yet here I am.*

She glanced around Rhoda's humble kitchen, with its linoleum floor, humming gas lamp overhead, and lack of microwave—worlds apart from Grandy Ellison's state-of-the art kitchen with computerized everything.

There's no comparison with the way this family does things at the table, she thought, having taken note of Earnest's head bowed in silent prayer before the meal and afterward, too, just as he had last evening at supper, the whole family joining in unison. For the longest time, it was silent around the table, except for the collective breathing. She had no idea how they knew when to stop and begin eating. Was there some unspoken clue she had missed? Or was this something they were so accustomed to, they all knew the expected amount of time to pray? As for herself, she hadn't actually ever prayed *per se* before a meal or otherwise. Although Adeline had once dared to ask God why He had taken both of her parents so prematurely, she felt foolish afterward. After all, why ask someone she wasn't sure was even there?

Licking her lips, Adeline studied the boys to her right, all sitting in stairstep fashion, with Ernie Jr. up near his father at the head of the table. It was sort of charming how every one of them dressed alike again today, suspenders over their short-sleeved pale blue shirts. *They're just as related to me as Liam,* she realized suddenly. *I have five half brothers!*

Like the boys and her mother next to her, Sylvia sat as straight as a pole, not saying much. Last evening, Rhoda also had been more talkative, and Adeline wondered if she might be overwhelmed today. Did the woman regret being so welcoming?

She did seem sincere about having me stay around, though, Adeline thought, more eager to find out about them and their lives than to actually sew.

Rhoda didn't want to come right out and ask Earnest if he was aware of the risk he was taking. But she had to make some suggestion about his hope to take Adeline out in the family carriage that morning.

"I'm done with secret keeping," Earnest told her in the clock shop after breakfast as they went around winding up all the clocks.

She nodded. "You don't have to convince me," she said, hoping she wasn't speaking out of turn. "I just think it might be best not to stir up more trouble. Adeline's an *Englischer,* after all."

"True, but what if I take Sylvie along?" Earnest replied. "They could sit together in the second bench seat, and Adeline wouldn't be seen."

"*Des gut, jah,*" she said, thankful he'd thought of a wise solution. She did not want to experience another shunning like the one her husband had just endured.

Earnest hitched up Lily to the buggy while Sylvie and Adeline waited on the back porch, seemingly still awkward around each other, although Sylvie seemed to be doing her best to break the ice. *As best she can, considering . . .*

When he was ready to go, the girls got themselves into the

second bench seat, quiet now as Earnest picked up the driving lines and they headed down the driveway to Hickory Lane.

This is mighty strange, he thought while driving the family buggy around the neighborhood. It felt like he was seeing the mule-drawn mowers in the fields, the towering windmills, and the water wheel for the first time, and he remembered how the Hickory Hollow landscape had looked to him when he'd first arrived more than twenty years ago. How odd it was to realize now that even as he had been inquiring about how to join the Amish church, his first wife, Rosalind, was secretly pregnant with Adeline.

The thought saddened him. *I missed out on her infancy, her growing-up years. . . .* Earnest sighed, not turning to look at Adeline. *Yet she's here now.*

"Do you ever miss driving a car?" Adeline asked Earnest as the carriage rolled past the bishop's blacksmith shop.

"I never think about it anymore."

She laughed softly, surprised. "I'm certain I wouldn't be able to do that."

"Makes sense why you'd think so." Earnest sat perched on the hard bench seat, the driving lines in both hands, eyes fixed on the road.

"What about electricity?" she asked, trying to imagine what it would be like to also abandon that huge convenience.

"It took some getting used to." Earnest paused and glanced over his shoulder at her and Sylvia behind him. He chuckled. "Okay, it was *very* hard."

"But you must have thought it worthwhile."

Earnest nodded. "I did. And for a lot of reasons that would undoubtedly seem strange to you."

He didn't attempt to explain, and she didn't probe further. Sylvia, sitting to Adeline's right, remained quiet as she stared straight ahead, like she was tired. Or perhaps she didn't really want to be there.

Not certain what to say to draw her out, Adeline turned her attention to the scenery, admiring the large farmhouses and even bigger two-story "bank barns," as Earnest called them. With both carriage doors open on this warm day, she had an unobstructed view as they rode past one roadside produce stand after another, and then the attractive but quaint General Store and harness shop.

Earnest slowed the horse when they approached what Sylvia said was the one-room Amish schoolhouse, where she had attended "for all eight grades."

"Only eight?" Adeline couldn't understand why Sylvia seemed so pleased about it.

Earnest spoke up. "Amish schoolchildren graduate after the eighth grade. After that, they go on to get vocational training by working with their parents in some capacity—girls with their mothers or aunts, or even working at a quilt shop or restaurant or as a nanny for a family outside the Amish community. The same goes for boys, who work alongside their fathers. Most become farmers or dairymen or learn the ins and outs of occupations like harness or carriage making, welding, carpentry, and such."

"But can they choose to further their education if they want to?" Adeline had to know; it seemed like a shame, otherwise.

Sylvia answered. "Very few of us go on to high school or college. The ones who do rarely remain Amish."

Adeline tried to let that sink in, finding it hard to imagine not being able to pursue as much education as desired. She thought of how her own mother had not completed college. *Because she had me. . . .*

At every turn, Amish farmers with their mule teams were out cutting hay—a remarkable sight. Adeline had never been anywhere quite so remote. She recalled how, while driving into Lancaster County yesterday, she had gone from traveling main highways to suddenly finding herself on the narrow back roads leading into Hickory Hollow, some unlabeled by her phone's GPS.

Several horse-drawn carriages passed by, and there were Amish people walking barefoot along the road. A few waved to Earnest. *My father is an Amish clockmaker,* she thought, studying him. She decided that Sylvia, Ernie, and Tommy most resembled him, while Adam and Calvin took after Rhoda. *Sylvia has his chin line,* she realized, wondering what characteristic, if any, *she* had from this man.

Unexpectedly, Earnest turned to glance back at her. She felt her cheeks warm, and she was rarely one to blush. "So, Rhoda says she plans to teach you to quilt," he said, adjusting his straw hat with one hand, the driving lines in the other.

"Rhoda's kind for offering," Adeline replied, fixing her eyes on the road ahead, aware of the rise and fall of the horse's head, the rhythmic bounce of its dark, thick mane.

"Well, if you're serious, she's one of the best quilters around." Sylvia nodded her agreement but again remained quiet.

Adeline wondered what they would think if she revealed how the bed quilt in the guest room had touched her, especially the intertwined hearts at the center. *Like Mom's pretty one.*

They doubled back to a road they'd passed earlier, and Earnest's horse pulled the carriage past a large spread of land where three quilts on a clothesline flapped in the breeze.

Adeline asked, "Do you know the names of those quilt patterns?"

Leaning forward, Sylvia squinted into the sunshine. "There's a Double Wedding Ring and an Ocean Wave." She shielded her eyes with her hand. "It looks like the last one's a Sunshine Diamond quilt."

Adeline loved the charming pattern names. "So who dreams up those designs?" she asked.

"Not sure, really. Some have been around for hundreds of years. Like with most things, there are lots of old traditions round here."

"You and your mother are amazing quilters," Adeline said to Sylvia. "You must enjoy working together."

Sylvia nodded. "Oh *jah*. 'Specially durin' the cold winter months."

Adeline saw what looked like a small greenhouse and, farther down the road, another farmhouse surrounded by rose arbors. "So many roses!" she exclaimed. "Those arbors must be gorgeous when the flowers are at peak."

Earnest gave a nod. "Until this past May, that was my old friend Mahlon Zook's place—his wife, Mamie, lives there as a widow now." Earnest paused long enough to sigh. "Mamie's deciding whether to move in with one of her married sons after the harvest. It's the way of the People to look after their widows and elderly."

Adeline felt a pang of emotion at hearing him speak about his friend and his widow. She couldn't help wondering if Earnest felt anything about her mother's passing.

"You seem very interested in quilts," he asked. "How did that come about?"

"Oh, my mom had a remarkably pretty one—a wedding gift

made by one of her in-laws. Mom never said who, though."
Adeline stopped a moment as a realization overtook her. "I'd
always assumed it was a gift to her and my stepdad, but it seems
more likely that it came from her first wedding . . . to you."

"Is that so?" Earnest seemed to come alive. "Did your
mother say anything about where it was made?"

"I was fairly young when she first showed me." She sighed.
"Now I wish I'd listened more carefully. There is so much I
don't know about Mom's past." *Or yours,* she added mentally.

Earnest shook his head. "A wedding gift, you say?"

Adeline nodded. "There must have been a seasoned quilter
in your family."

"Was there ever!" Earnest went on to tell about his grandmother Zimmerman, who had made beautiful quilts for his
mother. "Grandma died many years ago now."

For a split second, Adeline wondered if that sort of talent
was somehow passed on genetically. "I assume she would be
my great-grandmother?"

"*Jah.*"

Adeline pondered that, still envisioning the pattern and
meticulous stitches—so like those on the guest room quilt
at Earnest and Rhoda's farmhouse. The quilt seemed to
reconnect her to the life she had lived prior to her mom's
passing. Most days, Adeline felt displaced, even floundering.
My life is a crazy balancing act, she thought, aware her primary
focus now was on studying and making top grades, leaving
too little time for her fiancé or friends . . . and even less time
to process her grief.

Without a doubt, she had been fortunate to meet a guy
like Brendon Burgess two years ago. Her fiancé was not only
responsible and level-headed but also caring and attentive.

Even her mother had thought he was wonderful. They had both been glad when he'd chosen to stay in Georgia after graduating with his MBA—last winter he had landed a position with a prestigious Atlanta accounting firm.

Thinking of Brendon, Adeline hoped to find a way to contact him soon, as well as Grandpa and Grandy, to let them know she was all right and staying in an Amish community off the beaten path.

The last place I expected to end up!

CHAPTER
Four

The air hummed with the continuous drone of insects, and the pastureland around them was green and thick as Earnest took Adeline and Sylvia around in the buggy. He was mindful to take the back roads, not wanting to parade Adeline around, as Rhoda feared he was doing. While he preferred not to keep secrets any longer, he understood Rhoda's concern and appreciated where she was coming from. *Dear Rhoda . . .*

Earnest fell sober at the knowledge of all he might have lost this past May, when Rhoda had been so shocked—and deeply hurt—by the news of his first marriage and the details of the demise of that relationship. He had been wrong to keep the secret from her, and while at the time her request for some space had shaken him, he was thankful now that their relationship was on the mend. *I could not ask for a more forgiving wife. . . .*

Earnest slowed the horse when, some time later, Adeline pointed to a makeshift sign advertising local raw honey and asked if they might stop at the large roadside stand. "I would love to get some," she said.

Before Earnest realized where they were, he had pulled over onto the dirt shoulder and come to a halt.

"Dat," Sylvia whispered behind him. "Maybe just keep goin'."

There was such an urgency in her voice that Earnest looked about and groaned inwardly. *Where's my head?* he thought, recognizing the farm. So, instead of turning into the lane, he stayed put several yards back from the stand, where a young Amish couple were completing their purchase.

Earnest had always admired the small pond with the narrow walkway around it, and Preacher Amos Kauffman's expansive, rolling lawn. But it was too risky for him and Sylvia to get out with Adeline in tow, yet he didn't want to offend Adeline, either.

"What an attractive place," Adeline observed as she leaned forward to look out.

"Isn't it?" He glanced toward the preacher's house, thinking Amos was likely occupied in the barn or out in the field. Or so he hoped. *Maybe this won't be so bad after all.*

"What kind of bushes are those?" asked Adeline, pointing nearby.

"Redbud," Earnest said, still holding the driving lines, having half a notion to drive on. "They flower in spring."

"You know," he heard Sylvia say, "raw honey is much cheaper at the General Store. Let's go there."

"*Gut* idea." Earnest nodded his head, but it looked as though Amos's youngest daughter, Connie, tending the stand, might have already spotted them.

"We're here now," Adeline said, getting out of the buggy. "Please . . . I'll be just a minute."

Adeline hurried over to the long table, all smiles, and realizing there was no stopping her, Earnest halfheartedly climbed out, too, and tied the horse to the fence along the perimeter of the front yard. *How can someone so fancy be my daughter?* he mused, the idea still not squarely settled in his mind.

Momentarily, he hung back near the carriage with Sylvie, letting Adeline have a look at the ears of corn piled up on the table alongside the cucumbers, lima beans, tomatoes, and potatoes—many more varieties of vegetables than his family sold. In a couple of weeks, the watermelon would be in full swing, August being the month for the mouthwatering treat, and he could almost taste the sweet flavor. But the curly green vines and leaves of the plants hadn't yet begun to yellow and turn brown, signaling the ripening. So he would have to wait.

A mosquito bit his arm, and Earnest slapped at it—the nearby pond attracted the annoying pests. By now Sylvia was standing next to him, watching Adeline, too.

"She'll think we abandoned her," Sylvia whispered.

Earnest nodded and hoped this purchase Adeline was bent on would be quick. He and Sylvia made their way along the fence as Adeline set three honey jars aside, talking animatedly to fourteen-year-old Connie.

Sylvia waved at Connie when she looked their way, but the girl frowned slightly when she put it together that Adeline was with them.

"What brings ya to Hickory Hollow?" Connie asked, eyeing Adeline with curiosity.

"I'm exploring the area . . . hanging out for a little while."

Connie pointed to the various fruits and vegetables, as well as the jams and jellies, and Adeline seemed to take them all in. "Everything was picked fresh this mornin'."

She turned then to Sylvia and Earnest. "My wind-up clock is running real *gut* now." She laughed a little.

Earnest shrugged. "Didn't take much to repair it."

"Well, I'm grateful," Connie said, glancing at Adeline, then back at Earnest.

Earnest noticed that Sylvia remained quiet and close by his side.

"Did my Dat tell ya that he and Titus reseeded our pasture?" Connie asked, making small talk. "It's practically a thick carpet now. The cows are gonna love it."

The girl looked again at Adeline, clearly puzzled by their being together. "Uh, miss . . . do ya want these jars of honey?" she asked, moving down to where Adeline was still examining the options.

Adeline raised her head and smiled. "There are so many tempting choices, sorry." She paused a moment. "May I ask, is your fruit organic?"

"*Nee*, but you can prob'ly get that two farms over." Connie motioned behind her. "You'll pay more, though, and my Dat doesn't think there's much difference, really."

Seeing the two of them interacting, it crossed Earnest's mind that Rhoda had been absolutely right about not taking Adeline around in the buggy. *What was I thinking?*

"Does your wife need anything?" Adeline asked just then, startling him. "I'd like to get something . . . return the favor of your generosity in some small way."

Earnest hardly knew what to say as Connie's big blue eyes began to blink, and she again looked questioningly at Earnest. On top of that, here came her parents down from the house, Amos carrying a large crate of more ears of sweet corn, and his wife, Eva, tagging along.

Goodness, thought Earnest. *Now I'll have to make intro-ductions.*

Immediately, he felt ashamed for thinking that way. Of course he would introduce Adeline. English or not.

Sylvia tensed at the sight of her fiancé's parents. *Now what?* she fretted, wishing she had stayed home. Considering the shaky ground that she and Titus were on here lately, she was worried.

"*Willkumm,*" called Amos Kauffman as he and Eva made their way down the lane to the roadside stand. He set the box on the table, took out a blue paisley kerchief to mop his forehead, and went over to shake Dat's hand. "*Gut* to see ya this fine summer mornin', Earnest." The preacher looked Adeline's way, and a wave of inquisitiveness passed over his countenance.

Sylvia could see that her father was in a quandary. *Surely he's not thinking of telling them who Adeline is. . . .*

Dat removed his straw hat. Then, looking at Adeline, he said, "Adeline, this is Preacher Kauffman and his wife, Eva."

"It's very nice to meet you," Adeline said with a smile.

"Are you visiting in the area?" Eva asked Adeline, eyes bright with interest.

With an awkward glance at Dat, Adeline nodded. "Yes, but I haven't decided how long I'll be here."

Sylvia held her breath while Dat shifted his weight from one foot to another.

"Adeline is my daughter," Dat told them, a serious look on his face. "From my first marriage."

Titus's father didn't actually sputter, but Sylvia was fairly sure the preacher was on the brink of it. At the very least,

Preacher Kauffman hardly knew what to say. His eyebrows rose abruptly, then lowered. "Well, what a surprise, I must say."

Eva reached out her hand to shake Adeline's. "We didn't know Earnest had another daughter," she said, her eyes trained on Adeline's face.

"To be fair, he didn't know, either," Adeline said, giving Dat a faint smile. "So we're out getting acquainted while he shows me around your beautiful community."

"Oh, Hickory Hollow's a little bit of heaven on earth, for sure," Eva said, looking first at Adeline, then at Dat, as if trying to see a resemblance.

Then, thinking she should do something to halt the conversation and get Adeline moving along, Sylvia picked up a jar of blackberry jam. "Mamma loves this, and we don't grow blackberries, so this would be ideal, Adeline," she said, showing her. "That is, if you'd still like to surprise her, maybe?"

"I certainly would," Adeline said. To Connie, she added, "I'll take two blackberry jams, three jars of the raw honey, and those wonderful-looking potato rolls, please." Adeline opened her shoulder bag and removed her wallet.

Dat stepped back, not saying more, and Preacher Kauffman started talking about his plan to plant a rose arbor on the south side of the house. "In honor of Preacher Mahlon."

"I daresay he'd approve," Dat replied.

"He surely would." Eva bobbed her head, continuing to appraise Adeline as Connie made change for her. Thankfully, it wasn't long before Dat was saying "So long."

Adeline took her time to politely say how lovely it was to meet the Kauffmans before she fell into step with Sylvia as they followed Dat back to the horse and carriage.

Dat must've wanted to get things out in the open right away, thought Sylvia, *considering all he's gone through with the ministerial brethren recently.*

Then, just as Sylvia and Adeline were walking around the horse to climb inside the carriage, Sylvia happened to see Titus Kauffman coming their way in his father's spring wagon. Titus slowed up, gawked a bit, and then absently waved before making the turn into the lane.

It won't be long and he'll hear the news, Sylvia thought with a prick of concern.

Five

*D*o the Kauffmans typically sell their produce to—what is it you call us?" Adeline asked once they were on their way again.

Earnest smiled to himself. "*Englischers.*"

Sylvia spoke up from behind him. "They get plenty of tourists, just like the rest of us. 'Specially this time of year."

Adeline was quiet for a bit, then asked, "Will it be a problem for you? Them knowing I'm your daughter, that is."

Earnest drew a sigh. "A few months ago, it would have been, but hopefully not now." He wasn't ready to tell her about the six-week *Bann* the People had put him under for keeping his first marriage secret, but he wanted to offer some sort of explanation. "Suffice it to say, no one knew I had been married before I came here. Not even Rhoda." He shook his head, disliking the thought of dragging Adeline through all of this.

Adeline leaned forward in the back seat. "You didn't tell her?"

"Not a soul knew anything about my former life."

"Why not, though?" She sounded baffled. "Would telling have been such a big deal?"

"Definitely. The Amish don't believe in divorce," Earnest said, wondering how Sylvia was taking this conversation, quiet as she was.

"But some marriages do fail," Adeline observed.

"Not here, they don't. Not typically." Earnest sighed. "They take marriage vows seriously here, as the Good Book instructs." *Just like I always believed.* Now he'd opened up a Pandora's box—precisely what he had wanted to avoid. But keeping secrets had not served him well.

"Are you saying the Amish think they're perfect?" Her tone indicated she was upset.

Earnest shook his head. "To the contrary," he said. "They're people just like you and me."

"*They?*"

He felt foolish. "*We*," he restated.

Then Adeline asked, "Tell me again why you came here. I mean, what was going through your mind to make you want to live this radically different way?"

Earnest again mentioned that, had it not been for his experiences with his Mennonite grandparents, he might not have been drawn to the Plain life when searching for a fresh start. "I longed for a sense of community . . . a connection with a group of people who seemed reliable and stable. Considering all that I was struggling with, centuries-old Amish traditions were just what I needed." He paused suddenly, realizing that he didn't want to make her feel bad about what had happened between her mother and him. "And then after I'd joined church, and later, fallen in love with Rhoda, I couldn't think of living without her," Earnest said. "Once we started dating, I knew I would never be leaving Hickory Hollow."

"I can't imagine marrying for any reason but love," Adeline said.

Sylvia coughed a little, and Earnest wished the subject were not so sensitive. He still found it difficult to talk about this time in his life . . . the decisions he had made.

All the same, he had to ask, "Adeline, are you wondering if I loved your mother?" He hadn't planned to say it quite that way, but the words were out now.

Adeline sighed and leaned back in her seat. "You and Mom were young."

He nodded. "Too young, it turned out."

"Then maybe your relationship wasn't so much about devotion and true love as something else?"

Perceptive, Earnest thought, remembering how quickly he and Rosalind had married after dating for only a few months. But he wanted both of his daughters to know that he had been committed to that marriage for a lifetime. "Not to speak ill of your mother, but I couldn't believe it when she wanted a divorce."

"I presume you fought for the marriage," Adeline said.

This was a comment he hadn't expected. "At the time, I did everything I could think of: I called her repeatedly and sent her flowers. I did my best to reunite with her. Rosalind knew I loved her." Earnest stopped talking, determined not to say anything negative.

"I'm sorry," Adeline said, her voice sounding smaller just then. "I shouldn't have brought this up."

There were plenty of things wrong with the marriage. Earnest recalled Rosalind's materialistic side and their pinched finances, and how her parents had unhelpfully made it clear they were willing to provide her with everything that Earnest could not. Even so, he had said quite enough.

"I didn't come here to dredge up the past," Adeline said at last. "You're my natural father. And I came a long way to meet you. . . ."

He nodded, hoping she wasn't hurt by his lack of a response just now and wondering how Sylvia was holding up. Despite her continued silence, he was keenly aware of her presence.

"I don't mean to be pushy." Adeline's voice was soft and kind. "But if it's all right, I *would* like to get to know you." She paused, then again mentioned Rhoda's gracious offer to help her learn quilting.

"To be frank, I thought our way of living . . . well, I thought it might be difficult for you to accept."

"It *is* a little hard to get used to. But I can handle it for a visit. I guess I need to know if *you* want me to stay, Earnest."

He had never encountered such an inquisitive person. Except maybe Mahlon, gone to glory. But it had been different with his closest friend, who'd always asked practical questions, not pointed ones like Adeline seemed to thrive on. "It's all right, sure," Earnest said. "Besides, I'd like to get acquainted with you, too."

"Wonderful!"

Will she like what she discovers here, though? Earnest wondered as he directed Lily to trot toward home.

"I'm all thumbs with this thimble," Adeline remarked to Rhoda later that morning while trying to make beginner stitches on a piece of leftover fabric.

"You'll get used to it . . . and thank me later," Rhoda said as they sat together at the kitchen table. "I remember the first time my *Mamm* showed me how to sew. Soon as she left

50

the room, I took the thimble off. Well, come a half hour or so later, I had pokes and bruises on the pad of my third finger and realized it would prob'ly be bleeding, next thing."

Adeline smiled at how willingly Rhoda told on her younger self.

Rhoda leaned forward and observed the angle of Adeline's needle. She showed her how to adjust it to more of a horizontal slant. "Now you've got it."

Adeline laughed. "I might not be cut out for this."

"Practice, practice, remember?" And here Rhoda clucked like a hen.

"I'm thinking it's also patience, patience." Adeline glanced at her. "Am I right?"

Rhoda nodded and smiled, her cheeks growing rosier as the heat of the day pervaded the kitchen. "I say it's patience, determination, and practice."

Adeline could relate to that. "And passion, too?"

"*Jah*, for sure." Rhoda made several stitches on her scrap of fabric and showed them to Adeline.

"They're so small and straight."

"You'll make stitches like that, too, someday," Rhoda said. "But it's more important to make your running stitches straight than small." She made a few more example stitches. "Of course with quilting, it's also about community. Working with others, no one person trying to stand out or compete with another, just everyone doing their best to complete a project for someone to enjoy." She went on to also describe tatting doilies, crocheting baby booties, and knitting hats and sweaters. "Not all of these tasks are necessarily done in a group, mind you, but the finished product is almost always enjoyed by someone other than its creator."

Adeline wondered at that moment what her mother would have thought of Earnest's Amish wife. Would she have been impressed by Rhoda's seemingly unpretentious ways, her gentleness?

"It's more important to learn steadily than quickly," Rhoda added, getting up to go over to the counter and returning with a plate of the honey oatmeal bread she'd baked while Adeline had been out for the drive. "Work goes hand in hand with play at quilting bees and other work frolics. And we always set time aside for food and fellowship."

Adeline liked the sound of that.

"*Jah*, we womenfolk have ourselves plenty-a fun at our work frolics." Rhoda offered the plate of bread to Adeline, then took a piece herself.

Womenfolk, thought Adeline, drawn to Rhoda's homey choice of words. She found it more endearing than she would have thought possible twenty-four hours earlier.

Eyeing the plate of bread, Adeline's first inclination was to politely refuse, not so big on high-carb snacks. But, seeing the expectancy on Rhoda's face, Adeline reached for the smallest piece. "Thank you," she said, meaning it.

"And thank *you* once again for the goodies ya brought back," Rhoda said.

"I wanted to help in some way." Adeline savored the treat; the honey oatmeal bread nearly melted in her mouth. "What's in this?"

"Oh, it's a recipe Eva Kauffman gave me years ago—one passed down from her own *Mammi*." Rhoda rose to get some milk to go with their snack. "I understand ya met Eva and her preacher husband, Amos, today."

"Ah . . . yes, I did," Adeline said, wanting to decline the

fresh, rich cow's milk but figuring she was already in this deep, so what could a glass of milk hurt?

"Did you enjoy goin' to the Kauffmans' stand?"

"I certainly did."

"Well, I'm sure you've been to farmers markets before."

Adeline nodded. "But since I'm busy with my studies, it's mostly takeout for me these days. That and frozen meals."

Rhoda was nearly giggling as she sipped the milk and took a second slice of the delicious bread. "So comin' to Hickory Hollow's been quite a change of pace, I daresay."

Adeline agreed. "But I hope our stopping by your preacher's roadside stand didn't cause trouble for Earnest," she said quietly, glancing toward the hallway leading to the utility room and the back door.

Rhoda paused. "About bein' Earnest's daughter, you mean?"

Nodding, Adeline said, "They seemed pretty bowled over, yes—they kept giving me strange looks. Earnest didn't tell you?"

"He mentioned it, *jah*." Rhoda nodded, then said, "But he's not worried 'bout it and wouldn't want you to be, either."

Adeline didn't need to understand what was behind the Kauffmans' response to her. Of course they would be shocked, just as Earnest and Rhoda had been. So she dropped it.

Rhoda spoke up cheerfully, "I *do* know that Earnest is really lookin' forward to learning more about ya."

Adeline smiled, pleased to hear it. He was being the consummate host, showing her around the local farmland and making sure she felt welcome until she returned home. *Mutually beneficial,* she thought, feeling better about staying on longer.

CHAPTER

Six

*I*mmediately after the ride around Hickory Hollow, Sylvia walked to *Aendi* Ruthann's to purchase three dozen fresh eggs. It felt good to get out for some exercise after being cooped up in the buggy during Adeline's tour of the area. Goodness, Sylvia had learned things her father hadn't ever bothered to tell her. She wondered if even Mamma knew some of what Dat had shared about his first wife and how he fought to save the marriage.

On the way home from her aunt's, the sun beat mercilessly on Sylvia's neck and arms, and she wiped the perspiration from her forehead with the back of her forearm. Nearing the house, she prayed silently, *Please let Mamma be alone in the kitchen when I get back.*

Walking briskly now, she noticed the purple martins flying in and out of the tall white birdhouse Dat had built and erected years ago. To this day, she often wondered how birds could fly from their nest and return to the same spot to lay their own eggs a year later. "*God puts a homing device in their brains,*" Dat had once told her when she was a little girl.

Contemplating this, it struck her that God must have also given Adeline a sort of homing device to find her biological father. Outsiders didn't just happen onto Hickory Hollow; they had to know it existed.

As she neared the house, Mamma burst out the back door, waving a rag into the air.

"*Was in der Welt?*"

"Just gettin' rid of a big spider," Mamma said. "And I mean *big.*"

Sylvia disliked spiders, too. Farm girl though she was, she was not happy when they managed to creep into the house. "It didn't bite ya, I hope," Sylvia said, stepping onto the back porch.

"*Ach*, I'm all right."

They headed inside together, and as Sylvia put away the cartons of eggs, she asked, "Are the boys around?"

"Ernie and Adam are harvesting sweet corn."

"What 'bout Calvin and Tommy?"

"Picking cucumbers and squash. And Adeline's spending some time in the spare room, looking at our copy of *Martyrs Mirror.*"

"She's interested in Anabaptist history?" Sylvia was rather surprised. She went to the sink to lather up her hands.

"Seems so. She was practicing her stitching on the back porch when ya left to get the eggs, though," Mamma said.

She might also be texting her family or her fiancé, Sylvia thought, thinking how handy it would be to communicate with Titus whenever she wished. But as cell phones weren't permitted for any purpose but business, Sylvia dismissed that fleeting notion as fanciful.

Mamma eyed her soberly. "I know ya, daughter. Somethin's on your mind."

Sylvia nodded, drying her hands. "Dat seems more talkative than usual. Have ya noticed?"

"*Jah.*"

Sighing, Sylvia said, "He hasn't talked that much in months now."

Mamma frowned as she opened the fridge. "What're ya sayin', dear?"

She felt foolish, now that her thoughts were out in the open. "*Ach,* I don't know. . . ."

Looking baffled, Mamma closed the fridge without taking anything out. "Your Dat's just being friendly to Adeline, exactly as he should be."

It's confusing, Sylvia thought. *All the years I've tried to get him to open up about his former life without scarcely a word . . .*

"I know it's unsettling and will take some time to get used to, but it appears that Adeline's your father's flesh and blood." Mamma opened the fridge yet again and set out two heads of chilled lettuce, some radishes, carrots, and tomatoes. "And that makes Adeline yours, too, Sylvie."

"Honestly, she doesn't seem like kin to me." Sylvia opened the drawer for a white work apron.

"That will take time. This isn't easy for any of us, your brothers included."

Sylvia pondered that. "Is it easy for you, Mamma?"

"Showin' kindness to others is the right thing to do. The Lord instructs us about that in the Good Book."

"But Dat's Amish . . . and Adeline's worldly. An *outsider.*"

Mamma nodded. "But that doesn't mean he can't get acquainted with the daughter he never knew." She took down her big wood block and then spun around the lazy Susan, looking for her favorite chopping knife. Finding it, she began to cut up the heads of lettuce.

Sylvia glanced out the window, uncertain how to explain what she was feeling, even to Mamma. The conversation between Dat and Adeline during the carriage ride continued to replay in her memory.

"Remember, dear, that life is full of unexpected distress," Mamma said. "And ofttimes trials, too. This isn't easy for me, either, but I'm learning that it's not what comes our way that matters so much as it is how we react. Our heavenly Father is always with us. We're never alone." She went on to say that, from what she could tell, Adeline might have needed to come to Hickory Hollow. "Only the Good Lord knows for what reason. I'm sure, though, that she's still sufferin' from the loss of her mother." Mamma shook her head mournfully as she continued to chop. "I can't begin to imagine facing a grief like that at such a young age."

Now Sylvia felt terrible for bringing any of this up. Mamma was right—Adeline had to be carrying a deep sorrow within her.

Washing the radishes and then the tomatoes, Sylvia considered what Mamma had said. But it didn't change how she felt about Dat's sudden openness.

Later, when Adeline came into the kitchen carrying their large volume of *Martyrs Mirror*, Sylvia greeted her. "Mamma says you made lots of practice stitches today."

"I did." Adeline glanced at Mamma and returned the book to its spot on the corner cupboard. "All pretty amateur-looking ones. So I'm hoping for a breakthrough this afternoon."

Mamma opened the oven and checked on the roast, then looked over her shoulder at Adeline. "You'll get better in time."

"Patience, determination, and practice," Adeline said, parroting one of Mamma's pet phrases.

"*Wunnerbaar-gut*," Mamma said with a smile.

Adeline offered to set the table, which Mamma agreed to with a bob of her head. "Sylvia, do you mind if I ask how old you were when you learned to sew?" Adeline went to the utensil drawer and opened it.

Unsure, Sylvia looked at her mother. "Do you remember, Mamma?"

"Just four when I put a needle in your hand," Mamma said, a fond expression on her face.

Adeline shook her head in apparent wonder. "*Four?*"

"Well, round here, we teach our girls to sew and mend, and cook and clean, as soon as they can hold a needle or a broom," Mamma said, stirring the simmering beans on the stove. "Some of the little girls are helpin' dry dishes at three or younger."

"That is young," Adeline murmured, walking slowly to the table with a handful of utensils, as if lost in thought.

Sylvia blinked, amused. *She's unquestionably an* Englischer, she thought.

After the kitchen was spotless again following the noon meal, it was impossible for Sylvia not to notice how attentively Dat was regarding Adeline's efforts to sew straight stitches, out there on the porch. Perhaps he was at a loss for what to do with himself on a day he would normally have been at market selling his beautiful clocks to tourists and local customers.

Dat had actually pulled up a chair to sit beside Mamma as

she worked with Adeline and prompted her from time to time on things like the needle's position or the proper use of the thimble—all actions that were second nature to Sylvia. Trying to mind her own business and finish her mending, Sylvia wouldn't fret about the fact that she had no memory of her father ever sitting to watch *her* sew. She sighed, frustrated, and reminded herself of what Mamma had said earlier: Adeline hadn't wished for this awkward situation, and it wasn't her fault that she hadn't known her natural father all of her life. *Of course Dat's going to pay close attention to her while she's here*, Sylvia decided.

Later, when the sun had moved around to the west side of the porch, Sylvia offered to go in and get some cold water for everyone. "We also have some homemade lemonade," she suggested, aware of the intense heat.

"Water's fine for me, thanks," Adeline said. And Mamma said the same.

Dat, however, requested lemonade, just as Sylvia figured he would. *He likes sweet drinks.*

Once inside, Sylvia opened the cupboard for clean tumblers. As she did so, she heard one of her brothers cry out, sounding panicked.

Going to see about all the racket, Sylvia saw Tommy flying up the back steps to the porch, hollering that they needed some ice for Ernie. "He's lyin' on the ground in the garden!" Tommy told Dat and Mamma.

O Lord, please help my brother! Sylvia prayed, hurrying back to the kitchen to put some ice into a plastic bag.

Earnest got up immediately and ran with Tommy, thinking Ernie must be overcome with heat. The boys had probably lost track of time, out there picking the corn. . . .

Tommy scurried along, keeping up with Earnest's long strides. "Will he be all right, Dat?"

"We must get him hydrated and cooled down right away," Earnest said as they hurried to the large garden plot, where they found Ernie sitting up now with Adam's help, soil stuck to his black trousers and pale blue shirt. His eldest son looked awful red in the face. "Son?" He went to him, crouching to touch Ernie's forehead while the other boys looked on. Earnest reached for the bucket Calvin and Adam had brought from the well.

"*Sis mer kotzerich,*" Ernie said, holding his stomach and hunching forward. "I'm gonna throw up."

Sylvia came running with ice, which Earnest added to the well water before pouring it over Ernie's arms and hands. Then, when Ernie was ready, he gently poured the remaining water on his son's head and neck and back.

Drenched to the skin, Ernie coughed, still looking sick.

"Let's get you to the house," Earnest said, helping him to stay upright. Though unsteady on his feet, Ernie managed okay.

Now Rhoda and Adeline appeared, too, staying back to give Earnest and Ernie some space.

"Have him sit in the shade, and I'll run an' get an ice pack for his head," Rhoda suggested.

Ernie nodded, and Earnest had him put an arm around Adam's and Earnest's shoulders, one on either side, as they slowly made their way across the yard and over to the large tree near the walkway to the clock shop. Once there, the three of them lowered themselves onto the cool grass. Tommy followed and sat down in the shade, too, eyes on Ernie, whose soaked hair stuck to his head.

Promptly, Rhoda came with the ice pack and placed it on

the back of his neck, sitting on the ground next to him, looking very concerned. For several minutes, she continued to turn
the ice pack, at one point placing it right on his head.

His color is returning to normal, thought Earnest, relieved
as Ernie slowly sipped some of the water that Rhoda had
brought him.

Rhoda fanned herself with the hem of her black apron—in
this humidity, perhaps more out of nerves than because of any
hope for cooling. Even Adeline looked quite worried. Something about her concerned expression touched Earnest deeply
as he used his straw hat to fan his eldest son's face.

A few minutes later, a carriage rumbled into the driveway,
and Earnest turned to see Rhoda's brunette niece Alma Yoder
in the driver's seat.

Quickly, Sylvia ran to greet her. *"Kumme,* join us," Earnest
heard Sylvia say as Alma walked with Sylvia to the shade tree
and sat down.

Seeing Adeline there in the midst of his family, all of them
gathered around Ernie, something tugged at Earnest's heart-
strings, and he hoped she might indeed decide to stay longer,
if only just another day or so.

CHAPTER
Seven

*D*at introduced Adeline to Cousin Alma, and Sylvia saw that he was less on edge this time, compared to the rather uncomfortable moment at Preacher Kauffman's.

"How long can ya stay?" Cousin Alma asked, clearly curious about Adeline, but seemingly not shocked by Dat's admission that she was his daughter. *She must've heard it from someone already,* thought Sylvia, *maybe Titus or Connie.*

"I haven't decided." Adeline glanced at Mamma.

"Well, it's perfectly fine if ya stay till your college classes start," Mamma said, and Dat nodded in agreement.

That would be a few weeks, thought Sylvia, surprised.

But their attention soon returned to Ernie, who had revived enough to tell a joke, which their younger brothers seemed to enjoy. Sylvia asked Cousin Alma if she would go inside with her to help get the drinks Sylvia had promised earlier, including now some lemonade for her younger brothers.

In the kitchen, she realized how flushed Alma was in the

face. "You need a glass of cold water, too," Sylvia said. "And right quick."

Alma readily accepted. "It was terrible hot during the ride over here," she admitted. "But I didn't wanna complain, seein' how Ernie was suffering."

"He's much better now," Sylvia said. "And I'm so happy you're here!" She poured lemonade and water into tumblers. "What brings ya?" Usually Alma helped her mother at market on Saturdays.

Alma opened her pocketbook and removed an envelope. "Titus dropped by late this mornin' and asked if I'd give this to you."

"Titus did?"

"He seemed anxious for you to receive it today. Guess since he lives near me, it was more convenient."

Sylvia took the envelope, finding this odd, because Titus could have easily mailed it. Despite his apparent urgency, however, she would wait till Alma was on her way to read the letter in private.

Cousin Alma tilted her head, studying her. "I know he cares for you, Sylvia."

Sylvia smiled as she soaked up her cousin's soothing presence while they placed the tumblers on two separate trays. "You didn't seem at all shocked 'bout Adeline," she ventured.

"Titus mentioned her to me." Alma frowned, searching her face with her brown eyes. "So your Dat really had no idea? I can't believe his first wife didn't let him know she was expectin'."

Sylvia shook her head as they walked slowly through the hallway leading to the utility room and back door. "Believe me, it was a huge surprise to Dat."

"This must be strange for all of yous."

"It'll take some getting used to, for sure and for certain." Sylvia shrugged and thought of Titus's letter, which was burning a hole in her pocket.

She called for Tommy to open the screen door so they wouldn't spill the full tumblers. "So much has happened to our family this summer. Some families might've fallen apart, but thankfully, we're still together." Lately Sylvia had noticed less tension between her parents, especially at mealtimes, and felt that things were getting better all around. *Even Adeline hasn't changed that.*

Tommy dashed up the stairs to hold the door, and Cousin Alma said, "I'm glad we had a few minutes alone to talk."

Sylvia and Alma carried the trays out to the tree and distributed the tumblers, then sat in the grass with everyone else to enjoy the cold drinks.

"How's your Mamma?" Sylvia's mother asked Alma as sunlight dappled their faces.

"This minute, she's prob'ly busy with customers at market. Actually, she's expecting me to arrive within the half hour," Alma said before taking another drink of her water.

"It won't hurt to cool off some first," Ernie observed while Dat continued to fan him with his hat. "Take it from me."

Tommy nodded his head and set his tumbler of lemonade between his knees. Then, with brow furrowed, he began to roll his short sleeves clear up to his shoulders.

His brothers snickered at him, and when Dat did the same thing, everyone laughed.

It wasn't long before Alma stood and said she had to be on her way. She told Adeline how nice it had been to meet her, adding, "I hope you have a real *gut* time here." Then she helped Sylvia carry the trays of empty tumblers back to the house. "I'll keep you in my prayers," Cousin Alma said when she and Sylvia were alone again in the kitchen.

"*Denki.* Say, would ya want some cold water for in the buggy?"

"Oh, I'm fine now." Alma gave her a brief hug, smiling at her. "I care 'bout ya, Sylvie. I truly do."

"*Kumme* again soon, all right? I'd love to visit longer."

Alma nodded. "I'm awful sorry to fly," she said and headed toward the hallway to the utility room.

Sylvia said good-bye, anxious to see now what Titus had written.

The very second her cousin left the house, Sylvia dashed upstairs and closed her bedroom door. Sitting on her bed, she opened the envelope and held up the note.

Dear Sylvia,

How are you? It's been a while since we talked, but I'm not writing about any of that.

I'll get to the point. I would really like to see you, Sylvie. We need to discuss a few things. I will drop by tonight, after evening prayers. If that works, I'll meet you outside.

With love,
Titus

Sylvia put the letter down, frowning. *What's so urgent?*

With a sigh, she stood up and placed the letter on her dresser. Then, moving to the window, she wondered if Ernie was still feeling better after his dousing and rest in the shade.

She couldn't see him outside anywhere just now, but there was a young *Englischer* couple getting out of their car and walking toward the shop. The woman was laughing and looked ever so cheerful as she glanced around her.

Gut, Sylvia thought, *since Dat's missing out on sales at market today . . . and lost a lot of sales during the* Bann, *too*. In fact, some folk were still avoiding him even now.

Moving to the dresser mirror, she straightened her white head covering and looked forward to seeing Titus after nightfall.

CHAPTER
Eight

*T*hough Sylvia appreciated it, she declined Adeline's offer to sweep the porch and walkway that afternoon.

"That's Sylvie's job," Mamma said as she rinsed some of the fresh sweet corn the boys had brought in earlier.

"Okay, well, when you're done, would you like to go with me to the Tanger Outlet?" Adeline asked Sylvia. "I could use some help finding it."

Without thinking, Sylvia replied, "Oh, ya just go to Route 30 and head west. You'll see the stores on the left."

Adeline looked surprised . . . and a little disappointed.

Over at the sink, Mamma spoke up. "Sylvie, you can go with Adeline, dear."

Feeling she was being treated like a child, Sylvia wanted to point out that her baking responsibilities were not finished, and she had promised to help Mamma pick blueberries out back, as well.

But Adeline looked so crestfallen that Sylvia nodded. "All right, I'll go."

"When is the best time for you?"

"You can head out now, if ya like," Mamma answered. "I'll gladly tend to your pie baking and everything else, Sylvie. You girls go an' have a nice time together."

Adeline brightened. "Let's do this!"

A sense of unease nibbled at the edges of her mind, but Sylvia was determined to be pleasant. "It's been a while since I've been in a fast car," she said.

"Well, trust me, you'll *love* mine," Adeline promised. She grinned at Rhoda, who smiled back.

Oh goodness, Sylvia thought. *Mamma's all for it!*

From Sylvia's perspective in the passenger seat, it almost seemed like Adeline was starved for company. As they zipped through Bird-in-Hand and then traveled south to Route 30, Adeline was all talk, talk, talk, and then some. Sylvia learned not only that she needed extra clothing for the next few days but that she also craved a blast of air conditioning. "I almost wish I could sleep with my car running, just to get cooled off."

Sylvia hardly knew how to reply without smiling.

"Don't *you* ever need a break from the heat?" Adeline asked. "How can you be comfortable in those heavy clothes?"

"It depends on what I'm doin'. But really, I'm used to it."

Her hands on the steering wheel, Adeline shook her head back and forth, as if she could not begin to comprehend living this way.

"Summer doesn't last all year, ya know," Sylvia reminded her with a grin.

Adeline glanced at her. "You must be ready to party when fall comes."

Party? Sylvia wasn't sure what Adeline meant. "We rejoice over the harvest, *jah.*"

"Not for the cooler weather?"

"We're thankful for whatever weather the Lord brings our way," Sylvia said. "We don't complain that it's too hot or too cold."

Adeline nodded her head. "So you never wish you could put on a pair of shorts or a swimsuit and go swimming somewhere?"

"Oh, there's a swimmin' hole, all right."

"Really?" Adeline perked up. "Close by?"

"Just out behind Mamma's parents' barn, not too far from us. We ice-skate there, too, in the wintertime."

"Maybe I should also buy a swimsuit while I'm here," Adeline said.

Sylvia tried not to smile too much. "Sure."

Adeline looked happier than Sylvia had seen her. "No bikinis allowed, I assume."

Sylvia was quick to shake her head. "We strive to be modest."

"May I ask what your swimsuit looks like? Where do you shop?"

"Actually, I made it. Lots of the womenfolk do. It looks like a modest one-piece, but there's a skirt around the bottom edge."

Adeline was quiet for a moment. "Do the boys and your dad swim, too?"

"Of course. They wear old cutoff trousers."

Adeline laughed. "Well, I wasn't going to ask, but okay."

They slowed at the coming stoplight, and Adeline gasped. "Oh perfect! There's a convenience store. I left my phone charger at home, so I need to stop and get a new one. People might start worrying if they don't hear from me soon."

"You could use the phone shanty out in my uncle's cornfield."

"To *call* them?" Adeline shook her head. "It's much quicker to text. And to be honest, I'm not even sure I know their numbers, not off the top of my head."

Sylvia frowned a little, not sure why having a phone was so important if you couldn't actually talk to someone on it.

Adeline made the turn into the parking lot and stopped the car. She asked Sylvia if she wanted a cold soda or anything.

"*Denki*, I'm fine. I can wait out here."

"Are you sure? I could get you an iced tea or lemonade, if you'd prefer."

Sylvia smiled and declined again.

"Okay, if you're sure. I'll leave the car running so you don't die of heat." Adeline got out of the car and hurried up the walkway and into the store, her useless phone in hand.

Earnest caught himself whistling as he walked toward the house to tell Rhoda he'd sold two clocks. "And I didn't even have to go to market," he said, waiting for her to pour some ice-cold lemonade.

"God's kindness is shinin' down on us," Rhoda said. "He knows how we need to get your inventory moving again."

Stepping closer, Earnest smiled at her. "I don't want you worrying about that, love." He reached for her, and she let him embrace her. It was the first time they'd done so since he'd shared about his former marriage. But fearful he'd spoil the moment, he didn't say more.

"You were so nice to Adeline," Rhoda said, "takin' an

interest in her stitching an' all. Usually such things bore you silly." She reached for his lemonade and gave it to him.

He chuckled and drank some of the cold drink before saying, "The more I get to know her, the more curious I am about her."

"I'm not surprised." Rhoda put the pitcher of lemonade back into the fridge. "And she's curious 'bout you, too."

He gave her a look. "How so?"

"Oh, several times I've caught her starin' at you when you're talking to me or to one of the children." She paused and frowned. "But I can't help noticin' the sorrow in her eyes, too."

Earnest had noticed, as well. "It's been only five months since the loss of her mother—a short time to grieve such a deep loss. No matter how sickly or old they are, you never get over the loss of a parent."

"*Jah*, you know that, too," Rhoda said kindly. And for a moment, it looked like she had more to say.

"How are you doing, dear? I mean, with Adeline here?" He had to ask, now that Adeline appeared to be staying for a while longer.

"Well, she's your flesh and blood, Earnest. How are *you* doin'?"

Earnest scratched his head and glanced toward the window. "I guess we're both just finding our way."

"With the Lord's help."

He assumed something like that would be her response. "It's rather interesting that Sylvia wanted to go shopping with Adeline."

Rhoda grimaced. "That was the last thing Sylvia wanted to do."

"Why'd she go, then?"

Rhoda raised her eyebrows. "Because I nudged her—thought it might help them break the ice."

"Does it need to be broken?" Earnest asked, surprised Rhoda was so eager to encourage a relationship.

"It's inches thick," Rhoda said with a smile. "And smack-dab in the middle of Antarctica."

Earnest chuckled. "But they're kin . . . sisters—"

"And light-years apart," she murmured.

Earnest sighed.

"But give it time. Sylvia tends to be slow in warmin' up to new people," Rhoda said, turning to go to the pantry, where he could see her surveying the many jars of canned goods.

"Looks like you're busy, dear," he said. "I'll head back to work. There's plenty to do." He made his way out the back door, still relishing the tender embrace.

On the short walk over to his shop, he could only imagine the conversation Sylvia and Adeline were having right now. He had no concern that Adeline would try to influence Sylvia toward the world, but it made him uneasy knowing that Rhoda was so dead set on throwing the two of them together.

Sylvia was actually glad to see Adeline finally exit the convenience store. And when Adeline got into the car, she was all abuzz about finding a six-pack of sparkling Perrier. "My favorite," she said, placing it on the floor behind the driver's seat. "I also got to talking to the clerk inside about the Amish crafts they sell. I'm sorry for keeping you waiting." She went on to say that she wanted to take a minute now to text her family and fiancé, if it was all right with Sylvia.

"I'll give ya some time alone," Sylvia said while Adeline unwrapped a skinny white cord and plugged it into a socket in the car, then connected it to her phone.

"Why not go inside the store and get even cooler?" Adeline suggested.

"Okay," Sylvia said, opening her door, glad to give Adeline time to connect with her loved ones.

After fifteen minutes or so, Sylvia looked out the door from inside the convenience shop and could see that Adeline was now talking on her phone. *And here I thought she didn't use it to actually talk. . . .*

Looking around the store again, she spotted some magazines and picked up one that featured waterfront properties all over the world. *What would it be like to live near the ocean?* she wondered, staring at a picture of a location in faraway Tahiti, wherever that was. She didn't have any clue, although back when she was in school, she had learned most of the countries of the world. But Tahiti sure had a nice look to it.

She stared at the picture but didn't want to purchase the magazine, appealing as it was, and felt guilty looking at any more pages. So Sylvia returned it to the rack.

Then, spying some salted nuts in small bags, she decided to buy those to share with Adeline, who surely was finished with her call by now. *I'll purchase this and head out*, she thought, aware of the frigid temperature in the store. *I'm not used to air conditioning*, she thought with a little shiver.

When Sylvia left the store, she noticed Adeline getting out of the car, laughing as she spotted Sylvia. "I was coming to get you," she said. "I'm all caught up with my family . . . and Brendon, too."

They went back to the car, and Adeline started the ignition again with her magical little remote key. "Brendon surprised me," Adeline said. "I thought he would think I was crazy to stay in an Amish community, but he was really very interested."

"I wonder why," Sylvia said, opening the bag of salted nuts and offering some to Adeline.

"He didn't say, but I'm sure we'll talk more about it later." She reached into the bag, took two almonds, and popped them into her mouth. "Thanks . . . I love salty things."

"So you're engaged to be married," Sylvia said, making small talk.

"I am. We're planning a late May wedding, after my graduation."

Sylvia nodded. "I'm engaged, too," she said, letting it slip. "In fact, we were at my fiancé's parents' farm when ya bought the raw honey and treats for Mamma."

"Well, congratulations!" Adeline looked delighted. "But where's your engagement ring?"

"Oh . . . we don't wear jewelry."

"None at all?" Adeline looked shocked and glanced at the large diamond on her own left hand. Then she seemed to catch herself. "I mean . . ."

"It's all right . . . ya didn't know." Sylvia explained that engaged Amish couples made verbal promises to wed. "Our word is the only promise we need."

Adeline immediately fell silent, and if Sylvia wasn't mistaken, it looked like she was trying to conceal the sparkling ring on her hand.

"The longer you're in Hickory Hollow, the sooner you'll understand that our life is different from what's on the outside," Sylvia added, wishing she hadn't let Mamma push her out the door with Adeline. What *was* she doing riding to the outlet with a fancy young woman, anyway? *We may have a father in common, but almost nothing else.* . . .

CHAPTER

Nine

*A*fter supper, Sylvia went with Ernie and her younger brothers to pick the remaining sweet corn. Because of Ernie's scare earlier, Dat had suggested they work now, as the sun slipped lower in the sky.

Sylvia was eager to help, weary of sitting on the porch with Adeline, where Mamma kept asking one question after another, trying to include Sylvia, too, but she was too preoccupied with Titus's letter and impending visit to participate. Meanwhile, Dat had gone to help Mamma's parents with some repairs, though Sylvia suspected he'd mostly gone to tell them about Adeline.

"I heard ya went shoppin' with Adeline," Ernie said as they picked the ears from the stalks.

"*She* shopped. I just tagged along." Sylvia really didn't want to talk about it. She had merely been a sounding board in the dressing room for Adeline, who had tried on more than a dozen outfits before deciding on two pairs of cropped pants, three new tops, and a skirt and short-sleeved blouse. The young woman had been "*terribly challenged*," as she'd put it, to find a one-piece bathing suit. The way she'd said it led Sylvia to believe she thought of a one-piece as dull or unstylish.

"I thought you'd be with Mamma, enjoying the breeze on the porch," Adam said, working so hard the sweat rolled off him.

"She's busy with Adeline."

"Well, I'm glad you're out here, helpin' us," Tommy piped up. "We'll get done quicker. Then I can go in an' practice memorizin' *Das Loblied* with Ernie."

"*Gut*. Then once ya turn nine, you can walk into church by yourself with the rest of us boys," Calvin reminded him.

Sylvia remembered memorizing, with Dat's help, the twenty-eight-line hymn from the old *Ausbund* hymnal. While the choice of the first hymn they sang at Preaching varied, the second one was always the same and had remained so for generations. "The Praise Song" was something of an anthem for the People, and learning it was an important milestone for every child. "How far are ya on it?" she asked Tommy.

"I know five lines so far," Tommy replied, reaching high for an ear of corn.

"So just twenty-three to go," Calvin said from where he stood in the row of corn behind Tommy and Sylvia.

"That's nothin' to sneeze at," Sylvia said, hoping to encourage her little brother. "*Gut* for you!"

"How long did it take Dat to learn it?" Tommy asked with a glance at her.

Calvin chuckled. "A mighty long time, Dat said when he was helpin' me memorize it."

"Then I don't feel so bad," Tommy replied, smiling.

Sylvia agreed. "You'll have it memorized soon enough.

And once ya do, you'll never forget it." She paused. "Just think, when we're singing that hymn here in Hickory Hollow, many, many other Amish are singin' it in their Houses of Worship, too."

Twilight had come, and the blazing heat was replaced by cooling air and the distant rumble of thunder. Adeline could only hope that rain was in the forecast, and she checked her weather app to look at the radar. *Yay!*—an eighty percent chance of precipitation within the next half hour.

After her hours of practice, she felt a little more encouraged about her sewing efforts. Even Earnest had noticed her stitches were straighter than this morning's. *My fingers are sorer, too,* she thought, unaccustomed to such fine handwork.

Sitting in the guestroom, Adeline laid out her new outfits, still wishing she could have invested in normal summer clothes like shorts instead of the cropped pants she'd felt obliged to buy, as well as a flowing skirt that fell to her knees. The latter was in case she stayed around for what Sylvia called Preaching service, a week from tomorrow. Rhoda had shared that the Amish community gathered for house church every other week, which meant tomorrow's "Lord's Day" was not a churchgoing day, but a day set aside for visiting relatives and reflection.

So many unusual customs, she thought.

Earlier, Adeline had made a gaffe, though she hadn't known it at the time. She had mentioned to Rhoda that she was looking forward to doing more sewing tomorrow, but Rhoda told her that sewing was not permitted on Sundays, church or not. The Millers planned to read the Bible, write letters, take walks, pray, and go for a ride to visit relatives . . . the only acceptable options for activities.

It was too early to get ready for bed, so Adeline texted her brother for a few minutes. Liam had been out surfing all day and said his tan could beat up hers, adding, as he often did, a string of silly emojis.

We'll see about that, she responded.

You're nowhere near the beach. Liam inserted a winking emoji. *A serious disadvantage!*

True. And what I wouldn't give to be there to get cooled off. Try to imagine sleeping in a house without AC!

No way! he wrote. *Just skip out.*

Her brother had a point, but she wasn't ready to leave . . . not just yet, assuming the Millers' invitation to stay was good.

Later, while texting Brendon, she heard what sounded like a carriage rattle into the driveway and stop. The windmill was moaning and creaking in the wind now, and the summery scent of the fragrant pastureland drifted in through her open window. She wouldn't have bothered to look out at that precise moment, but she heard a clicking sound outside above her and crept over to peek beneath the green shade, rolled only partway down so as not to block the breeze.

Surprised, she saw someone in black pants not far from her window, tossing a pebble up. "Won't ya come down, Sylvie?" a man's voice called up to Sylvia's window.

Sylvia's small voice floated down. "I thought you were comin' earlier, Titus."

"I got tied up—came as soon as I could," the young man answered, sounding apologetic.

"Okay then . . . I'll meet ya in the barn in a jiffy," Sylvia told him, and Adeline heard the upstairs window slide closed.

How odd, Adeline thought, wondering why Sylvia's fiancé hadn't just gone to the back door and knocked like a typical visitor.

Sylvia quickly smoothed her hair and put her *Kapp* back on, anxious to see Titus, still troubled by his apparent urgency. *What can be so important?*

She glanced in the mirror, wanting to look nice. *We haven't been alone with each other in quite a while. . . .*

Then, stepping out of her room, she made her way down the hall. Just as she was turning toward the staircase, Mamma peeked her head out of her bedroom. "You goin' out?"

"*Jah*, Titus is here."

"Well, have a nice time," Mamma said. "Maybe take along an umbrella, though. Dat says a storm's comin'."

"Oh, we won't be out riding." Sylvia headed down the stairs, thinking it kind of Mamma to wish her well.

At the bottom, she noticed Adeline's door opening, and when she appeared, she looked concerned. "I heard a guy outside talking to you," Adeline said with a tilt of her head.

"*Jah*, my fiancé, Titus Kauffman."

Adeline nodded slowly, her eyes meeting Sylvia's. "Are you seeing each other secretly? Why didn't he just come to the door?"

Sylvia had to smile. "It's tradition for an Amish fella to toss pebbles at his girl's window to get her attention. Titus prob'ly doesn't need to do that since we're engaged, but so far only our parents and friends know." She quickly explained that the rest of the community would officially learn the news two weeks before their November wedding day. "That's when my father will announce it at the end of the Preaching service, to invite everyone."

"I guess it could be nice to know exactly when and how to tell people," Adeline said, as though trying to understand. "Well, I should let you go." She wiggled her fingers in a wave.

As Sylvia hurried through the kitchen and into the hallway leading to the back door, it occurred to her that Adeline could sometimes be rather nosy.

Lightning flickered all around them as Sylvia ran with Titus to the shelter of the barn. The temperature was dropping quickly, and Sylvia knew that Adeline would be relieved at the cooler weather. One lightning strike seemed to take direct aim as they worked together to slide open the heavy barn door, and once safely inside, Titus quickly pulled it shut.

Rain began to pelt the barn roof as they climbed the ladder to the hayloft, still warm from the day and just light enough for Sylvia to see Titus's face. The sweet, subtle scent of hay filled the area as they each found a seat on a square bale of hay.

"This rain's a blessing," Titus said as he removed his straw hat and shook it off, even though no moisture had fallen on them. His light brown hair looked freshly shampooed.

"*Jah*, farmers will be thankful," she said, wondering more than ever why he had wanted to see her on such short notice.

Titus's hazel eyes turned serious now. "I hope ya know how much I've missed seein' you, Sylvie."

She smiled. "I missed ya, too."

He reached for her hand. "Ain't so *gut* for us to be apart too long, *jah*?" he said, looking ever so thoughtful.

She nodded, glad to have this time with him in the privacy

of the hayloft, where the wonderful smell of rain came in the open window.

Titus placed his straw hat between his knees. "As ya know, I saw you this mornin' with the fancy young woman who's visiting here. My father says she's your half sister."

Sylvia tensed and let go of his hand.

He cleared his throat. "I had no idea 'bout her. Just wonderin' what this means. . . . Are there more surprises to come, Sylvie?"

She sighed. "I know what ya mean, but none of us knew 'bout Adeline, let alone expected her to show up here," she said right out. "I'm doin' my best to show her kindness, considerin'. She had no idea what she would find when she came searching for her father."

For several seconds, Titus looked at her as though uncertain what to say. Then he went on, "I'm just concerned, coming so soon after your father's shunning and all."

So this is why he came.

A frown flickered across his brow. "You surely understand what I'm getting at."

"*Jah*, you're worried how all this looks to others. . . ."

He suggested that her acquaintance with Adeline could become close as time went by, exposing Sylvia to a worldly perspective that he and his family wouldn't be comfortable with.

Ach, Sylvia thought. *He's already done a lot of thinking.* Clenching her jaw, she said, "Just to be clear, I'm not close to Adeline. And she doesn't mean to stir things up—she's only here to get acquainted with Dat." She paused. "Can ya think how you'd feel if you hadn't known your father, and then suddenly, you found out who he was? Wouldn't you want to get to know him, to spend time with him?" It stunned her that she was defending Adeline and the young woman's time there.

Titus glanced down at his hat. "I hear what you're sayin', but it doesn't change the fact that she's an *Englischer*. Even my Mamm was worried."

Sylvie could hear the horses stomping in their stalls in the adjoining stable, one of them neighing loudly. She recalled how Titus's mother, Eva, had made earlier demands on where she and Titus were going to stay the first weeks after the wedding and whatnot. And Sylvia suspected that Titus's parents might be behind some of what Titus was saying just now.

Titus's eyes searched hers. "I'm caught between wanting to go ahead with our plans to marry and my concerns for what might come next. After all, I have to consider my family, too, what with Dat bein' an ordained minister. But it's an awful spot to be in."

At the mention of his father, Sylvia remembered the times she had been so impressed by Preacher Kauffman and his sermons—not necessarily idolizing him, but always looking up to him. If what she suspected was true, she no longer knew how to think of him, or of vivacious Eva, who had been so welcoming to Sylvia on the day Titus proposed beside the beautiful pond on their property. *The most perfect day . . .*

In that moment, Sylvia wanted Titus to long for *her* and to stand by what he'd lovingly declared months ago—that nothing would ever come between them. Most of all, she wanted him to trust her. But sadly, it was obvious he was waffling about marriage because he sought to protect his own image as a preacher's son.

The rain was beginning to slow some, and Sylvia felt no need to talk this to death tonight. "I'd best be getting back to the house," she said softly, wanting some time alone to process all of this.

Titus stood up, too, still clutching his hat like a buffer between them. "I care 'bout ya, Sylvie, I do."

He leaned in awkwardly, as if to kiss her cheek. But not wanting him to reach for her and hold her now, she turned to climb down the haymow ladder and ran through the gentle rain to the house.

CHAPTER

Ten

*A*deline could hear bare feet padding through the sitting room and assumed it was Sylvia. While curious, she did not open her door to try to engage her in conversation. *What a strange way to date,* Adeline thought, turning over in bed, still thinking of the quaint way Sylvia's fiancé had gotten her attention.

It had been difficult to relax tonight. Sylvia and Titus's relationship, and all the unfamiliar traditions that surrounded it, reminded her yet again of how foreign this world was from her own.

She had texted a while with Brendon, who was full of questions about the Amish. There was much to learn and understand, she'd told him, both good and bad. *I don't know how my father made the transition!*

Adeline closed her eyes and thought tenderly of her mother. One of the last, most vivid memories she had was of sitting on her hospital bed as Adeline squeezed her mother's weak hand, careful not to disturb the IV and oxygen tube.

They had been talking quietly about things that were important to Mom, things she needed to tell Adeline related to
faith, making an attempt to put into words what she had
only recently come to believe. *"I've started keeping a journal,"*
she told Adeline that day. *"Sometimes, I jot down random
thoughts, and other days, I admit my stupidity. But I want you
to wait to read it till after I'm gone. And please, try to read with
an open heart. . . ."*

At the time, Adeline had been uncomfortable with the
direction of the conversation, but seeing how very frail her
mother was, Adeline hadn't questioned her. It still struck her
as ridiculous for her mother to apply the word *stupidity* to someone like herself. Now and then, when this particular memory
came to mind, Adeline would wonder when—or if—she would
ever feel ready to see what Mom had written.

She sighed as tears slipped down her face and onto the
pillow.

"I think I just heard someone come upstairs," Earnest said
as he and Rhoda sat in their chairs near the open bedroom
windows. Even though the earlier downpour had been heavy,
the wind was blowing from the opposite direction, so Earnest
left the windows open to admit the cooler air. "Do you think
it could be Sylvia?"

"*Jah.*" Rhoda glanced up from her devotional. "Maybe I'll
go an' check on her."

Earnest agreed. He remained there, recalling once more
how wonderful it had felt to embrace his wife earlier and wondering if they were getting back what they had lost. Cautious
not to assume anything, he decided to let Rhoda make the
next move.

He returned to reading his paper, hoping all was well between Sylvia and Titus. For the longest time, he'd worried that word of his first marriage—and his decision to keep it secret—might cause problems for her with Titus and his prominent family. *And now here we are. . . .*

When Rhoda returned, she came over and dropped into her chair with a sigh. "I wondered if this might happen," she said. "Adeline's comin' has caused a ruckus with Titus."

"Sylvia said that?"

Rhoda nodded. "Sylvia argued that Adeline doesn't mean to cause a stir or pose a threat. It's not as if the poor girl's to blame."

Earnest found himself agreeing wholeheartedly. *If anyone's at fault, it's me,* he thought.

"Sylvia's understandably upset at his reaction."

"Our girl has a *gut* head on her shoulders."

They talked more about this, but after a time, Rhoda asked, "By the way, how did my parents take the news about Adeline?"

Earnest frowned. "As I suspected, they'd already heard some rumblings yet didn't believe it was anything but hearsay. So I came right out and told them how shocking it's been for me to learn that I have another child. I didn't hold anything back."

"It's best they heard it directly from you."

He nodded and they returned to reading, not saying anything more on the topic.

As Earnest was closing his book, Rhoda said quietly, "All of us are really just tryin' to adjust."

He smiled at his wife, pretty in her soft pink nightgown and matching duster. "You, dear, are doing better than the rest of us."

She shrugged her small shoulders. "Well, it's not as easy as you may think."

"*Jah?*"

Frowning slightly, she said, "I've tried to put myself in her shoes and honor the Golden Rule." She turned to look at him. "And don't sell yourself short, Earnest. I've noticed the kind attention you've given to the dear girl. It's just what she needs."

"She needs *all* of us. We're her family," he said, reaching for Rhoda's hand.

"I doubt Adeline realizes that yet."

"True."

When they retired for the night, Rhoda asked, "Do ya think Titus and Sylvia's relationship will survive?"

"I daresay we're seeing that fella's true colors. Much as I hate to say it, I wonder if she would be better off without him." He hoped he wasn't letting his temper get the best of him.

"We'll just leave it with the Lord. What else can we do?"

Earnest didn't reply, thinking there were things that *could* be done. For one, he could ride over and talk with Amos Kauffman, help him understand that Adeline had nothing to do with Sylvia and Titus's relationship.

Sitting in bed in her summer nightgown, Sylvia understood why Adeline had complained nearly all day. Despite the falling temperature outside, the heat trapped in the house had risen to the upstairs, and for the first time since last August's dog days, Sylvia coveted a fan. *Or even air conditioning,* she thought, remembering how she had actually shivered at the convenience store.

She went to the dresser drawer for Titus's letter, picked it up, and reread it slowly yet again. Their conversation in the haymow had been distressing. Briefly, she thought of praying about it, but then again, what was the point? Her many prayers hadn't seemed to make a bit of a difference when it came to Dat's shunning earlier that summer. *Why would things be any different now?*

CHAPTER

Eleven

The next day, a no-Preaching Sunday, Sylvia got up earlier than anyone else except Dat to shower and dress. She wanted to help make breakfast, enjoying having Mamma to herself in the kitchen early in the morning.

Together, she and her mother moved about the airy space, each knowing what to do without saying much. Mamma gathered ingredients to make buttermilk pancakes while Sylvia got the blackberry jam out of the pantry and made toast, expecting Adeline to wander in at any moment. *She won't be around forever,* thought Sylvia. *Then things will return to normal.*

It was impossible to glance out the window toward the barn without nagging thoughts of last night's meeting with Titus. Unsettled feelings continued to brew within her.

"Good morning," Adeline announced when she entered the kitchen wearing her new cropped pants and the breezy sleeveless yellow top.

"*Guder Mariye* to you, too," Mamma replied with a smile. "You look like a sunbeam, ever so bright."

90

Adeline dipped her head before looking over at Sylvia. "How are *you*, Sylvie?"

Sylvie? she thought, surprised.

"I hope you don't mind if I call you that," Adeline said quickly. "I heard your brothers refer to you that way yesterday."

Sylvia forced a smile. "It's okay," she said, catching Mamma's eye. Her expression indicated, *"Be nice."*

Adeline, who seemed to have read the temperature in the room, was already backtracking. "I'm sorry, I don't mean to—"

"No, really . . . it's fine." Sylvia broadened her smile. "I like the nickname."

"I do, too," Adeline said a bit sheepishly.

"So do I," Mamma added brightly, mixing the pancake batter by hand. "By the way, Sylvie, Dat will be stayin' home with Adeline 'stead of goin' visiting," she said. "So if you'd like to stay, too, you may. Your brothers and I will go an' see my parents and stay for the noon meal." Mamma also mentioned taking along the two blueberry pies she'd baked yesterday while Sylvia and Adeline had gone shopping.

Dat surely wants more time with Adeline, Sylvia thought, figuring she would be in the way here. "*Nee*, I'll go with ya to visit *Dawdi* and *Mammi*," she said.

Mamma looked her way. "Well then, you and your brothers can go together," she said. "And I'll stay home."

Now Sylvia felt bad about Mamma not getting to see her parents, something she so looked forward to, but Sylvia wasn't going to argue in front of Adeline.

For her own part, she also hoped to visit Cousin Alma that afternoon. *I'll see how long we're at Dawdi and Mammi's,* she mused, assuming Dat had told them yesterday about

Adeline. *Surely . . . otherwise Mamma wouldn't send us kids over there alone.*

Though Adeline had decided not to bring it up, she wanted to charge her phone in the car after breakfast and reach out to Brendon. She missed him and wanted to follow up on their conversation yesterday, when he had shown surprising interest in her sudden immersion into Amish culture. *Eager for more details*, she thought, glancing at Sylvia while the two of them set the table. He had also asked a series of questions about their beliefs, which was strange, considering his general indifference to religion.

She considered the peculiar interaction between Rhoda and Sylvia earlier, when Rhoda had suggested Sylvia stay home while Rhoda and the boys went to visit the grandparents. But Sylvia had immediately shot it down. *Is she upset with me?* Adeline wondered, realizing that she *had* barged into their lives. *Without an ounce of warning.* And it wasn't as if she found it easy to fit in around here.

The strangest thought occurred to her: *Is Sylvia threatened by me?*

The idea was laughable, and Adeline dismissed it as absurd as she poured orange juice into eight small glasses while Sylvia poured coffee for her parents and herself. Adeline had never enjoyed the taste of coffee, having been raised to drink herbal or green teas—hot or cold. Mom thought it was far healthier . . . better for the brain. *"Drink it at breakfast and lunch,"* Adeline remembered her saying.

Glancing at Sylvia, she noticed dark circles under her eyes and decided it must have been a restless night for her. *She's not quite herself*, Adeline thought, wondering if Sylvia and her mother were close enough for heart-to-heart talks. Rhoda certainly seemed like someone who could be trusted.

When at last the family sat down to eat, Adeline's gaze took in everyone there, all of them dressed in their Sunday best. Earnest and his wife and kids were the proverbial picture of a happy family, though a decidedly old-fashioned one. *And devout,* she thought as they bowed their heads simultaneously for the mealtime blessing.

While the prayer was taking place—today it seemed extra long—she mentally tallied up the things she wanted to tell Brendon the next time they were in touch. If only she dared to send him a photo of Earnest and his family . . . but she was reluctant to do that without their permission, and she certainly would not inquire.

Finally, the blessing was finished, although she still didn't know exactly how that was determined. *Why doesn't Earnest just pray aloud?* This and other questions filtered through her mind as she took a single pancake from the platter, noticing that each of the boys had taken at least two larger ones, including little Tommy.

Ernie and Adam were more talkative at this meal, and Adeline assumed they were more comfortable with her presence. There was the usual table talk between Earnest and Rhoda, niceties from Earnest about how delicious everything tasted, and Rhoda smiling in response and asking him about things around his clock shop.

Sylvia, however, made only inconsequential small talk—a comment about last night's rain and all the lightning. *She hasn't mentioned meeting her fiancé after dark,* Adeline thought, guessing there was a reason. Perhaps she didn't want her personal business to become everyone else's business, too.

Suddenly, Ernie spoke up. "Onkel Curtis told me recently that courting carriages weren't always open back in the old days."

Earnest gave his son an amused look, as if he sensed he was trying to shift the conversation to something he thought might interest Adeline. "That's what I've heard, too. It wasn't till the late 1800s that people really took to the open carriages."

Ernie poured more maple syrup onto his pancake-filled plate. "Onkel Curtis also said that, back in those days, Amish weren't allowed to hitch up on Sundays, so people had to walk to Preachin', no matter how far away they lived."

Earnest's eyes widened. "Is that so?"

"*Jah.*" Ernie grinned as though he was proud of himself for knowing something his father did not.

"Where'd Curtis hear this?" Earnest glanced at Rhoda, a hint of a twinkle in his eye.

"His Dawdi Mast told him, and Aendi Hannah asked Ella Mae, the old Wise Woman, to confirm it." Ernie took a large bite of pancake, then forked up a bit of sausage, as well.

Adeline, meanwhile, was quite entertained, wondering why Ernie was so interested in courting buggies at his young age. And she wondered, too, who among the women of this area had earned the remarkable title of Wise Woman.

I really should be keeping a journal of this visit, she thought.

Even though she rarely ever helped with hitching up on a Sunday, Sylvia was thankful that Ernie and Adam managed the task without her assistance. Ernie did surprise her, though, by getting into the driver's seat on the right side of the buggy and reaching for the driving lines, and Adam climbed in beside him.

Sylvia didn't mind sitting in the second bench seat with Calvin and Tommy, glad for some time with her brothers. After the heavy rains last night, the air had a freshness to it, and she breathed in deeply.

It wasn't long before Calvin asked why Dat and Mamma had wanted to spend time alone with Adeline today.

"Maybe Dat has somethin' on his mind to discuss with her," Ernie said with a glance over his shoulder.

"Like what?" Tommy asked, looking up at Sylvia from where he was squished between her and Calvin.

"Maybe to ask her not to dress so fancy round us kids," Adam suggested.

Sylvia doubted that. When *Englischers* visited, they weren't expected to dress Plain. As she listened to her brothers speculate aloud as to why they might have been sent to visit their grandparents, Sylvia did find it a little odd that Mamma had expected Dat to stay home with Adeline, although she didn't admit it out loud. After all, wouldn't Dat want to introduce his firstborn to his in-laws? Or was he uncomfortable around them, perhaps even embarrassed, coming off his recent shunning?

Something our family must never go through again, she thought, realizing just then how very concerned Titus and his family must be about Adeline.

CHAPTER
Twelve

$\mathcal{E}$arnest was looking forward to showing Adeline his beautiful spread—the garden and berry patch out back, the expansive meadow, and the hayfield. It was his idea to include Rhoda, as well, and he shared with Adeline how he'd stumbled upon this fantastic land back twenty years ago, when he'd purchased it from Isaac Smucker, a local clockmaker. "Isaac's great-uncle built the farmhouse where we now live," he noted.

Adeline seemed fascinated, and when they wandered toward the family's garden, she commented on the maze that the pumpkin plants had made as they wound their way into the cherry tomatoes and squash vines. Like a child seeing this for the first time, she was full of questions about what they grew and how, and she asked why this garden was the responsibility of Rhoda and the children.

"It's just the way things are here," he said, understanding why she would ask. He'd had similar questions upon his arrival in Hickory Hollow.

"An Amishwoman's domain is mostly the house," Rhoda

said as she walked on the other side of Earnest. "Besides that, we're expected to care for the children, of course, and plant and cultivate the vegetable garden, mow the grass, and keep the potting shed tidy."

"So the men do the farm work?" Adeline asked.

"*Jah*, and in my case, make and repair clocks." Earnest glanced at Adeline to his left, thankful the weather had turned in the night. It was an ideal day to be outdoors, although by high noon it would likely be scorching again.

Just then, he spotted Andy Zook coming their way across the pasture, carrying a paper sack and looking spiffy in his black Sunday frock coat and trousers. His exceptionally blond bangs shone in the sunlight beneath his best straw hat with its black band.

"Hullo, Andy," Earnest called to the grandson of his deceased friend, Preacher Mahlon Zook. "*Wie geht's?*"

"Oh, real *gut*. Nice to see yous!" Andy was swinging his long arms like he was in a hurry.

"Where are you headed?" Earnest asked.

Andy slowed his stride as he neared. "On my way home. Was just over visiting Mammi Zook." He held up his sack, a grin on his face. "She makes the best homemade candy."

"How's your Mammi doin' today?" Rhoda asked, glancing at Earnest as if waiting for him to introduce Adeline.

"She seems fine, but I doubt she'd let on if she wasn't," Andy replied.

Rhoda nodded. "She just goes and goes, doesn't she? It's the Lord's strength in her, I daresay."

Andy smiled now at Adeline and opened the sack to offer each of them a piece of candy.

"*Ach*, sorry—I should've introduced my daughter," Earnest

said, taking one and explaining quickly that Adeline was visiting from Georgia.

"That's a long way from here," Andy said as he reached to shake her hand. "*Willkumm* to Amish country." He seemed unruffled by her fancy appearance and the fact that Earnest had introduced her as his daughter. Word had obviously gotten around about Adeline.

"Adeline, meet Andy Zook," Earnest told her.

Andy pointed in the direction of the cornfield that separated Earnest's house from the Zooks' stately brick farmhouse, where Andy's grandmother resided. "Yous should go over and see Dawdi's Old Garden roses bloomin'. I've never seen 'em so pink or so hardy."

"We'll have to do that," Earnest said.

Andy turned now to Adeline. "Are ya lookin' to become Amish, maybe?" he asked.

"Oh no," she demurred politely.

"Well now, are ya sure?" Andy pressed, still grinning.

Adeline nodded and smiled in return. "I'm quite sure I'm not cut out for it."

Rhoda changed the subject. "Ernie and the boys'll be sorry they missed seein' ya, Andy. They're over visiting my parents."

"Sylvie too?" Andy asked.

"*Jah*," Rhoda said.

"It's a *gut* day to go visiting," he said, tapping his straw hat. "Well, it's *wunnerbaar* to meet ya, Adeline. Enjoy your time with us." Then he was on his way.

Earnest continued walking with Rhoda and Adeline, wondering what Adeline might say, if anything, about Andy.

"Is he always that friendly?" Adeline asked a few moments later.

"No question about that," Earnest said. *Like his Dawdi Mahlon,* he thought as Rhoda nodded her agreement.

"Does Sylvia know him well?" Adeline asked, surprising Earnest.

"All the young folk round here know each other well," Earnest told her, wondering why she'd asked and still smiling at how quickly Adeline had responded to Andy's question about her becoming Amish.

No, she won't be following in my footsteps, he thought drolly. But Adeline's mention of Sylvia reminded Earnest of her plight—and what he had been pondering since last night. Perhaps there *was* a way he might lessen the damage he'd caused to Sylvia and Titus.

Then again, maybe not, he thought. *But I need to try something.*

He turned his attention back to Adeline, and the rest of their walk was taken up with a fresh supply of questions she posed. *She's very curious. Much like I was at her age,* he thought, taking in her latest inquiry. "Why don't you use tractors?"

Most *Englischers* questioned the old-fashioned methods the Amish still used to farm, and Earnest began to explain that one reason for those was that the church ordinance prevented farm equipment with inflatable tires. "If an Amish farmer takes to driving a tractor, it won't be long before a car will look mighty enticing, too. Besides, tractors don't make manure." He chuckled.

"I see your point," she said with a smile. "But you talk so much about farming. I know you have a little farm here, but what about Amishmen who don't want to farm or who maybe can't find land to do so? Can they have other jobs?" asked Adeline.

"Most definitely," Earnest said. "Especially in the past several decades." He told her about traditional trades of blacksmithing and harness making, as well as about the newer cottage industries begun by both men and women. "The People also make a living doing everything from welding and carpentry to selling quilts and building solar panels."

"Don't forget clockmakers' shops," Adeline said with a grin.

"Well, those are few and far between amongst the Plain folk.

"And do Amishwomen have much of a say in how they live their lives?"

This conversation was probing deeper than Earnest had expected. "Rhoda, would you like to answer that?" He slowed his pace, watching their mules graze nearby.

"Guess no one's ever asked me that before," Rhoda said, looking thoughtful. "We're expected to be the 'keepers at home,' just as it describes in the New Testament in Titus, chapter two, verse five . . . and we grow up thinkin' that way. You could say there's some freedom to choose the way we live our lives as faithful wives and nurturing mothers." Rhoda paused a moment. "In my experience, the Amishmen who love their families don't make demands on their wives and children or rule with an iron fist . . . like ya might read in the news sometimes."

Earnest didn't inquire why Adeline had asked this, but he did find Rhoda's answer quite revealing, considering the awful wedge that had come between them after his long-kept secret was disclosed.

"This is all so intriguing," Adeline said as they made the turn at the west end of the meadow to head back toward the house. "I hope you don't mind my prying."

"*Nee*," Earnest said. "If you can't ask us, who can you ask?" Adeline smiled.

"Is there anything else?" Rhoda said, leaning her head forward to glance at Adeline as they walked.

"Well, since you asked . . ."

Oh boy, thought Earnest. *What now?*

"When you pray silently before and after meals, are you all thinking the same thing?" Adeline sounded a bit hesitant.

Earnest explained that young children were taught to say the Lord's Prayer at mealtime and at bedtime, and as they grew older, they memorized passages from the *Christenpflict*, a treasured German prayer book, to pray at meals. "Other Amish families teach children to pray a silent prayer of gratitude of their own."

Adeline matched her stride with Earnest's and Rhoda's. "Your way of life is so unique."

Earnest didn't immediately reply, but when he did, he simply said, "It certainly is."

She looked at him quickly, and a smile spread across her pretty face, reminding him once more of his dear sister.

"The fact that you were able to wholeheartedly throw yourself into Amish life is really something," she went on to say. "You must've had a lot of great support."

Earnest nodded as he remembered those days, especially the caring way Mahlon Zook had taken him under his fatherly wing. "I couldn't have done it without the assistance of established church members." He glanced at his wife, his heart full. "Rhoda was also a big part of helping me learn the ropes here."

The sky was nearly white with the brilliance of the sun as they neared the stable. And seeing the lone driving horse foraging with the mules made Earnest wonder how the visit with Rhoda's parents was going for his other children.

For the noon meal, Sylvia helped her Mammi serve a warmed-up chicken and rice casserole, along with plenty of summer squash and a second side dish of chow chow. The manner in which Mammi moved about the kitchen, from the gas range to the table and to the fridge and back, was so similar to Mamma's own pattern that Sylvia felt at home working alongside her.

She remembered how Mammi once told her that a home was all about the people who filled it. And pouring water into all the tumblers just now, she wondered how her parents were faring with Adeline. Were they truly just getting better acquainted? Or was there something more important that Dat was itching to talk about?

It was still mind-boggling to think how her father must feel, getting used to the fact that he had another child, a grown young woman on the verge of starting her own life with her fiancé.

Adeline may make him a Dawdi one day, she thought, feeling more uncertain than ever where she stood about her own future, with or without Titus.

As they skirted the barnyard, Adeline felt compelled to ask Earnest one final question. "This may sound strange to you, but considering your radical lifestyle change, what's the most profound thing you've learned by being Amish?"

Earnest laughed a little. "That's quite a question, I'll say."

He drew a breath. "Well, I can tell you that most of what I've learned is about living with less." He went on to say that this approach had been a big factor in his settling so well into Amish life. "When all's said and done, it's people, not things, that bring the most joy."

Wondering if he had guessed that one of her passions was shopping—as had been her mom's—Adeline didn't know how to respond. She wasn't a compulsive spender like some of her friends, but she did find great pleasure in shopping for the fun of it, and not necessarily with a list of things she needed.

"Does that make sense?" Earnest asked.

"Sure, I agree that people are important, but I've never really thought about paring back," she replied, thinking of all the material things that brought her joy—the new furniture she'd purchased with some of her inheritance, her fabulous new car, and certain pieces of jewelry she took pleasure in wearing.

"That's okay," he said. "Maybe it's just something you want to think about."

I could never live this hard, regimented life, she thought. *Or embrace all these religious dos and don'ts.*

Thankfully, no one was asking her to.

CHAPTER
Thirteen

*E*arnest didn't waste any time asking Sylvia to talk with
him when she arrived home with her brothers. She followed him into the shop, and he mentioned what he was
planning to do. "Normally I wouldn't stick my nose in, but
I've been thinking that it's time for me to talk with Preacher
Amos," he said, sitting in his work chair, surrounded by the
gentle ticking of many clocks.

"Oh, Dat." Sylvia grimaced where she stood in the doorway.
"I wouldn't want Titus to think I put you up to it."

"I'll make that very clear."

Sylvia frowned and glanced toward the window. "I don't
know how to say this, but Titus has changed so much since
he proposed marriage. It's just odd."

"Well, a lot has happened to our family since then."

She nodded. "But I don't blame anyone for that."

"Not even me?"

"No, Dat—not you, and not Adeline, either." She sighed.
"I told Titus when we talked that Adeline doesn't change

things between him and me." She drew a long breath. "Or at least it shouldn't."

Earnest agreed, nodding his head and wishing she might come in and sit down, the way they used to have their father-daughter talks. "So you don't mind if I test the waters to see what Amos says?"

Sylvia was still for a moment. Then, shrugging, she said, "If ya feel it's the right thing." She looked down at her bare feet as if there was much on her mind, but she turned and headed out the screen door without saying more.

Earnest walked over to the back porch, where Rhoda was sitting and reading her Bible. "I'm goin' to Preacher Amos's right quick," he told her.

"Does Sylvia know?"

He said she did.

"Might be a *gut* idea," Rhoda murmured. "Then again, might not."

"I'll be mindful what I say."

Rhoda looked up at him from the willow rocker. "I'll pray that all goes well. When we ask humbly, the Lord guides His children in the way they should go."

"*Denki*. I shouldn't be gone long." He hurried down the steps and out to the waiting carriage, where he picked up the driving lines. Then, signaling the mare to move forward, he headed for Hickory Lane, realizing once again that Rhoda's prayers were the mainstay of his and their family's life. Without her strong convictions, he would be a floundering mess. Some days, he still felt like he was just going through the motions of his Amishness, although he wouldn't admit that to a soul, not after all he'd gone through during the six-week *Bann*.

Riding along, Earnest took in the beauty of the landscape, where some livestock rested under shade trees or drank from the stream. Mentally, he prepared what he was going to say when he saw Amos, then let his mind wander back years ago, to Amos's ordination as a minister . . . a time when everything seemed to change for the Kauffmans. Almost immediately, there had been a noticeable difference in the family. Amos promptly traded in his carriage for a more conservative one. He also bought a wider-brimmed hat, and soon his wife, Eva, was wearing plainer and longer dresses, as well as more conservative black shoes. Over the weeks that followed, Amos had even grown his beard longer and kept it less trimmed.

The ordination had not only altered Amos's and Eva's outward appearance, but their children had been affected by the divine lot, too. Titus and his younger siblings were being raised in a very strict manner and were expected to set an example of piety. "Forever trying to be more devout than other church members' kids," Earnest murmured as he rode past the ivy-covered farmhouse of David Beiler, son-in-law to the Wise Woman.

He fleetingly wondered what Ella Mae Zook might say about his interfering with Sylvia's engagement. But conferring with the Wise Woman was for womenfolk. *If only Mahlon were still around to ask . . .*

Leaning back in the bench seat, Earnest tried to relax, but he was worried even though the decision to go ahead with the marriage was ultimately up to Sylvia and Titus. When it came down to it, he wanted his daughter to be judged on her own merits, independent of his past mistakes. *I just need to see what Amos thinks about what's going on between our children,* he thought. *Is he a part of the problem, or is it more about Titus?*

But above all, it was the potential of heartbreak for Sylvia that compelled Earnest to pay Amos a visit today.

Sylvia walked up to Cousin Alma's, wanting to get her mind off Dat's visit to Preacher Kauffman and to spend time with Alma. *She will give her honest opinion on what Titus and I discussed last evening,* she thought, knowing her cousin would also be reasonable.

When Sylvia arrived, the Yoders' watchdog was standing out near the road, barking and wagging his long tail. She called to him, clapping her hands, and he bounded over. After she had given his neck a good rub, he followed her up the driveway and toward the back of the house, where he playfully lunged at a grasshopper near the walkway.

The place seemed almost too quiet, and when she knocked on the rear screen door, there was no sign of anyone. She called several times with no answer, so she walked out past the stable and peeked into the small carriage house, finding it empty.

They must be out visiting, she thought as she headed back down the driveway to the road.

An occasional breeze cooled her some as she walked more slowly now, recalling that Ella Mae Zook had once said that a walk was as good for the soul as for the body. And, realizing she hadn't seen the Wise Woman out and about lately, Sylvia wondered if the dear woman was suffering from the heat, much like Ernie yesterday. *Older folk mind muggy summers,* she thought, hoping all was well.

As she strolled along, she noticed dairy cows wandering amongst the trees, seeking shade. She did her best not to fret over what Dat might be saying to Titus's father right about now. Truth be told, Sylvia didn't think Dat would have gone over there if she'd asked him not to. *So why didn't I?*

Recalling her conversation with Titus in the haymow, she felt sure that he had not understood why she cared about trying to put herself in Adeline's shoes. *She only wants to connect with her natural father. Titus cares more about how something looks than the people actually involved,* she thought, dismayed and feeling terribly frustrated.

One gray enclosed horse-drawn carriage after another rolled along past Sylvia as she walked. Most people recognized her and waved or called out a greeting, but there were a few who were undoubtedly from other church districts, traveling home after visiting Hickory Hollow relatives.

A carriage slowed up suddenly, and the horse pulled over onto the shoulder in front of her. She was surprised when Andy Zook's face appeared in the back opening of the buggy. "Need a ride, Sylvia?" he called, smiling broadly as he often did.

"Is there room?" she asked, going to the open door on the driver's side, where Andy's father, Benuel, sat holding the driving lines.

Rebecca, Andy's mother, motioned her around to the other side, and when Sylvia got there, she could see that there really was no space for her to sit other than balanced precariously on the very edge of the front seat. Even so, she climbed in, leaning in and holding on to the seat back for support. "I'm all set," she announced with a laugh. *"Denki!"*

Andy's younger brother, Michael, fifteen, was telling her that their father had gotten stung by a bee when they first got in the buggy.

"Oh, I hope he's not allergic." Sylvia glanced at Benuel and saw the telltale red bump surrounded by a white patch of skin.

"'Tis just an annoyance is all," Benuel told her, and Rebecca nodded and said her husband was a tough one.

Rebecca looked now at Sylvia. "Your face is nearly purple with the heat, dear," she said. "*Gut* thing we came by to give ya a lift."

"I appreciate it." Sylvia was surprised they'd taken time to stop, given how crowded their buggy was.

"Say, how's Ernie doin'?" Michael asked, jumping into the conversation. "Is he lookin' forward to going to Singings next winter?"

Sylvia recalled a conversation she and her brother had had not so long ago, but she wouldn't reveal that Ernie didn't think he was ready to start seeing girls home just yet. "It's a big step," she said.

"Well, Andy's been tellin' me how much he enjoys it," Michael added.

She nodded and thought again of Titus, wondering if he still enjoyed attending, considering they weren't even seeing each other at Singings or on Saturday night dates, like before.

"Are ya goin' next Sunday night?" Andy asked, surprising her.

"I might," she said, conscious that his parents and siblings were overhearing everything.

"Your Aendi and Onkel are hosting it," Andy continued.

Just the way he said it made her think he was about to suggest she go.

"They're planning a big picnic on the grounds before the Singing starts," Andy added.

Michael snickered a bit, as if trying to stifle a laugh at his brother's persistence.

"Sounds nice," she said, not wanting to give the wrong

impression. It was a bit unusual for Andy to mention this, all things considered.

Andy brought up an upcoming volleyball game, too, but Sylvia just listened. Then, thinking she ought to clarify what she'd said earlier about possibly going to the Singing, she said, "If Adeline's still here, I'll stay home with her Sunday night."

Nothing more was said on the subject after that, and Sylvia was relieved when her house came into view.

At the end of the driveway, Benuel halted the horse, and she got out. "*Denki* again!"

"Anytime," Rebecca replied with the sweetest smile.

Sylvia waved and turned to head toward the house. *Goodness*, she thought. *That was unexpected!*

CHAPTER
Fourteen

*A*deline was pleased to be invited to tag along with Rhoda to visit her youngest sister, Hannah Mast.

"Hannah has a Double Wedding Ring quilt on her bed you oughta see while we're there," Rhoda told her as they walked along the road. "It's possible that it's more like the one your mother was given."

"I'd love to have a look at it," Adeline said. She'd changed out of her cropped pants and into the new skirt she purchased yesterday, thinking it might be a good idea, since Rhoda was dressed in a plum-colored dress, full black apron, and crisp white head covering.

When they arrived at the back door of the neighboring farmhouse, Hannah seemed surprisingly eager to meet Adeline, opening the door wide and welcoming her and Rhoda inside. "*Mamm* told Curtis and me about your visit here," Hannah said, smiling brightly at Adeline, then offering to shake her hand. "*Willkumm* to our family," she said, ushering her and Rhoda through the kitchen after Rhoda mentioned Adeline might like to see her quilt.

What a warm greeting! thought Adeline as she followed the sisters to Hannah's upstairs bedroom. *Rhoda and Hannah are alike in more than just their appearance.*

There, Hannah showed Adeline the most beautiful bed quilt. While the pattern was the same as that of her mom's and the quilt in the Millers' spare room, this one was done all in pastel pinks, blues, and yellows, with an off-white background. "May I look at the stitching more closely?" she asked.

"Go right ahead," Hannah said, lifting the quilt's border on one side for her to inspect.

The stitching, in the shape of many small hearts, was so perfect it seemed impossible that anyone could have done it by hand. "You must be grateful to have it," Adeline said, marveling at the workmanship.

"It's a treasure to me 'cause Mamm and my sisters made it," Hannah told her.

Adeline quietly observed how neither Rhoda nor Hannah vied for attention, simply taking turns talking with her. It was refreshing.

"Would ya like some homemade root beer?" Hannah asked as they headed downstairs to the kitchen.

"Sure," Rhoda said, "if Adeline wants some."

Adeline agreed, touched by how Rhoda was including her in the decision to stay.

As they took a seat at the long table, Adeline was completely charmed by Hannah's sincere warmth and welcoming spirit. *Are all Amishwomen like this?*

"I'm not here to cause trouble, Amos," Earnest said as they sat outside the Kauffmans' stable on overturned buckets. "But

I'd like to know what Titus intends to do about his engagement to Sylvia."

The men slapped at flies, neither saying a word.

After a time, Amos breathed out a long sigh, then said, "I s'pect Sylvia knows you're here."

Earnest gave a nod of his head. "She does, but my coming wasn't her idea."

Amos considered this while scratching his beard. "I'll admit Titus has questions. We both do. Guess it comes down to this, Earnest: How can it be that ya didn't know about your first child?"

"That's a question I've asked myself." Earnest paused. "I don't know why her mother didn't tell me, but for whatever reason, she didn't."

Leaning back, Amos was quiet, nodding his head as if pondering this.

"If I'd known, I would've told you about Adeline when I confessed earlier this summer."

Amos looked away toward the barnyard. "Fair enough. Yet it's one thing to have this young woman track you down and quite another for her to have an influence over your children while she's visiting." He removed his straw hat and began to fan himself.

"Do you fear Sylvie isn't steadfastly rooted in the faith?" Earnest had to ask. "That she might be led astray by Adeline?"

Amos shrugged. "None of us likes the idea of Sylvia spending time with an *Englischer*. The way I see it, everything hinges on what Titus is thinking now. I've counseled him several times—Eva and I both have, actually—and we feel protective of him and his future. Frankly, all this has Titus worried what other unpleasant surprises might be coming his way. Don't get me wrong: We think Sylvia is a nice girl, but we're concerned that Titus might come to regret his decision."

Earnest fell silent. After hearing Amos's opinion, he was beginning to see the man's point, though from the opposite side of things—that *Sylvia* might regret marrying Titus.

"It's up to our children to do what they feel is right 'bout their relationship," Amos continued. "We've encouraged Titus to be prayerful and certain the two of them are on the same page." He leveled stern eyes at Earnest. "I'm sure you've done the same with Sylvia."

Truth be told, Earnest had not mentioned praying to Sylvia, though he knew Rhoda would be quick to do so. It was the People's way, after all.

"I'm sorry ya felt ya had to come over here and leave your family behind on the Lord's Day," Amos said more kindly now.

"From past experience, I've learned it's best to clear the air sooner rather than later." Earnest rose and thanked Amos for his time.

"No need to spread this around," Amos said, walking with him to the waiting horse and carriage. "I'm sure you agree."

"Well, I agree that Titus and Sylvia need some breathing room to decide whether to stay the course or to break off the engagement," Earnest answered, more convinced now that Titus was not a good match for Sylvia, after all.

Since Mamma and Adeline had gone somewhere together, and the boys were out in the meadow eating ice cream under a tree, Sylvia sat on the back porch sipping iced tea while trying to keep her attention on her Bible reading. Instead her mind continued to wander from one scenario to another as she wondered what was taking place between Dat and Preacher Kauffman. She could feel her heart beating too hard and, taking several deep breaths, she looked out toward the barn and silo, the peaceful landscape of meadow and grazing livestock.

At long last, Dat came rolling into the driveway, taking the carriage clear up next to the stable to unhitch Lily. While she waited for him, she noticed how very serious he looked, walking tall and straight, his stride quick.

As he led the mare into the stable to curry her, she decided to give her father some time to himself. She willed herself to read three more psalms until, finally, he walked over to the clock shop, bypassing the porch. She assumed he hadn't seen her sitting there, which was all right, considering his grave expression.

She sighed and wondered about his demeanor. Then, when she could no longer keep still, she wandered over to his shop, where she found him sitting and staring into space.

"Okay if I come in, Dat?" she asked softly as she peered in through the screen door.

He jerked his head her way and waved her inside.

Going to sit down, Sylvia hardly knew what to say. "Not such *gut* news, I guess," she said, her stomach in knots.

Dat leaned forward for a moment, then rose and walked to the screen door, where he stared out. "Ah, Sylvie, I don't like to see you hurt over Adeline's arrival . . . or what I did in the past."

"But the People have already disciplined ya for that, Dat." It pained her to see him beat himself up. "And as for Adeline, well . . . Titus shouldn't judge me for that. Not if he loves me. He's just *ferhoodled* by everything, I think. After all, we've all been a bit off-kilter lately."

Dat wandered back to his chair and sat. "I would do anything for your happiness, Sylvie." He inhaled audibly. "Unfortunately, there are some things I can't change." He went on to say that he had been unwise in rushing into marriage to Adeline's mother. "I should have paid closer attention to troubling signs in my relationship with her . . . signs not unlike those I'm seeing in your relationship with Titus." He shifted in his chair. "I would hate to see you make the same mistake, Sylvie. The cost is too great."

She listened, understanding his concern. "I want a strong foundation for our marriage," she told him. "I honestly thought Titus and I were right for each other, but now I'm not so sure."

"Well, it's critical to choose wisely." Dat paused. "And to pray about that choice, too."

It was the first she'd ever heard her father say anything like this about prayer. "Maybe I should talk to Ella Mae 'bout some things," she said softly, glad for his loving counsel. "*Denki,* Dat," she added in almost a whisper. "This did my heart *gut.*"

Monday morning was ideal for getting the clothes out on the line early, this being their usual washday. A steady breeze came from the west, and with not a cloud in the sky, Sylvia expected another scorcher. *Perfect for drying laundry,* she thought, noticing an abundance of grasshoppers while she and Mamma carried out the wide wicker basket full of newly washed clothes. Adeline had offered to make veggie omelets for all of them while Sylvia worked outdoors with Mamma. It was a kind and unexpected treat, having someone doing one of their regular chores.

"She seems a bit more at home, don't ya think?" Mamma

asked Sylvia as they pinned the clothes on the line. "And not quite as puzzled by our ways."

"Maybe *we're* the ones getting used to her," Sylvia suggested.

Mamma smiled. "You may be right."

Earlier that morning, Sylvia had offered to show Adeline how to use the wringer washer to do her own clothing. But Adeline had politely refused, saying she preferred to wash things by hand. Sylvia certainly understood, considering how very new the old-fashioned ways were to Adeline.

Much of the rest of the day was consumed by the family's laundry, which also entailed taking it off the line and folding it, then distributing it to all of the correct bedrooms. By the time Adeline's own laundry was hung on the line, it was time to think about making supper. Sylvia suggested they make a haystack dinner.

"It'll be another new experience for Adeline," Mamma said while Adeline chatted on the porch with Dat. Presently she was getting a feel for stitching through two layers of fabric.

"I still can't imagine bein' in her shoes, not knowing what kind of family she was walking into," Sylvia said as she gathered some of the many ingredients for the meal—crackers, rice, corn chips, carrots and cheese to shred, onions and peppers to dice, lettuce, raisins, black and green olives, walnuts, and sunflower seeds. "And to think she's already makin' such progress in learnin' to sew."

"She could use a lot more practice, but even so she's quite determined," Mamma said as she went to the pantry for some taco seasoning and spaghetti sauce. Then she began to fry the lean ground beef in her big black skillet.

Sylvia washed the carrots in the sink and recalled her discussion with Titus about Adeline's staying. *None of this is her fault,* she thought, feeling guilty for not making her half sister feel more welcome.

"Your Dat'll be happy we're havin' haystacks," Mamma said from where she stood near the gas range.

"It's Adam's and Calvin's favorite meal, too." Sylvia glanced toward the windows. "There are never any leftovers."

Mamma agreed. "And one way to clean out the fridge."

Sylvia nodded. She could hear Dat outside talking with Adeline and was grateful that he had shared so openly about his visit to Preacher Kauffman's. *He's awfully worried about Titus and me,* she thought, knowing full well he was not alone in that.

CHAPTER
Fifteen

The next morning, in better spirits after helping her mother with a bit of ironing, Sylvia invited Adeline to go with her to Quarryville to BB's Grocery Outlet after the noon meal. "Bents, Bumps, and Bunch of Bargains," she said, quoting their slogan.

"Wait . . . that's a real place?" Adeline looked baffled.

"You'll have to see it," Sylvia said, going on to describe the amazing discounts. "It's always packed with customers."

"If shopping's involved, then count me in," Adeline said, sounding enthusiastic.

"Okay. I'll go an' call a driver," Sylvia said, motioning to the cornfield where the local phone shanty stood hidden.

"*I'll* drive us," Adeline offered. "Why not?"

"Well . . ." Sylvia didn't want to keep taking advantage of her, although it was nice to have a vehicle so handy.

"No, seriously—let's take my car."

Still a bit hesitant, Sylvia agreed. "*Denki.*"

Adeline waved it off. "It's the least I can do when your family has been so kind to me."

So after Mamma, Sylvia, and Adeline made and served a noon meal of macaroni and hamburger, the young women headed southwest toward Quarryville.

"It's their second outing together," Earnest remarked when he came in for a thermos of cold meadow tea and Rhoda mentioned the girls had gone to BB's. "They must be warming up to each other."

Rhoda smiled. "Maybe so."

"Who would've guessed?"

"Let's not jump to conclusions," Rhoda said, pouring the cold tea carefully into the large thermos.

He wanted to lean down and kiss her cheek but winked at her instead. Then, glancing at the thermos in his hand, he said, "This should keep me goin' till suppertime."

"If ya run out, come back," Rhoda said with a laugh. "There's more where that came from."

He nodded and hurried toward the hallway to the utility room. Thus far, he hadn't told Rhoda of the Kauffmans' concern that Adeline might possibly influence Sylvia toward the world. Truth be told, he didn't see the point.

Nothing to worry about there, he reasoned as he made his way toward his little shop. *Our Sylvie has a good head on her shoulders. . . .*

As Adeline drove, Sylvia stared at the dark clouds building up off to the west, above the area's rolling green hills.

Adeline turned to glance at Sylvia through her sunglasses. "If you don't mind my asking, where do you purchase the clothes you don't sew? Or do you make everything?"

"*Nee*, I don't make everything." She smiled. "Things like socks, underwear, and even pajamas come from Walmart or wherever I can get the best price. There's even a row of hitchin' posts in the Walmart parking lot. They know we Amish shop there for basics."

She glanced in the direction of the Welsh Mountains again and pointed out the coming storm.

"You seem more aware of the weather than most people I know," Adeline commented. "More in tune with nature, too."

"Dat says that Mother Nature is a show-off, always remaking herself for our enjoyment." She laughed a little. "And Mamma likes watchin' all the birds that come to nest every spring."

"I noticed your tall birdhouse with four openings—like mini condos."

Sylvia nodded. "Oh *jah*, that's for the purple martins. Our Dawdi Riehl makes lots of those to sell," she said, going on to talk about how she was taught to appreciate and observe nature. "When we were little, Dat would take Ernie, Adam, and me on winter walks . . . 'specially on snowy days. '*What animal tracks do you see?*' he'd ask, then get us to identify the animals that made them. From then on, we kept our eyes wide open to the outdoors. There's always something new to see."

Adeline appeared to consider that. Then, after a moment, she said, "You must really enjoy your life."

Surprised, Sylvia nodded. "Don't you?"

Adeline frowned. "Some days."

The lukewarm way she said it made Sylvia's heart go out to her.

Adeline sighed loudly. "Mom's death took my breath away, and I think I'm still finding my way back to normal . . . whatever that is."

Sylvia bit her lip, trying to imagine losing her own mother.

"It feels like I've lost part of myself," Adeline said, shrugging a little. "It's hard to explain."

Her openness touched Sylvia. "I'm awful sorry," she said softly. "I really am."

Adeline glanced her way again, as if she wanted to share more. "There were times after Mom became sick that I wished I had a sister, someone who could get inside my head . . . you know . . . understand what I was feeling."

I've always wanted a sister, too, Sylvia thought, *but Adeline's not exactly what I had in mind.*

"Maybe you don't get what I'm saying." Adeline stared ahead at the road. "I wouldn't wish what I'm feeling on anyone."

For the longest time, Sylvia contemplated that. She recalled how very sad Dat had been when Mahlon Zook died. She also remembered how she'd felt when Dat finally told her about his first marriage—all because of the pocket watch she'd found in his heirloom tinderbox. She let out a little sigh.

"You okay?" Adeline asked, looking concerned.

"I might know just a smidgen of what you're goin' through," Sylvia admitted as the farmland whizzed by. She told about the day she'd learned of Adeline's mother. "The secret Dat had been hiding for so long sure caused an *Uffruhr.*"

Adeline looked befuddled. "What's that?"

"An uproar. Dat was shunned for six long weeks because of it." Sylvia softened her voice. "Truth be told, it kinda felt like we were, too."

"Your dad told me some about that."

"It was the worst time for him. For Mamma and us kids, too."

Silence enveloped them as they rode. It was hard to focus on the landscape around them with everything flying by so fast. In the car, Sylvia noticed the screen and all the buttons and dials on the console, so different from Titus's courting carriage. She bit her lip at the thought of her and Titus being in such limbo.

After a time, Sylvia had the urge to know something more about Adeline. "I hope I'm not being too snoopy if I ask ya somethin'."

Adeline laughed lightly. "I've been the one picking *your* brain. Ask whatever you like."

"I'm wonderin' if you were nervous 'bout meeting Dat . . . when ya first arrived."

"Actually, I was terrified." Adeline described how she'd broken out in a sweat, despite her car's air conditioning, the minute she pulled up to the vegetable stand last Friday. "I was close to a panic attack. What if he doesn't want to be found? What if he's angry to find out about me only now? I asked myself these and a dozen more questions. I almost bailed."

"How'd ya get up the courage?" Sylvia asked.

"I had to know the other half of the story . . . from his perspective."

Sylvia listened, then found herself nodding.

"And I didn't really gather the courage. I took mini steps—turned off the ignition, took a deep breath, opened the car door, and stepped out. And then I met you, and there was something about you, Sylvie, that helped me go ahead with it."

Sylvia couldn't believe her ears. And here she'd thought Adeline had seemed unruffled, at least at first. "*I* helped you?"

Adeline nodded. "You were so kind, so willing to hurry off

to get your father for me." She drew a breath. "Life can be hard. And you know what? I think this world needs more people like you." She smiled.

Embarrassed, Sylvia turned quiet, surprised at how very candid they had both been just now.

Adeline was still thinking about her conversation with Sylvia as they turned into BB's large parking lot, crammed with cars. She drove down one row after another, looking for a spot to park.

When finally she spotted a place somewhat removed from the store's entrance, Adeline quickly claimed it, pulling in and sitting there a moment before turning off the ignition. She looked at Sylvia. "You know . . . your dad is talkative enough, but at the same time, he seems quite restrained. Like there's this whole world in his mind that he doesn't reveal."

"*Jah*," Sylvia said, then looked away.

"I'm sorry. He's your father, and I don't mean to . . ."

"He's *yours*, too," Sylvia said, surprising Adeline. "But are ya thinkin' he might be hiding something . . . holding back?"

"No, I'm not getting that," Adeline said, then tried to explain that she felt as if she were seeing tiny pieces of an enormous puzzle, when what she really wanted was the whole picture.

Sylvia nodded. "I've experienced that, 'specially when it comes to Dat's former life as an *Englischer*." She was shaking her head. "I'd like to know more, too."

Adeline considered that. "How long ago did your dad's shunning end?"

"Just days ago, actually."

Adeline groaned. "Wow, I have lousy timing."

"Maybe it's for the best," Sylvia assured her. "Certainly it's better now than earlier." She reached for the door handle. "Let's talk more later."

Adeline smiled, feeling strangely close to this long-lost sister, although their lives couldn't have been more dissimilar.

She reached for her purse, their conversation echoing in her mind, and she wondered how things stood between Sylvia and her fiancé. But Adeline wouldn't think of asking. *I've been too nosy as it is.*

Getting out of the car, she noticed the huge brown-and-white sign, *BB's Grocery Outlet*, against the store's dark brown siding.

"I've got my list," Sylvia said sunnily, patting her shoulder bag as they hurried across the jam-packed parking lot.

"Great. And I'll grab a cart," Adeline offered, still marveling at the seeming breakthrough she and Sylvia had just had. *How did it happen?* she wondered, puzzled.

CHAPTER
Sixteen

In the middle of aisle seven, Sylvia and Adeline soon located dented cans of mushroom soup, something Sylvia's mother didn't care to make from scratch. And while Sylvia was counting out the twenty-five cans Mamma had requested, Adeline was looking for green olives, also on the list.

Just ahead of them, an elderly Amishwoman was reaching for the top shelf, standing on tiptoes but unable to reach the cans of mandarin oranges. After the woman's second attempt, Adeline must have noticed, because she hurried over to ask if she might help. Just then, the woman turned slightly, and Sylvia saw that it was Ella Mae Zook.

With hardly any effort, Adeline got down several cans of mandarin oranges and placed them in Ella Mae's cart. "They put them up high enough, don't they?" Adeline noted cheerfully.

"It'd help if I were a smidge taller," Ella Mae said with a chuckle.

"Well, I wouldn't mind being a bit shorter!" Adeline laughed. "Anything else I can do for you?"

Ella Mae thanked her, and Sylvia's heart was touched by

Adeline's kindness. When Adeline returned to their cart, Sylvia commented on how thoughtful it was.

"Well, she seemed so determined, I had a feeling she might keep trying to reach, no matter how many times she didn't succeed."

Sylvia smiled. "You just helped our dear Wise Woman," she whispered as Ella Mae headed up the aisle and turned out of sight.

Adeline's eyebrows rose. "The woman your brother Ernie mentioned?"

"*Jah.*"

Adeline straightened a bit, smiling now. "Will you introduce me?"

"We'll catch up with her in the next aisle." Sylvia was tickled at this. *If anyone will be gracious and accepting of Adeline, it's Ella Mae,* she thought.

However, other customers and their carts were ahead of Sylvia and Adeline now, so Sylvia suggested they just keep working down Mamma's list until it was more convenient to talk to Ella Mae.

Dark gray clouds blanketed the sky and thunder rolled as Rhoda removed three golden-crusted loaves of bread from the oven. Breathing in the familiar aroma, she glanced out the window and felt she ought to alert Calvin and Tommy to the coming storm. Ernie and Adam had gone to town with Earnest to run some errands, and she was glad they had taken the enclosed family buggy.

"*Kumme!*" she called to the younger boys, out on the back porch. "Ya don't wanna get struck by lightning."

"*Uff em Weg.*" Tommy replied they were on their way as he glanced over at Calvin, who was coming now, too.

The two of them scurried inside the house just as big drops of rain began to fall. Heavier thunder boomed, and Tommy laughed, saying he liked how it felt as it rumbled through him.

"This seems like a *gut* time for some ice cream," Rhoda announced as they washed up at the deep double sink before coming over to the table.

"Cookies too?" Tommy asked, eyebrows high.

"Well, you two *have* been workin' hard."

"We worked up an appetite, *jah,*" Calvin said, uniting with his brother in apparent hope.

"Cookies and ice cream it is." Rhoda smiled.

Tommy playfully tugged on Calvin's suspenders as they went to sit on the long wooden bench at the table.

"I was thinkin', Mamma," Calvin said with a glance at her. "Would Adeline wanna learn to milk?"

"Might frighten Flossie," Tommy said, frowning a bit.

"Well, you'd have to ease the cow into it, make sure Adeline moves slowly and quietly in the barn," Rhoda told them. "But it *would* give yous a chance to get to know her better." Dishing up their vanilla ice cream with chocolate syrup and placing a cookie on the rim of the bowl, she felt proud of her young sons for considering ways to include Adeline.

Calvin leaned back and stretched out his arms. "She *is* our sister, after all."

Tommy kept his hands in his lap till Rhoda carried over a dish for each of them. Then he picked up one of the spoons Rhoda had brought and scooped up a big bite. "*Appeditlich!*" he announced.

"Delicious, for sure," Calvin agreed, digging in.

Rhoda dished up some ice cream for herself and hoped Sylvia and Adeline didn't get caught in this fierce downpour on their way back from BB's.

The wind had picked up significantly, and the gray clouds had turned charcoal while Sylvia and Adeline were shopping. There hadn't been an opportune moment for Sylvia to introduce Adeline to Ella Mae, so they made their way to the front of the store, where all the cashier lines were quite long.

"This place is as packed as you predicted," Adeline whispered to Sylvia.

"It's almost always like this. The discounts are one of the main draws, and the cashiers are all so friendly—many are Plain, as you can see."

While they waited, Adeline asked Sylvia what she thought about destination weddings, but Sylvia didn't know what she meant.

"Oh, sorry . . . it's basically a wedding celebrated someplace where people vacation, sometimes many miles away from where the couple lives," Adeline explained. "Only a few family and friends are invited—the people you feel closest to and really want to come. Everyone spends a few days together relaxing and having fun." She paused. "Supposedly it takes the stress out of planning a wedding by making it small and a lot more manageable."

Ain't for me or any Amish, thought Sylvia, though of course she didn't say that as Adeline continued to describe some of the ideas she was exploring. "I went with my parents on vacation to Mackinac Island when I was little, before my brother was born," Adeline said. "Seeing the pretty brides and their handsome grooms riding down Main Street in quaint horse-drawn carriages has stuck in my head all these years." She also mentioned the possibility of getting married on a yacht on Lake Tahoe. "Brendon and I have also talked about Bow Bridge in New York City's Central Park. It's a beautiful spot."

Such different-sounding options! "Honestly, I'm prob'ly not the best person to ask about any of those," Sylvia replied.

Adeline looked confused. "Why not?"

"Well, I've never seen any of those places."

"Where will *your* wedding be held?" Adeline asked as they moved forward in the cashier's line.

What with the way things stood with her and Titus, Sylvia felt awkward answering that question, and she felt she should also be mindful of what she said with so many folk nearby. "Amish weddings usually take place at the bride's parents' home or in a rented white tent pitched outside the house."

Adeline's eyes blinked. Then, smiling, she whispered, "You must think I'm a romantic dreamer."

"Aren't we all?" Sylvia wanted Adeline to know she was interested. "It's fun to hear your ideas."

"Well, I appreciate your humoring me," Adeline said. "So which of the settings I mentioned would appeal most to you, if you weren't Amish?" Adeline asked, flipping her hair over her shoulder.

"I'd have to think on that."

"Just give me your knee-jerk response," Adeline insisted cheerfully.

Sylvia thought over each of the locations, then said, "Maybe the island you mentioned."

"Ah yes, the one with the horse-drawn carriages." Adeline laughed a little. "Of course you would choose that."

Sylvia enjoyed seeing Adeline so bubbly and talkative. She wished she, too, felt as happy and settled about her future as Adeline seemed to be.

After paying for the items, Sylvia suggested they wait out the heavy rainstorm; the clouds were quickly moving off to the east. As Adeline pushed the loaded grocery cart toward the side near the exit, Sylvia spotted Ella Mae Zook sitting beside her cart on one of the benches. *Now's our chance,* she thought, motioning for Adeline to follow her.

"Hullo, Ella Mae." Sylvia mentioned that she'd seen her earlier but wasn't able to catch up to greet her. "I happen to be shoppin' with the young woman who helped ya out earlier."

Adeline stepped forward to shake her hand. "I'm Adeline Pelham, Sylvie's half sister."

Lest Ella Mae wonder, Sylvia spoke up quickly. "Maybe you've heard already. Lately I have no idea what the grapevine's spreadin'."

"Well, it's *wunnerbaar* to officially meet ya, Adeline—and what a perty name," Ella Mae said, smiling up at her and Sylvia. "As for the grapevine, what can ya expect when there's potential for a scandal?"

Adeline smiled, but Sylvia didn't know what to say. *Leave it to Ella Mae to make a joke. . . .*

Straight-faced, Ella Mae continued, "'Tis human nature, ya know. We Amish ain't perfect." She smiled again, this time at Adeline. "Are ya havin' a pleasant visit so far?"

Adeline confirmed that she was. "It's nice to meet you, Mrs.—"

"*Ach*, chust call me Ella Mae. No need to be so formal when I'm an old widow lady."

Looking out at the sky and seeing the rain beginning to subside, Sylvia asked, "Are ya waitin' for your driver? If so, we can help you out with your groceries."

Ella Mae shook her head. "Actually, my daughter dropped me off while she went to Quarryville to take some sewing to a customer, so I'll just sit here and wait for her to mosey on back."

"I'm glad we saw ya," Sylvia said. "Adeline really wanted to be introduced."

"Well then, why don't you come to Preaching with Sylvia's family on Sunday?" Ella Mae suggested, blue eyes brightening. "Maybe I'll get to talk with ya again, Adeline."

Sylvia nodded and turned to Adeline. "Of course, you're welcome to join us if ya want to."

"We'll see," Adeline answered. Then she added, "I enjoyed meeting you, Ella Mae."

"Hold your head high, dearie," the Wise Woman said to her, looking more serious now. "You have an extraordinary family in Hickory Hollow, as I'm sure you've discovered."

With Dat's shunning still so fresh, hearing that made Sylvia fight back tears. *What a thoughtful thing to say!*

CHAPTER
Seventeen

I'm glad ya met Ella Mae," Sylvia said as they walked across the parking lot to Adeline's car. The rain had slowed to a sprinkle now, and the sun was already making an attempt to peek through the diminishing cloud cover.

"She's just like I imagined her." Adeline unloaded the canned goods into her trunk with help from Sylvia, then closed it.

Sylvia was ever so curious. "What do you mean?"

Adeline paused a moment. "Well, she looks like everyone else in your community, as far as being Amish. But there's something about her eyes." She shrugged. "I don't know, maybe it's the way she looks at you . . . makes you feel accepted."

Sylvia was touched by Adeline's assessment. She was right: It wasn't just that Ella Mae was wise—her appeal was also in how she made you feel.

"I know what ya mean." Sylvia wondered how it must look for her to climb into the sporty fire red Camaro dressed in her traditional Amish garb. *Quite a contrast!* she thought wryly.

Adeline hurried off to return the grocery cart as Sylvia

fastened the seatbelt. And in that moment, recalling Ella Mae's nonchalant remarks, Sylvia realized she didn't care how Adeline's relationship with her and her family might look. *If the Wise Woman can make light of the gossip about Adeline's relationship to Dat . . . why should I fret?*

A beautiful rainbow was visible during the trip back through Bird-in-Hand and up toward the village of Intercourse. After they had taken the Y to the left to stay on Route 340, they turned south onto Cattail Road, past the Amish schoolhouse on the left. Then they took the right-hand fork and drove past the old waterwheel on the right.

"You're starting to find your way around, *jah?*"

"I'm getting there."

There was a lull in the conversation, after which Sylvia said, "I meant what I said . . . if ya want to go to church with us on Sunday, we'd be happy to have ya."

Adeline hesitated, then caught Sylvia's eye. "It's just that I rarely attend church," she said politely.

Sylvia almost didn't know how to respond to that—not going to church was unthinkable in Hickory Hollow. Sylvia wondered how she could phrase things so that Adeline wouldn't feel put off. "For us, it's a way to worship with those we love . . . encourage each other on this life journey."

Adeline nodded. "Right, but it's all related to God, isn't it?"

"Sure, but goin' to Preaching service also means learnin' how to live and make good choices." She mentioned their church ordinance, the *Ordnung*, which laid out the rules for their community life. "Church really is central to everything we Amish do."

Adeline seemed stumped by this. "I'm sorry. This is so foreign to me. You must think I'm a pagan."

"We were raised worlds apart," Sylvia said at last.

"That's very apparent," Adeline agreed.

Sylvia felt sorry for Adeline in that moment—she was missing out on one of the most important things in life.

When they pulled into the driveway, Calvin and Tommy waved at them from the narrow petunia garden along the back walkway, where they were weeding. "I wonder why they're doin' the work Mamma likes to do," Sylvia said as she got out and motioned for them to help carry in the bags of canned goods.

Calvin went over to the well pump to rinse off his hands, but Tommy stood there, staring at Adeline's car. "Must be fun to ride in it," he said, stroking the side near one of the rear tires.

"I'll take you for a ride, if you'd like," Adeline offered.

"Sure! That is, if Dat lets me," Tommy said, going now to the well pump to clean his hands, too. Then, drying them on his work pants, he hurried to the trunk to help Calvin.

Sylvia didn't know what to think of her little brother's interest, but she figured that if Tommy really wanted to, Dat might just let him. She carried a large bag of mushroom soup cans into the house.

In the kitchen, she found Mamma baking a batch of sticky buns to sell at their roadside stand. And, while organizing the canned goods in the large pantry, Sylvia overheard Tommy talking to Adeline again. From what she could tell, he and Calvin had plans for her in the barn, once they were finished unloading.

"It'll be an adventure," Calvin said, his voice sounding enthusiastic.

"Tell me more," Adeline encouraged him.

"Well, you'll have to wear Sylvia's old work boots," Calvin said as he came to hand two more grocery bags to Sylvia in the pantry.

"And a kerchief on your head," Tommy added, his face beaming.

"If work boots and a kerchief equals adventure, then I'm in," Adeline said, laughing merrily.

It sounded so good to hear her laugh, Sylvia thought, hurrying to keep up with her brothers now. *We've come a long way in a few days,* she thought, beginning to see that a relationship with Adeline might offer more positives than negatives. *Even if an Englischer half sister isn't something I would've asked for!*

Not in a million years would Adeline ever have imagined herself standing in an Amish barn, or any barn, waiting to touch a cow's udder with her bare hands. Following Tommy's instruction, she stood back at a respectful distance from the cow while Calvin secured Flossie's head in the single stanchion. Then Calvin gave the cow some hay to munch on as he pulled up a wooden stool to sit on while washing her udder and teats.

Tommy quietly gave Adeline the play-by-play as the two of them slowly inched toward the cow. "It's important not to upset Flossie, or her milk won't come down."

Adeline nodded and opened her mouth to speak, but Tommy quickly raised a finger to his mouth.

"Don't say anything," he explained. "Flossie doesn't know your voice."

Staying quiet isn't my strong suit, she thought as she watched Calvin place the clean milk bucket under the cow, then massage the teats. He demonstrated how Adeline was to squeeze and pull straight down, and after a few rhythmic pulls, he stopped and moved off the stool to let her try. "Your turn," Calvin said quietly. "Always stay to her side here, so ya don't get kicked. It's no picnic, trust me."

Adeline followed directions, feeling totally out of her league. Yet if young kids like Calvin or Tommy could milk a cow, why couldn't she? Placing her hands exactly the way Calvin had shown her, she was surprised at how soft the cow's udder was. And she was even more surprised when absolutely nothing happened when she squeezed.

"Try a little harder," Calvin encouraged softly.

She felt foolish. *How hard?* she wondered, not wanting to hurt Flossie.

Then, shifting forward a bit on the short stool, she nearly knocked over the milk bucket. She opened her mouth to apologize but, just in time, remembered not to speak.

"Try again," Calvin said, his voice so soothing, it sounded more like he was talking to the cow than to her. "And relax . . . this isn't too tough, really."

Maybe not for you, she thought, squeezing harder, and then, in what seemed like a sudden miracle, a long white stream flowed into the bucket. A few more pulls and she slowly got the hang of it, and the rhythm, too.

If only Brendon could see me now! she thought.

After several dozen times with each hand, she felt her fingers growing weak and realized that whoever milked Flossie twice a day must have super strong hand and arm muscles. She grimaced. *I'm obviously not a farm girl.*

Later, when her little adventure was finished, Adeline got a kick out of washing her hands at the well pump before going inside to do a more thorough washing in the Millers' only bathroom. Secretly, she was glad she hadn't had any mishaps.

Adeline found Sylvia in the kitchen making a pencil drawing for a Nine Patch pattern quilted wall hanging. She was pleasantly surprised when Sylvia said it was a project for Adeline to do. "If you're interested."

"Are you sure I'm ready?" Adeline asked.

"Oh *jah*, it's time to move forward," Rhoda said from the kitchen counter, where she was flipping through her recipe file.

Adeline felt happy, ready to graduate from obsessively making small, straight practice stitches on random bits of fabric.

"I can show ya the fabric scraps we have on hand, and you can choose a color scheme for this layout," Sylvia told her, beckoning her to follow her to the sewing room upstairs.

One adventure after another, thought Adeline, eager to proceed with something less barnyardish.

The next day, Sylvia suggested to Ernie, when they were out digging potatoes, that maybe he'd like to ask Adeline to help him at their roadside stand that afternoon.

"She's helpin' put up pickles with Mamma over at Aendi Hannah's," Ernie protested, as though he wasn't so interested in having Adeline around.

Sylvia knew this well enough—Adeline had seemed altogether pleased about the prospect of helping to make her first batch of pickles. "Well, just ask her when ya see her next," Sylvia urged, saying how much fun Adeline had had yesterday milking Flossie.

"*Jah*, that was risky business. You know what Dat and Mamma always say 'bout not havin' strangers in the barn during milking."

"Thankfully, it worked out just fine," she said.

"This time, but did the boys ask Dat first?"

"I don't know." Sylvia felt a little put out at Ernie, but she didn't press the matter.

"Well, maybe you should ask Dat what he thinks of havin' an *Englischer* tend his roadside stand."

"What's it matter, Ernie?"

Ernie looked away and kept digging, saying no more.

And Sylvia did the same.

That afternoon, once Mamma and Adeline returned with many jars of pickles, both sweet and dill, Adeline asked if it was all right to work on her Nine Patch quilted wall hanging.

"After your chores are done," Sylvia agreed.

Mamma turned quickly to gape at her. "What in the world?"

Sylvia smiled. "Just kidding!"

Adeline set the jars of pickles on the counter and turned to her, hands on her hips. "*Ach*, Sylvie, you're such an Amish taskmaster."

The three of them had a good long laugh.

Sylvia happened to see the mail truck come while she was mowing the side yard with their old push mower late that afternoon. To her surprise, Ernie had taken Sylvia up on her idea, and he and Adeline were working together at the family's roadside stand.

It was a pleasant day, with a temperature in the low eighties,

as one car or buggy after another stopped for fresh produce—
primarily corn and tomatoes today. Like yesterday, Mamma
had also given Ernie some freshly baked loaves of bread, as
well as several dozen sticky buns to sell, knowing that the
tourists in particular could never resist anything homemade.

Sylvia quit mowing and went to check the mail, finding
a letter from Titus. Her heart trembled at the sight of his
handwriting, but she patiently waited to open it, first carrying the rest of the mail into the house. If it was bad news,
she would have to veil her reaction if anyone was around,
and if it was good news . . . well, she wasn't sure she wanted
any from him.

She went out to the stable, sat on a hay bale across from Lily's
stall, and opened the envelope. Inside, she found a short note.

Dear Sylvie,

*Would you like to meet me Saturday evening at our usual
spot, down from your house? If it suits you, I can be there
around seven o'clock.*

With love,
Titus

Seeing how he had signed off, she had mixed feelings about
this. But she remembered her talk with Dat and knew she had
to have an honest conversation with Titus. *Looks like it will be
sooner rather than later. . . .*

Adeline enjoyed helping Ernie but was unable to follow the
conversation when some Amish customers stopped by and

talked very fast in Pennsylvania Dutch. A couple of times they gave her a sideways glance, as if questioning her presence there, something Ernie seemed to find humorous.

One Amish guy in a black open buggy pulled over and got out. He waved at her and came up to the vegetable stand to purchase a half dozen ears of sweet corn. "Hullo again," he said. "Adeline, ain't?"

She removed her sunglasses and realized this was the same young man whom she had met last Sunday while walking with Earnest and Rhoda. "Yes, it is . . . and you're Andy Zook, if I remember."

He nodded with a good-natured expression. "I see Ernie's got ya workin'."

Ernie waved at him and kept bagging tomatoes for another customer.

"We're working together," Adeline said, pleased to say so.

"S'pose Sylvia's busy, then," he said, glancing toward the house.

"Oh, she's around somewhere." Adeline wondered if he would follow up on that.

"Well, just tell her hi for me, okay?" he said with a smile.

"I certainly will." Adeline accepted Andy's payment for the corn and placed it in the money box over near Ernie. "Thanks for dropping by."

As Andy returned to his horse and buggy, she remembered that he had asked her last Sunday if she was looking to become Amish.

Never, ever, she thought once again, although it had never occurred to her that she could have this much fun in Hickory Hollow.

While Adeline was still tending the roadside stand with Ernie, and after getting Mamma's permission to go walking awhile, Sylvia hurried down the road to visit Ella Mae. She found the Wise Woman sitting out on her little white porch, fanning herself with a newspaper.

"Hullo," Sylvia called to her.

"Well now, I was just thinkin' about ya, dearie." Ella Mae motioned her up to the porch with a bright smile. "Wonder if the Lord put ya on my heart."

Sylvia didn't know quite what to make of that, but she took a seat in the rocking chair next to the woman, already feeling cared for, as Ella Mae had a special way of doing. "I hoped ya might be able to sit and talk a bit."

"I'm all yours." Ella Mae slowed her rocking. "What's on your heart, Sylvie-girl?"

"I haven't told anyone, but I'm about to do something I hope I won't regret."

Ella Mae reached over to pat Sylvia's hand. "Well, what could cause ya to think that?"

"I feel so frustrated here lately." Finally she'd admitted part of what was bothering her.

"Frustration is usually toward someone or something." Ella Mae stopped rocking altogether. "Might this be concerning your visitor?"

Sylvia smiled fleetingly. "When Adeline first came, *jah*, it was. But not any longer. Now it's much more about Titus . . . my fiancé."

A soft breeze blew across the little haven of a porch, and

the potted geraniums fluttered slightly. "Are things off-kilter with him?"

Sylvia glanced at Ella Mae, pondering whether she really dared to say all that was on her heart. "I'm finding that I can't forgive him."

"Can't?"

Sylvia shook her head. "It goes back to when Titus reported my father to the ministers—remember when Dat and Titus were in Maryland earlier this summer? It's a long story," she added quietly, hating to bring it up yet feeling she must.

"Doesn't matter how long a story 'tis . . . not if it needs to be told."

So Sylvia shared that, while in Maryland, her father had sought private counsel from his great-uncle Martin Zimmerman, a retired Mennonite minister. "This was before Dat told the deacon about his first marriage to his college sweetheart."

"I see." Ella Mae began to rock slowly again. "I daresay Titus ain't solely to blame for how things went after that point, considering the real cause of your father's *Bann* was the secret he kept from the People."

"Oh, I know that," Sylvia agreed. "What bothers me most is that Titus wouldn't admit the truth of what he'd done when I asked—he pretended like he had nothing to do with it." She sighed and shook her head. "It makes me wonder if I know him as well as I thought."

"It could be ya missed some early warnin' signs. Sometimes when we first fall in love, we see the other person more as we want them to be than as they actually are."

"*Jah.*" Sylvia was thankful Ella Mae had brought that up. "That could be, but it still doesn't change how I'm feelin' toward Titus right now." She stared at her hands in her lap.

"You prob'ly think I should ask God to soften my heart, to forgive him."

Ella Mae smiled ever so sweetly. "That wasn't my first thought, but *jah*, 'tis mighty important if you're goin' to marry this young man."

"That's just it—I'm not sure anymore. I mean, if I can't forgive him, and neither of us really trusts the other, how can I be his wife?"

"I s'pose that's what I would've said, if you'd asked." Ella Mae was nodding her head thoughtfully. "Seems to me you've answered your own questions, dear girl."

Sighing, Sylvia wasn't quite sure. "To tell the truth, I've struggled with doubts about the relationship for months now. I just don't see how I can wed with things how they are."

"Is something keepin' ya from telling Titus good-bye?"

"Love . . . I guess." She inhaled slowly. "If that's even what I'm feeling."

"Well, but love isn't only patient, it's also prudent."

Sylvia hadn't thought of love being wise. And in that moment, it came to her that she had been standing still, simply hoping things would work out. "Ella Mae, I honestly don't understand how ya do it, but I feel now like I know what to do."

Ella Mae patted her hand. "I'll be prayin' the Good Lord will help ya say just the right words when the time comes. And someday soon, I hope He'll help ya forgive Titus, too. Letting go of anger and just plain forgiving is ever so much better and stronger than holdin' on to it. It's the path to God's peace."

"I need peace 'bout this, for sure." Now it was Sylvia who reached out, not just to pat Ella Mae's hand but to clasp it. "You don't know what this means to me." Getting up, Sylvia leaned against the pretty white railing and looked down at Ella Mae. "All this, and we didn't even have tea."

"You're right!" Ella Mae giggled. "Now, ain't that somethin'!"

Sylvia thanked her again and waved before turning to head down the few steps and over the flower-bordered footpath. *Why did I wait so long to open my heart like this?*

CHAPTER
Eighteen

*T*hat evening, Earnest invited Adeline over to his shop while he worked on a new clock featuring a mariner's compass in fruitwood. "Calvin and Tommy are still talking about teaching you how to milk Flossie," he said, wanting her to know how much he appreciated her humoring them.

She was inspecting the two grandfather clocks, both unique in style and wood choice. One, his favorite of the two, had a hand-rubbed Windsor cherry finish. "It was fun—and quite a challenge, to be honest," she admitted. "Your boys were so helpful and sweet. I mean, most kids their age wouldn't give me the time of day. . . ." She paused. "I don't know. Maybe the ones I know all have their noses in their phones. Kids don't really make their own fun anymore, like I did growing up. It's kind of sad."

Earnest listened, glancing at her as she traced the smooth cherrywood, as if transfixed by its beauty. "Are you interested in owning a floor clock someday?" he asked.

She stepped back to appraise it. "I never thought I would,

but yes . . . this is lovely." She came to sit down near his work-bench. "Maybe after I'm married and have a house."

He nodded and smiled. "They do take up space."

Adeline laughed lightly at that.

"By the way, Ernie was impressed with how you interacted with the customers at the roadside stand—Amish and English alike. He said you were a *gut* coworker."

Adeline seemed pleased and said she was glad to help. "Oh, and Andy Zook came by and bought some sweet corn."

"Did he, now?"

She nodded, then, looking a bit sheepish, added, "And asked about Sylvie."

Earnest shook his head. "Well, she's spoken for, as I'm sure Andy knows."

"Maybe he's just interested in being her friend."

Chuckling, Earnest replied, "Friendships between fellas and girls round here don't stay that way for long."

"Do you mean Sylvia can't have a platonic friendship with Andy or any other guy while she's dating Titus?"

"Sylvie's *engaged* to be married," Earnest told her, yet even as he said it, he realized that he wasn't sure what Sylvia was going to decide about that.

"Okay . . . I won't bother telling her."

They began to talk about the new clock he was making—where he got his ideas so that each creation was one-of-a-kind. He showed her its inner workings, and Adeline leaned closer, clearly intrigued.

Then she said, "I wanted to follow up on something you mentioned earlier. And not to be too philosophical or any-thing, but did you come to the Amish searching for answers? You may be tired of all my questions, but—"

"Not at all," Earnest reassured her.

She hesitated. "I still can't wrap my head around why you, as an educated man, would join the Amish. I mean, some people in my generation live what they think is a minimalist lifestyle, but this takes that to another level." She sighed. "I guess what I'm trying to say is, what was it you were really searching for?"

He wasn't prepared for such a serious question. "I can't say I had any idea what I was looking for other than an escape. My old life, at least as I knew it, was over. But after running across Hickory Hollow and meeting some of its people, living as an Amishman really appealed to me. And for two decades now, it's allowed me to heal and focus on the essentials—my family, a slower pace of life, work that I enjoy, and a sense of community."

"Are you really satisfied with less?" she asked, letting him know that she had paid attention last Sunday. "I've actually thought a lot about that."

"Well, let's see . . . how can I say this so you'll understand, because I doubt I would have when I was your age." He paused and set the clock case and chisel he was holding aside on his workbench. "Life is about so much more than material things. If we're too busy in the pursuit of those, we don't take time to develop the close friendships we need in order to thrive." He was thinking of Mahlon again, and his own dear Rhoda. "Nature does wonders for me, too. Being Amish, I'm less cut off from it and the natural rhythms of life than I was as an *Englischer*. I take time to appreciate the seasons and the different aspects each has to offer. All of this—and meeting Rhoda—was healing to me after my divorce."

She studied him. "So your newfound faith didn't heal you?"

Earnest was momentarily struck silent—she'd hit the nail on the head. "Well, I know God is a loving heavenly Father, and He created nature for our benefit. He doesn't want us to live alone, without community. But I have to admit, I'm not the best Amishman when it comes to faith, though I've given it my best shot."

Adeline seemed to consider that. "The Scripture verses you read each night . . . some of them are jarring to me," she admitted. "Do they ever jump out at you, too?"

"Sometimes." He nodded, feeling inadequate and wishing Rhoda or Sylvie were here.

"You don't seem comfortable talking about this." Adeline sat back in the chair. "I get that."

"I'm still finding my way," he was quick to say.

"If that's what you want, I guess it's better than giving up."

He didn't have the nerve to press Adeline for where *she* was as far as religion stood. It wasn't his place, as short a time as they'd known each other. And wanting to change the subject, he reached for his chisel and the clock case again. "If you could have any clock in this shop, which one would it be?"

Adeline's face broke into a smile. "That's an impossible question. Each one is beautiful in its own way."

This was unexpected; most people coming in to purchase a clock took little time to find something that caught their eye.

She glanced over at the two tall floor clocks again. "I can't believe how much I've learned here about things I never bothered to think about before."

"Like making pickles or milking a cow with your bare hands?" he asked.

"Exactly." She smiled. "I've learned so much from Rhoda

. . . and Sylvia, too. It still blows my mind to think I have a *sister*." Adeline folded her hands over her knees.

Earnest chuckled. "Sylvia probably thinks the same."

"Well, I'm sure it hasn't been easy having me around, not when Sylvie's been the only girl."

Earnest was moved by her observation. "Sylvie's heart is pure gold. I can see that she and Rhoda are doing all they can to make you feel at home."

"Which is amazing, if you think about it." Adeline looked away, and Earnest thought she might have tears in her eyes. Then, glancing up at one of the nearby mantel clocks, she said, "Isn't it about time for evening prayers?"

"You're right." Earnest smiled.

And together, they walked over to the main house.

Following family prayers, after Mamma served everyone homemade ice cream and hermit cookies rich with cinnamon, chopped walnuts, and raisins, Sylvia asked Adeline if she'd like to see her room. "Since it's presentable," she said, leading the way upstairs. "I have a summer quilt to show ya." Sylvia motioned for Adeline to enter the room and pointed out the pale blue, green, and lavender spread.

"It's different than any I've seen," Adeline said, going to look at it.

"Go ahead and sit on the bed, if you want." Sylvia sat down, too. "Mamma and I worked on this for nearly half a year, a little at a time," she told her.

"I like it," Adeline said, gently running her hand across the quilt. "You must be so proud of your handiwork."

"When I look at this Hearts and Nine Patch pattern, I

remember all the hours talking with Mamma, listening to her tell stories about her childhood."

Adeline nodded. "I have happy memories with my mom, too, just not doing anything like this." She paused a moment and leaned closer to inspect the quilt. "Your mother seems to thrive on making lovely things, doesn't she? On baking, too."

Sylvia agreed. "I think it's 'cause she knows her purpose and place in life, as most Amishwomen do."

"Your parents are such good people, Sylvie." Adeline paused a moment. "I catch myself wondering what it would have been like to be raised by someone other than my mother and step-father." She stood then and went to the window to look out. "If I had been raised here in Amish farmland, I wouldn't have been a very well-behaved Amish girl."

"You don't know that," Sylvia said from where she still sat on the bed. "If you'd grown up knowing our ways, you would've fit in. We all do, sooner or later. At least most of us, anyway."

Adeline turned to look at her, a question in her eyes. "Do you really think so?"

"Without a doubt."

Coming to sit again beside her, Adeline asked, "Do you ever wonder what your life would be like if you had been born to an Englisher?"

"*Nee*, never."

"That's amazing." Adeline sighed audibly.

"Why?"

"In your place, I would . . . but I guess that's just me. You have no frame of reference for a life outside the world of Hickory Hollow."

"That's true, but I honestly don't want anything else."

Adeline shook her head in apparent wonder, and Sylvia

went to open her hope chest, at the foot of her bed. "Would ya like to see the things I've made or been given as gifts to use when I set up housekeeping?"

"Are you sure?" Adeline looked surprised. "I mean, aren't they rather personal?"

"Every young woman I know has a hope chest like this, but *jah*, this one holds some things that are very special to me. I don't mind showin' you, though." Sylvia opened the large oak chest.

"Sure . . . thanks." Adeline got up and knelt on the floor with her.

This is a big step, thought Sylvia, knowing as she reached for the topmost gift that sharing her life like this with Adeline was the right thing to do.

CHAPTER
Nineteen

*T*itus's mother made this for me," Sylvia said as she
showed Adeline the pretty dresser runner with color-
ful tulips embroidered at each end. "She gave it to me the
morning Titus proposed." Sighing inwardly, she recalled her
recent conversation with Ella Mae.

Adeline marveled at the workmanship. "I might be hesitant to use it," she said, kneeling beside the hope chest next
to Sylvia.

"Well, I haven't yet. I've been waiting till I marry."

Adeline nodded as Sylvia refolded the runner and reached
for a set of white doilies her grandmother Riehl had tatted.
Again, Adeline seemed awestruck by the handiwork, com-
menting on how very tiny and delicate the stitches were.

There were also bedsheets and embroidered pillowcases,
blankets, a set of bath towels and washcloths, quilted potholders, tablecloths, tea towels, more doilies for dressers, two
handmade work aprons, and a large crocheted afghan. A large
box of twelve sets of flatware, plus serving spoons, a meat fork,

butter knife, and gravy ladle to match, completed the contents of the trunk.

"There's even more stored in the sewing room closet," Sylvia said. "Pots and pans, a set of carving knives, and glassware, too. I don't have room for everything here, as you can see."

"So have you already had a wedding shower?" Adeline asked, her expression puzzled.

"*Nee*, these are just things Mamma and I have picked up over the years. Wedding showers happen much closer to the wedding day." Sylvia felt glum in that moment.

"Well, whenever the time comes, will I get a wedding invitation?" Adeline gave her a hopeful look.

"Of course I'll send you one," Sylvia replied quietly.

Adeline helped by handing Sylvia each item as she refilled her beloved hope chest. "Thanks for showing me your lovely things," Adeline said. "And your room and the quilt, too."

Sylvia nodded, and they walked down the hall to the sewing room, where Adeline set to work on the squares for the wall hanging, using the running stitch Mamma had taught her.

"Maybe you'll add this to your own hope chest," Sylvia suggested as she sat at the table with Adeline, repairing a hem on Mamma's black apron.

Adeline smiled. "Well, I don't exactly have a hope chest, but the few things I have are stored at my grandparents' place in Hilton Head," she said. "My girlfriends plan to have a personal shower for me, as well as a wedding shower, closer to the time of the wedding. Of course, Brendon and I need to set up a wedding registry prior to that."

"You have much to look forward to," Sylvia said, wondering what on earth a wedding registry was.

Sylvia got up quickly the next morning since Thursday was the day she and Mamma usually cleaned house upstairs and down in preparation for the weekend. The Preaching service would be held this Sunday at Onkel Josh and Aendi Ruthann Yoder's farmhouse. *I should run over there and help with last-minute raking or weeding,* she thought as she put on her green dress and matching apron. But she wouldn't leave Adeline behind unless Mamma could spend time with her.

After breakfast, Sylvia cleaned the entire upstairs, including her brothers' bedrooms—dusting, wiping down the wide windowsills, dry mopping and then scrubbing the floors on all fours. Several of the windows needed washing on the inside, so she did that, too. And after the noon meal, she ran over to Aendi Ruthann's, where someone was giving the horse stable a fresh coat of white paint as she arrived. *It's always an honor to host church,* she thought, offering to tidy up the flower beds, as well as to sweep the walkways and porches.

That evening, after family prayers, Sylvia sat with Adeline again while she worked on her squares for the wall hanging. Adeline seemed eager to talk about her mother's parents, who had picked up the pieces for Adeline and Liam after the passing of Adeline's stepfather first and then their mom.

"Do ya think you'll end up livin' near the ocean like they do?" Sylvia asked.

"I hope so, at least someday, but Brendon has a very comfortable condo in Atlanta, so I'll move to his place after we're married. I'm hoping to land a job right away so that we can pay off our student loans."

Sylvia inquired about Adeline's upcoming classes and, at one point when Adeline was describing her studies in great detail, Dat poked his head in. Seeing him there, Sylvia wondered how much he'd overheard but didn't have to wonder long, because he moseyed in and asked Adeline about certain professors he had studied under twenty years ago. Lo and behold, two of the instructors were still teaching, much to Dat's pleasure and amazement.

It wasn't long before Adeline and Dat were caught up in conversation, and Sylvia was glad she had some sewing of her own to do. But today, as the two of them talked together, she didn't feel left out. Her perception of the relationship between her father and Adeline had changed in the last week, and she actually enjoyed seeing Dat connect with her. *He has room in his heart for both of us.*

On Friday afternoon, Sylvia assessed the boys' church clothes, as well as her own, making sure each garment was in good repair and hung up neatly. Mamma tended to Dat's black for-good trousers, white shirt, and frock coat. Sylvia also polished every pair of black shoes, all the while thinking about seeing Titus tomorrow night.

After Dat's shop closed for the day, he washed the family carriage inside and out, and later shined up all the buggy windows, too, while Ernie checked the brake fluid and made sure the solar battery that powered the road lights was charged up.

Mamma called Ernie in for a haircut, which she gave out on the back porch. Then, one after another, each of the boys got a trim for the Lord's Day.

That evening, Mamma's parents arrived for supper, and

Sylvia smiled at their reaction to meeting Adeline. Almost right away, Mammi Riehl made over Adeline's light brown hair—saying how thick it was—and calling it short, even though fancy folk didn't consider shoulder length short at all.

They stood around at one end of the kitchen talking before the meal was served, and Adeline seemed to take a liking to them. She asked what type of farm they had, which appeared to impress Dawdi Riehl.

"We used to run a large dairy farm when Rhoda was growin' up," Dawdi told her, "but we're down to just eighty acres, mainly for growin' crops."

Sylvia could see that Adeline wasn't the only one enjoying the conversation as Dawdi asked her how she liked Amish country so far.

When the food was steaming hot and placed on the table, they all sat down for the silent blessing. Afterward, Mamma passed the large platter of baked ham with a sugar and mustard glaze first to Dat, following with scalloped potatoes in a cheesy sauce. Chow chow, a carrot salad in an orange gelatin with crushed pineapples and raisins, and buttered lima beans rounded out the spread.

Ernie mentioned how hectic it had been at Dat's showroom today, and while he didn't actually brag, he came close to it when he said they'd sold four clocks and taken two custom orders. "It was a real *gut* day." He grinned at Dat, who shrugged it off as if embarrassed.

"Now, son," he said as Dawdi Riehl nodded and smiled his congratulations.

"Earnest does build the nicest-looking clocks," Mammi Riehl commented as she looked over at Adeline.

"I second that," Adeline agreed as she passed the platter of ham to Tommy and held it while he forked up a large helping, smacking his lips as he eyed the meat.

"And I can speak from experience that they keep perfect time, too," Dawdi Riehl added.

Sylvia wasn't surprised at how gracious her grandparents were to Adeline, but she couldn't help wondering what they privately thought about Dat and Mamma hosting a newfound relative who was the furthest thing from Plain.

Sylvia spent Saturday morning cooking while Dat, Ernie, and Adam headed to market to sell more clocks. It was their practice to talk there with everyone, even folk who were just roaming up and down the aisles. The whole family was thankful Dat's clock sales were starting to pick up again after the marked lull during the shunning. Sylvia honestly wondered if folk might be coming over to Dat's shop not just to look at clocks but to catch a glimpse of his fancy daughter. She couldn't know for sure, though.

With some help from Adeline, Sylvia and Mamma made a large tuna macaroni casserole for the weekend, as well as a hamburger, potato, and green bean dish that would be easy to simply warm up on tomorrow's Lord's Day.

Then, to help Ruthann and her daughters with the fellowship meal, they rolled out dough for twenty-five snitz pies, using the applesauce and apple butter they'd canned last fall to make the delicious filling. Hannah and another neighbor had offered to make the remaining twenty-five pies needed to feed everyone, so Aendi Ruthann had plenty of help making food for tomorrow.

Midafternoon, Sylvia showered and washed her hair to prepare for her after-supper date with Titus. She didn't know how to think about this first real date in weeks, except that they absolutely had to have a frank discussion about their relationship. With November not so far away, it was essential.

She wrapped her waist-length hair in a thick bath towel, knowing it would dry in plenty of time once she sat out in the sun. *I'll let Dat and Mamma know I'm seeing Titus tonight*, she decided, hoping her parents and brothers might teach Adeline how to play Dutch Blitz or another game while she was gone.

After supper, when it was time to step out the door, Sylvia could hear her brothers in the stable, undoubtedly busy with their usual chore of cleaning and oiling the horses' hooves for tomorrow's ride to church. They would also oil the harnesses to make them shine.

All the familiar sounds of a Saturday date night, she thought, taking a deep breath, trying to calm her nerves.

At the appointed time of seven o'clock, Sylvia didn't have to wait for Titus at their specified location. She could see his black courting carriage gleaming in the sunshine as he halted the horse just down from Dat's property. *One more hour till sunset*, she thought, glad they would be riding while it was still light.

Titus waved to her and jumped down to come around and greet her. "Hullo, Sylvie," he said, offering his hand to help her into the buggy.

"How've ya been?" she asked as he stepped into the right side and reached for the driving lines. She wondered if Titus might bring up her father's visit with his father.

"Oh, all right. I've been busy diggin' potatoes and getting ready for a big watermelon harvest," he said. "How 'bout you?"

She mentioned having stocked up on canned goods at BB's,

as well as tending to the usual chores in the house and garden. She didn't mention helping Adeline lay out her quilted wall hanging, thinking it best not to bring her into the conversation.

Sylvia couldn't help but notice the mare's leisurely pace and wondered if Titus had taken the horse out somewhere earlier. But, too nervous to ask, she sat back and tried to enjoy the relaxed pace, the pink evening sky, and the warm air, thick with the fragrance of honeysuckle.

Adeline was pleased the Millers wanted to spend time playing a game with her. "I'm sure you have other things to do," she told them.

"Once you're back at college, we'll be glad we took every opportunity to be with ya," Rhoda said, and Earnest nodded.

Rhoda's remark was sweet, and Adeline smiled as Ernie got the Dutch Blitz cards. "You've all made this visit incredibly special for me," Adeline said. "I don't know how I'll ever thank you."

"Well, I can think of something," Rhoda said, pressing her lips together now. "*Kumme* see us again, maybe?"

Tommy was quick to nod his head in agreement, and the other boys brightened, too.

"You're very kind," Adeline said.

"All of us would enjoy seein' you again . . . and meeting Brendon someday, too," Earnest said.

"I'd like that." Adeline remembered that Sylvia planned to send her a wedding invitation.

"Never forget that our door is always open to ya," Rhoda said.

"Thank you," Adeline said, feeling genuinely accepted.

Not far from the bishop's farm, Sylvia spotted an Amish-woman sitting in the back of a spring wagon, selling sweet corn. "Where could her horse be?" she murmured.

"I noticed that, too." Titus wondered aloud if the woman might need a ride home. "Let's stop a minute."

Agreeing, Sylvia sat there waiting while Titus hopped down and went to talk to the middle-aged woman, whom she did not recognize. But in a jiffy, Titus came running back and climbed into the carriage. "Her son's comin' for her soon," he said.

"I've never seen her before. Have you?"

Titus shook his head. "Sometimes Amish from other areas with fewer tourists bring their produce here so they can sell it more quickly."

"Who can blame them?"

Titus added, "I'm not sure why she's still out at this hour, though."

"*Jah*, seems strange."

Titus turned onto Hershey Church Road and slowed the horse even more as they came upon a sheltered patch on the right-hand side. He stopped the horse and got out to tie the mare to a tree. Then, coming around for Sylvia, Titus said, "Let's walk for a while. It's such a nice evening."

"Okay," she said, ready for some exercise.

He reached for her hand as the sun sank, a large red ball on the pink horizon. They walked for a good quarter mile before he spoke. "Sylvie, I hope you've never doubted how much I love ya, despite all that's happened this summer."

She listened, feeling uncomfortable holding hands.

"That's what makes this next thing hard," he said, pausing

to look away. "I'd like to postpone getting married till things calm down with your family . . . as hopefully they will."

Sylvia's temper rose at the suggestion.

"Also, I've recently heard from others that you've been drivin' around with Adeline in her car, at the mall and even down to Quarryville."

Sylvia took a quick breath. "Regardless of her background, she's *family*, Titus. I've just been getting to know her."

"But after everything that's happened with your father, don't ya realize how that comes across? And with baptism so near, you oughta be extra careful to make a *gut* impression as a devout young woman." Titus gave her a serious look. "After all, as you know, my family has a reputation to protect."

She released her hand from his, and everything that had been building in her mind, including her recent talks with Dat and with Ella Mae, seemed to come together. "Well, I'm planning to keep in touch with Adeline after she leaves, so if you can't understand that or my spending time with her during her visit, then I think it's best we call off our engagement."

He stopped walking, shock on his face. "Sylvie . . . you're choosin' Adeline over me?"

"I don't see it that way. Anyway, she's just the last straw for you, ain't so?"

Strangely, he reached for her as the sun's last rays shot sprays of light high into the sky.

Shaking her head, she pulled away. "Titus, you don't trust me to do what's right, and you're much too worried 'bout what others think."

"Let's talk this through," he protested. "We have nothin' to lose by waiting a year, seein' what happens."

Why put it off when this isn't true love? she thought, tired of arguing. *He can't accept me or my family as we are.*

She stared at the fading sky. "I see no benefit in waiting."

"How can ya say that?" His tone was disbelieving.

She looked up at him, her heart a mixture of sadness and relief. "Because we have no future together, Titus. Not anymore."

With that, she turned to walk back to the waiting horse and carriage.

CHAPTER
Twenty

Gaslight glimmered through her father's shop windows, and instead of going to the house, Sylvia walked across the backyard to talk with him. Lately, their relationship had become better, stronger. *Because of Adeline and his sharing so openly with her, I know much more about his life before he became Amish,* she thought. She never could have foreseen that this would happen.

Crickets chirped all around as she tapped on the screen door. She stood there looking in at the pretty new clock Dat was working on.

"*Kumme* in," he said absently, then turned to see her there. "Oh, I thought it was your Mamma." He smiled and welcomed her in. "You're home early, Sylvie."

"I went ahead an' broke up with Titus," she announced even before she sat down. She mentioned Titus's suggestion they postpone the wedding for a year. "But there was no point in draggin' it out any longer while he scrutinized our family further."

Dat looked at her, his eyes searching her face. "Are you all right?"

She nodded. "To be honest, we've been fallin' apart for some time." She scrunched up her face. "When that all began to happen last month, I felt real sad and cried a lot, but not now."

"I know something about the kind of pain you're experiencing." Quietly, he told her how distraught he'd been when Adeline's mother had broken up their marriage. His face displayed compassion. "I just want to see you happy again, Sylvie."

They sat there surrounded by the ticking of Dat's clocks, the sounds of time hanging in the air.

"I've decided something else," she said, gathering herself. "I don't think I'm ready for baptism next month. My heart's not right . . . it hasn't been all summer."

Dat reacted like he'd been hit. "*Ach*, Sylvie, are you sure?"

"*Jah*. I plan to let Deacon Peachey know tomorrow before class begins."

"Shouldn't you take your time and contemplate this, since you're coming off this difficult evening with Titus?"

A shake of her head was the only response she could give just now.

Her father drew a long breath, then rose and walked to the back of his showroom, where he stood in front of one of the two tall floor clocks. He stared at the clock's face, and then after what seemed like minutes, he turned and trudged back to his chair to sit down. "I'd be mighty lax if I didn't caution you not to be hasty in this decision."

"Deacon Peachey and the other ministers will surely counsel me to put it off till I'm ready. They won't pressure me to continue—I know that for certain."

Grimacing, Dat glanced at the ceiling, like he was letting that settle in. He had to know that what she said was true.

"I haven't forgiven Titus for reportin' you to the ministers,

Dat, and I'm still angry with him for actin' like I'm somehow damaged goods because of my family. I know I shouldn't be angry, but I am. Until that changes, I can't go forward with baptism in *gut* conscience." She stopped for a moment. "I'm just bein' honest with ya."

He nodded, his expression solemn. "Honesty is the best path," he said, sounding like Ella Mae. "If I'd walked that path twenty years ago, we wouldn't be sitting here talking like this." Dat went on to say that he understood it was important not to continue the classes when she was in such a state. "But why say anything to the deacon tomorrow? Why not think a little more about your decision over the next two weeks?" he suggested, his voice shaky. "Will you do that?"

"I'm sorry to disappoint ya." She shook her head. "But I don't think two weeks will change anything."

"You might pray about this, daughter. Please."

"I should prob'ly head over to the house now," she said, getting up. Then, wanting him to know how much it meant for him to sit with her just now, in the depths of her discouragement, she added, "I'm grateful to ya, Dat." She smiled through tears. "*Denki . . .*"

"We've been through the fire and back again, haven't we?" he said, walking her to the screen door.

"*Gut Nacht*," she said, nodding, then made her way across the porch to the back door.

In her room, Sylvia turned on the gas lamp near her bed and sat there, still trying to get a grasp on all that had happened tonight—her breakup with Titus and her most open-hearted talk ever with Dat. It had appeared that her father was fighting back tears of his own when she left to come back to the house.

He understands me. . . .

She read several psalms before getting ready for bed, merely going through the motions, doing what she always did. But the words of Psalm twenty-five, verse sixteen, seemed to stand out: *Turn thee unto me, and have mercy upon me; for I am desolate and afflicted.*

Once she had washed up and changed, she outened the gas lamp and slipped into bed. She recited her rote prayers silently, with very little heart. Lying there, staring into the darkness, she did not understand why God was letting her life fall apart like this. The past months had been so chaotic.

My heart's out of tune, she realized again, struggling greatly with the knowledge.

Earnest walked out to the stable to check on the livestock, thinking that Sylvia was behaving impulsively. *One of my own worst flaws,* he thought, recognizing that if he were as devout as Rhoda, he would have spent this time in prayer.

After twenty minutes or so, he returned to the house and showered before heading upstairs, preparing how he should tell Rhoda about the end of Sylvia's engagement—the very thing they had once been so concerned about that, for a time, they had made a pact to keep his secret. *What we feared has come to pass,* he thought, *though not at all in the way we expected.*

Rhoda was reading the Good Book as he opened the door and stepped in. She glanced at him, looking exceptionally pretty tonight. He walked silently to his chair and sat down, thankful to this day that she hadn't kicked him out when he was going through the *Bann* and all that led up to it. A *remarkable woman*, he thought, trying not to stare at her where she sat with her open Bible in her lap, the dearest expression on her face as she read to herself.

Yawning, Earnest reached for the *Family Life* magazine he often enjoyed before bedtime. Yet after reading only one short article, he closed it and sat quietly looking out the window, gazing now at the dark sky filled with many bright stars. He felt torn over poor Sylvia's breakup, even though it was for the best.

"You look troubled," Rhoda said, setting the Bible on the table near her chair.

Turning, he paused. "There's no easy way to say this."

"Oh?"

"Sylvie called off her engagement tonight."

Rhoda nodded, eyes suddenly moist. "I guess I'm not surprised," she said. "Is she upset?"

"She seems to be all right, but there's something else." He told her that Sylvia was not ready to join church next month. He shook his head. "I wish she'd rethink it, but who can blame her?"

"Aw, poor girl . . . so *ferhoodled*. I feel for her." Big tears rolled down Rhoda's cheeks, and she got up and went to her dresser for a tissue.

Pained to see her like this, Earnest rose and opened his arms to his dear wife, and she moved toward him, weeping softly. He stroked her long hair, saying not a word, his heart breaking with hers.

Long after the gas lamps in the Millers' house were out, Adeline made her way into the house, having sat in her idling car to charge up her phone. She had enjoyed several rousing games of Dutch Blitz, then talked for a while with Tommy and Calvin. Later, when she excused herself to go out to her car, she texted her best girlfriends, Callie and Piper, then talked with Brendon, who joked about her getting sucked into Amish life. She'd laughed but assured him that the longest she would stay in Hickory Hollow was a few more days. Then it would be time to start the fall semester at Georgia Tech. That seemed to satisfy him, but when she called her grandparents, they didn't seem at all interested in hearing about the tranquility of Amish farmland or her quilted wall hanging, so Adeline talked around those topics. Later, Liam got on their landline, as well, showing a little curiosity in her cow-milking experience before going on to talk about body surfing and playing beach volleyball with his friends earlier that day.

Strangely, by the time she returned to the spare room, she felt lonely for the Millers. *At least Brendon enjoys hearing about my experiences here*, she thought, deciding at that moment to attend church with the Millers tomorrow, surprising herself. *If for no other reason than to show gratitude for their wonderful hospitality.*

CHAPTER
Twenty-One

The sky was partly cloudy the next morning, lessening the sun's heat, at least for now. Sylvia was thankful to be riding in the open spring wagon, the fresh air on her face and neck, while Adeline sat beside her and Ernie held the driving lines up front with Tommy.

To accommodate the rest of the family, Dat had taken the enclosed carriage with Mamma, Adam, and Calvin as passengers. Everyone was pleased that Adeline had decided to join them for church.

When they arrived at Onkel Josh and Aendi Ruthann's farm, Sylvia noticed Preacher Kauffman and his wife getting out of their buggy several carriages ahead. A knot twisted in her stomach at the sight of them.

The People began to gather outside the farmhouse. And as a few churchgoers cast glances in their direction, Sylvia felt obliged to remain with Adeline, since she was the only *Englischer* present. Occasionally, outsiders would come at the invitation of Amish neighbors or friends, but Sylvia assumed that Adeline would be the only one today. Quietly, she explained to Adeline what was taking place outside the temporary House of Worship, noting especially where to line up near the women's and children's entrance at the back of the house. All the while, Sylvia kept watch for Deacon Peachey's arrival. She hoped to locate him well before the morning baptismal instruction class, to let him know she was bowing out.

With Sylvia heavy on her heart, Rhoda turned to look for her and saw her standing at the very back of the line with Adeline, who wore a modest skirt and blouse. Recalling Earnest's revelation before bedtime last night, Rhoda was encouraged by how attentive Sylvia had become toward her half sister. *Adeline will be a good distraction for her today.*

Early that morning, Rhoda had slipped into her daughter's room to tell her how truly loved she was, and that she could depend on Rhoda's prayers for God's comfort and peace during this trying time. *"And for wisdom, too,"* she'd added, hoping against hope that Sylvia might change her mind about quitting baptism classes. *O Lord, may it be so,* she breathed, sending another entreaty heavenward even now.

Deacon Peachey and his wife had just pulled into the driveway, and it was all Rhoda could do to stay put in line there with her sisters Ruthann and Hannah and not rush back and plead with Sylvia to rethink this important decision. She tried to keep her focus on her sisters, glad to see that Hannah's health had returned after two miscarriages in two years. *Dear sister,* she thought.

Then Rhoda saw Eva Kauffman with her teenage daughters, Lavina and Connie, their matching royal blue dresses brushing their ankles as they came this way across the yard. Difficult as things might be now, she knew it was only right to forgive Titus's parents for whatever part they might have played in Sylvia and Titus's breakup. *Grant me Thy help in that, Lord God,* she prayed.

Sylvia stood very still, staring at the wall hanging in the upstairs hallway just outside the room where the baptism class was to take place in a few minutes. Already a number of youth had gone in and taken their seats to await the rest of the candidates, as well as the ministerial brethren. She hoped she wouldn't have to encounter Titus, but even with that in mind, she was determined to stand there and wait for Deacon Peachey.

She kept looking at the wall hanging made by Cousin Alma years ago, noting that it wasn't quilted piecework like the one Adeline was working on, but rather a Scripture verse done in needlepoint. *Thou wilt keep him in perfect peace, whose mind is stayed on thee: because he trusteth in thee.*

How can I trust again? she wondered. *After everything that's gone wrong.*

Behind her, she heard heavy footsteps on the stairs, likely the deacon. Turning slightly, she saw that it was the bishop, who paused and admired the wall hanging with her. "Trusting our heavenly Father is the key, Sylvia Miller," he said, startling her. "That's a verse to remember." With that, he turned and walked into the room for the start of the class.

Does he suspect I'm dropping out? she wondered, practically wringing her hands now. *And where's the deacon?*

Just as she'd hoped wouldn't happen, Titus came running up the stairs with his cousin, who hurried ahead into the room. Titus, however, remained.

"What are ya doin' out here, Sylvie?" He frowned as his eyes searched her face.

"I'm gonna tell the deacon that I'm droppin' out."

Titus's face fell. "What? Why?"

She shrugged and looked away, wanting to avoid his piercing gaze. "I need more time," she said, hoping he wouldn't inquire further. It was going to be hard enough to do this.

Titus stepped closer. "Honestly . . . Sylvie, why would ya do that?" He studied her. "Are ya mad at me 'cause I wanted to postpone our wedding?"

"It's not about you and me, Titus."

"Then listen to reason and follow through with baptism," he urged. When she made no reply, he turned and slipped into the room for class.

Sylvia hoped they hadn't been overheard. Then, wondering where the deacon was, she thought of simply going downstairs to join Adeline and talk to the deacon at another time. But then here he came at last, making his way slowly up the steep flight of stairs. His ruddy face was solemn above his long, straight beard, and he looked out of breath.

At the landing, she stepped forward to quickly inform him that she was quitting classes.

Oddly, he seemed unsurprised by her announcement, almost as if he had been expecting her news. "You do realize that you're more than halfway through the instruction?" he asked.

"Jah . . . but I need to be in *Rumschpringe* a little longer," she said quietly.

He raised his eyebrows. "Is that so?"

Sylvia nodded. "An earnest candidate should demonstrate sincere fruits of repentance and alter their lives, just as the Dordrecht Confession says." She went on to say that it wasn't the right time for her to be baptized. "There's something I need to repent of, and I'm afraid I'm not ready to let it go just yet."

"I'd hate to see ya regret this, Sylvia."

She momentarily bowed her head. "Even so, the Lord God would not be pleased if I continue . . . not now." Sighing, she added more softly, "I don't mean to disappoint ya, Deacon."

He glanced toward the ceiling. "'Tis not I you should fear disappointing."

She nodded slightly, then headed downstairs as swiftly as she could, hoping Adeline had saved her a place in the back row with all the other unbaptized youth and any *Englischers.*

Adeline did her best to remain attentive as the congregation sang the hymns, many of which Sylvia said dated from the sixteenth century. She attempted to follow along as Sylvia's pointer finger moved across the pages of the thick hymnal printed in a Gothic German script. After the first few verses, each one sung unaccompanied by any instrument, she realized there must be at least twenty identical-sounding stanzas to the hymn. The painstakingly slow melody kept repeating like a Gregorian chant. But something about the ultra-simple melody made her feel peaceful while standing there surrounded by Amish young women her age and younger, many of them wearing royal blue or plum-colored dresses and long white organdy aprons, as well as the white see-through head coverings that formed the shape of a heart.

"We sing the songs of our martyred forefathers," Sylvia whispered after the near-endless hymn came to an end.

Martyred . . . Several days ago, Adeline had taken time to look through the enormous book *Martyrs Mirror* that Rhoda kept in her corner cupboard. She had perused a few of the accounts of the dreadful suffering and the execution of Anabaptists during their persecution by the Holy Roman Empire in the 1500s.

During the sermon, Adeline noticed how quietly some of the small children sat not far from her and Sylvia, either on their mother's laps or on the bench next to them. Occasionally, an older sister or mother would give one a white handkerchief, and soon they were making something that resembled a baby in a cradle.

The Scripture readings were in High German, so Adeline was able to understand words and phrases of those, thanks to her high-school German classes. But when the minister gave his sermon, he reverted to Pennsylvania Dutch, the dialect Adeline had become accustomed to hearing at the Millers' home.

After two solid hours of sitting, then kneeling for prayer one time—a wonderful change of position—she wondered how she would manage to sit for another hour and a half. When Sylvia had mentioned to her earlier how long the service would last, Adeline had hoped she wasn't serious, but it was clear that Sylvia hadn't exaggerated. And the fellowship meal was still to come. *More sitting!*

Adeline took a deep breath and fought to stay awake in the warm, crowded room, where she could see other women, mostly older, nodding off. It was good to be sitting in the back row, she realized, because while the benches were hard, those seated in the last row could lean against the wall behind them. *One of the perks of being a visitor,* she thought.

Next to her, Sylvia was a model of reverence and attention. Had she been programmed to do this every other Sunday since she was a baby? There *were* quite a few infants in the service, nestled in their mother's arms, and if they whimpered in the slightest, they were taken out and presumably nursed elsewhere.

Thinking back to the few times her parents had taken her to church as a child, Adeline realized that those paled in comparison to what she was experiencing this morning. Yet she could not put her finger on why. Sitting up straighter, she tried to see where Earnest and Tommy were over on the men's side. Eventually, she also spotted Ernie, Adam, and Calvin, the three of them in a row, just as they sat for each meal. Smiling, she recalled how enthusiastic they had been the other day at the prospect of introducing her to their farm life and daily chores. *Thoughtful kids . . .*

Daydreaming now, Adeline recalled the day her mom first told her about her biological father. It was a week after the man whom Adeline had always thought *was* her father had passed away, and she was completely shocked to learn otherwise. Her mother, on the other hand, had seemed relieved to set the record straight after twelve years, all of Adeline's young life up to that point. *As if she were waiting for the right time to tell me . . .*

Just then, Sylvia bumped her as she turned to kneel for the second prayer, and Adeline quickly knelt, too, embarrassed she had been so checked out. *I've just about survived this nearly endless service!* she thought as she leaned against the bench and a minister offered a prayer in German. *Shouldn't three and a half hours of this count for something?*

The clouds had long since shifted off to the east as, following the service, Sylvia and Cousin Alma walked to the nearby shade tree. The lilac-like scent of the crepe myrtle trees filled the air as they waited for Adeline, using the indoor restroom, and Sylvia whispered to her cousin that she wasn't going to be baptized this year, after all. "And Titus and I broke up last evening, too."

"Oh, Sylvie." Alma's dark eyes grew serious. "I'm so sorry."

Sylvia motioned for her to walk back around the other side of the tree, where she filled her in on more. "It's all for the best."

Tears welling up, Cousin Alma placed her hand on her chest. "And this is because of Adeline?"

Sylvia admitted that her half sister's presence had set off Titus's alarm bells. "But I don't think it was just 'bout Adeline. Titus isn't willing to associate his family with anyone who falls short of their ideals."

The dinner bell rang just then, and Cousin Alma suggested they head back.

As they came around the tree, there was Adeline, frowning, her eyes intense. "May I talk with you, Sylvie?" It sounded urgent.

"They're callin' the youth inside," Sylvie protested uneasily.

"I'll go in an' save us seats," Alma said, hurrying away.

To Sylvia's chagrin, there she stood with Adeline, who seemed to have overheard at least part of the conversation with Cousin Alma.

"Did I hear correctly that your engagement is off?" Adeline asked, clearly concerned.

Sylvia nodded, worried now.

"But you seemed so happy." Adeline looked at the ground and shook her head.

"Honestly, I'm happier now."

"It's likely my fault for barging in here . . . and for staying this long."

"I'm glad you did." Sylvia reached to touch her arm and explained that there had been growing problems between her and Titus for some time. "They had nothin' to do with you."

"But my being here hasn't helped." Adeline groaned softly. "I'm your big sister, after all. This is terrible. . . ."

Sylvia appreciated Adeline's seeming protectiveness, unexpected though it was. "Really, it's too late to salvage anything between Titus and me," Sylvia said, moved by Adeline's caring. "I don't want you to leave just when you're getting acquainted with Dat and the rest of us." She felt like crying now, when moments before, Cousin Alma had been the only one shedding tears. "*Kumme*, let's go eat. We can talk 'bout this later, *jah?*"

CHAPTER

Twenty-Two

*F*ollowing Preaching service and the shared meal, Earnest was looking forward to another peaceful Sunday afternoon. He quickly changed his clothes and then, after seeing to the animals, went to sit on the back porch. *Ah, these calmer hours,* he thought, gazing into the distance as he sat there with Rhoda.

"Mamie Zook told me something interesting at Preaching today," Rhoda said, touching his arm. "I think ya might be surprised."

"*Jah?*"

"She's changed her mind 'bout selling the farm and decided to move into the *Dawdi Haus* to be near Mahlon's rose arbor— I guess the downstairs bedroom windows overlook it. And she says she likes the idea of living next door to her daughter-in-law Rebecca."

"So Benuel and Rebecca must be taking over Mahlon's farm?"

"According to Mamie, *jah.*"

Earnest was happy to hear it. Benuel had always been close

to his father, and he and Earnest enjoyed a solid friendship. *Almost like brothers,* he thought.

The back door opened, and Adeline walked over to them as though wanting to talk but too shy. He motioned for her to join them. "Please . . . pull up a chair."

Studying her now, Earnest noticed she looked shaken and gloomy. "I'm afraid I've caused terrible trouble for Sylvie," she said, glancing at her feet. "I've decided it's best for me to leave tomorrow morning."

Earnest looked at Rhoda, who was clearly as surprised as he felt. "You certainly don't have to, we hope you know."

Adeline looked away for a moment, toward the area of the meadow where a cluster of trees provided enough moisture for purple coneflowers to thrive into early October. A place where she had enjoyed walking in the recent days. "I've had the best time here," she said quietly, turning to look at them again. "Your farm is amazing, and so is your family, but I need to get back to my life. Hopefully then Sylvia's guy will get his head on straight and go ahead with the wedding."

"The breakup really ain't your doing, dear," Rhoda said. "Please don't think that."

Adeline nodded like she knew all about it. "Sylvie and I talked after church and just now in my room. She said the same thing, but I have a feeling they'll get back together once I'm gone."

Disappointed to hear it but not wanting to urge Adeline to stay if she was determined to go, Earnest excused himself to his shop. He had something he wanted to do.

Out in the stable, sun flooded the nearby window as Sylvia gave Lily a sugar cube, talking softly to the horse. "Adeline thinks what happened with Titus and me is her fault," she said. "But I was the one who took matters into my own hands. . . ." While she had no regrets about ending her engagement, it *had* been awfully impulsive to quit baptism instruction. *The deacon was correct to admonish me like he did. Even so, I'm doing the right thing. The Lord would be displeased otherwise,* she thought, having been taught in class the importance of a contrite heart when going into the sacrament of holy baptism. After all, baptism meant making a lifelong vow to follow God and the Amish church all the days of her life.

A public confession of my abiding faith, she thought, knowing she was sorely lacking in that area right now. Yet she was glad she'd had the opportunity to be forthcoming with the deacon, at least on that point. What she still wasn't ready to do was forgive Titus.

All the same, she wished everything could have been different these past months. *For all of us . . .*

Carefully, Earnest leaned down to open the bottom cupboard and lift the tinderbox out of hiding. Carrying it to his workbench, he opened it and emptied out the contents to get to the bottom, where he unwrapped the gold pocket watch. Holding it carefully, he looked at it through new eyes, then carried it outside and over to the back porch, where Adeline was talking with Rhoda.

"I want you to have this," he said, handing the watch to Adeline.

Her eyes widened, and she gasped. "It's lovely."

"It's not a grandfather clock, but it's a treasure."

Rhoda's gaze caught his, and she smiled approvingly.

Adeline held it, looking at its beautiful, clear face. "It's absolutely gorgeous." She held it out to him. "But I think you should keep it, Earnest. Seriously. It looks valuable."

He shook his head and refused it, his palms up. "Look on the back," he told her. "You'll see why it should belong to you."

Seeming puzzled, Adeline turned it over and read the inscription—*To Earnest, with all my love, Rosalind*—her mouth dropping open. Then she looked up at him. "My *mom* gave you this?"

Earnest nodded. "A Christmas gift from her the year we eloped." He mentioned that he had been thinking recently of selling it, but something had kept him from doing so. "And then when you came, I forgot about it . . . till just now." He paused and smiled. "Think of it as something of your mother's . . . from across the years."

Tears filled Adeline's eyes. "This is wonderful," she whispered. "I'll always cherish it. Thank you."

"You're holding time in your hands, so to speak," Earnest said to her gently.

Wiping her eyes, Adeline smiled at him. "May I ask why you kept it this long?"

Earnest remembered how this had been the question of the day for weeks on end this summer. "It's really not important." He didn't want to stir up any sadness or misunderstanding in dearest Rhoda, not with the small strides forward their relationship was taking. "Just know that it belongs with you."

Adeline looked again at the inscription on the back and shook her head, visibly moved by the gift.

"I have a soft cloth to wrap it in for safekeeping, if you'd like," Earnest offered, and Adeline rose and followed him to the shop.

Sylvia sat through Bible reading and prayers that evening, mindful that this was the last time they would gather with Adeline present. To think that in this very room Dat had shared with all of them, before Adeline's arrival, about his marriage and divorce from a young college student named Rosalind. Sylvia remembered how devastated and confused she'd felt as Dat humbly asked for their forgiveness.

Recalling that earth-shattering Sunday afternoon eight weeks ago gave Sylvia pause as she looked at her brothers, then at Dat and Mamma, who sat side by side on the cane-backed sofa. *We managed to weather the storm,* she thought, her heart thankful.

For a moment, she tuned out the Scripture verses Dat was reading, instead rehearsing the nine days she'd shared with this very modern half sister on the chair next to her. One thing stuck out in her mind, especially: When they'd run into Ella Mae Zook at BB's, the Wise Woman had told Adeline to hold her head high because she was a part of this family. At the recollection, Sylvia smiled so broadly that, when Mamma caught her eye, she had to quickly suppress her smile.

After the short prayer, Dat quietly informed the boys that Adeline would be heading home tomorrow.

Tommy turned to look at Adeline, his forehead instantly knitted into a deep frown. "Do ya *have* to?" he asked, eyes pleading.

Adeline got up and sat down beside him on the floor. She slipped her arm around his shoulders. "Don't forget me, okay?"

Tommy shook his head, and a tear trickled down his cheek.

"Hey, kiddo . . . I didn't mean to make you cry," Adeline said softly.

Tommy wiped his cheek and shook his head. "You didn't," he said, giving her a little smile.

Ernie, Adam, and Calvin said nothing as they observed this. Ernie, however, looked like he might have wanted to speak, if not for the fact that Dat and Mamma got up right then, which signaled the end of their time together.

As their parents left the front room, Ernie and Adam went over to Adeline and leaned down to shake her hand. "We'll miss seein' ya round here," Ernie said, and Adam nodded his agreement.

Calvin, meanwhile, took it all in, still perched on the wide windowsill in the corner. Sylvia wasn't sure if he wanted to be left alone or not, but she walked over to him. "You all right, Calvin?"

He seemed to force a smile. "Why wouldn't I be?"

"Just checkin'," she said, noticing Adeline coming their way now.

"So, Calvin," Adeline said, "I'll never forget our little milking adventure. It was super fun." Her voice cracked, and she held out her hand. "This is the hand that milked a cow, thanks to you," she said with a laugh. "But seriously, I understand that, here in Hickory Hollow, it's thought of as a *wunnerbaar* thing to shake hands with a friend . . . or a brother."

Calvin nodded and shook her hand. "It sure is."

Adeline turned to Sylvia. "Thanks for all you did—hanging out with me, enduring my questions, and helping with the wall hanging."

"I was glad to," Sylvia said. "And you'll enjoy completing that project when you're home."

They talked about the remaining steps, and Adeline said she would have to take it slow since her studies would dominate her time.

"That's the best way, anyway," Sylvia said. "Inch by inch, everything's a cinch."

Adeline reached to hug her, and Sylvia couldn't remember being so moved.

Very early the next morning, Sylvia carried Adeline's wall hanging out to the car as Dat took the luggage and Mamma brought an insulated carrier packed with ham and turkey sandwiches, sliced apples, celery and carrot sticks, and chocolate-chip cookies for Adeline's long trip home.

Her brothers stood from tallest to shortest, forming a line with Dat once he finished loading Adeline's bags into her trunk. Sylvia handed Adeline her project, wrapped in plastic to keep it clean, and Adeline placed it in the back seat behind the driver's side.

"Thanks again for everything," Adeline said, smiling at them.

Will we ever see her again? Sylvia wondered as she tried to keep her chin up.

Slowly, the red sports car backed out of the driveway and turned onto Hickory Lane, heading north to Cattail Road. Sylvia stood there with the rest of her family, all of them waving good-bye to the young woman who had come such a long way to find them.

Once they'd seen Adeline off, Sylvia trudged down the cellar steps and began to sort the dirty clothing tossed down the laundry chute . . . white clothes first, colored ones next, and the darks last of all, as Mamma had taught her.

When the first load of whites was in the wringer washer, she made her way upstairs and went to look in the spare room. Seeing it empty, she got a sudden lump in her throat and went to sit on the quilt that Adeline had so admired. "She would've stayed another week if she hadn't overheard what I told Cousin Alma."

"Talkin' to someone, dear?"

Sylvia turned and saw Mamma standing in the doorway. "Oh, just to myself," she said, going to give her a hug. "I'm really gonna miss her."

"We *all* will," Mamma said, beckoning her toward the kitchen. "What if we made a special breakfast today?"

Sylvia agreed. "Chocolate-chip pancakes, maybe? The boys will love it."

"So will your Dat." Mamma smiled extra big, and Sylvia guessed she was trying to get everyone's mind off Adeline's leaving. It was no small task. For Sylvia right now, the loss of her half sister weighed more on her than the loss of her fiancé.

When it came to her breakup with Titus, Sylvia still felt surprisingly settled, considering the course their courtship had taken and how it had slowly but surely crumbled apart. *I'll wait for true love, whenever it comes,* she thought. *The Good Lord willing.*

As mile after mile passed, Adeline relived her time with Earnest Miller and his family. "*Wunnerbaar-gut,*" she whispered with a smile as she fondly recalled sitting at the big kitchen table with everyone.

It'll be lonely in my small apartment, she thought, *and the food won't be as good, either.* She had thoroughly enjoyed getting to know each one of her half siblings, as well as her natural father. And Rhoda—what an amazing woman she was.

But, sighing now, Adeline faulted herself for having brought destruction to Sylvia's longtime relationship with Titus. No matter what Sylvia had said, Adeline knew that she was the ultimate cause of their breakup.

CHAPTER
Twenty-Three

The entire next week, Sylvia spent her days picking peaches and some pears, canning them with Mamma and Aendi Hannah at the next farm over. There was scarcely a moment when the big canner wasn't on the stove, jars gently rattling in boiling water, and many hands making light work. Each woman was calm and relaxed, taking care with every step of the process. And because Sylvia was so busy, there was hardly any time to miss Adeline. Although at night, she would lie awake and remember what Adeline had said when they were alone in the spare room before saying good-bye. *"You have a really special family, Sylvie. And to think, I was so reluctant to stay here."*

The last Saturday in August, while Earnest and Ernie were at market, Deacon Luke Peachey and his wife, Lois, dropped by to see what new clocks were available. Deacon came right over to Earnest and asked if they might talk. Agreeing, Earnest suggested they walk down the aisle, over toward the kettle corn. "What's on your mind, Luke?"

"Your daughter." The deacon rubbed the tip of his nose. "Has she come to her senses yet?"

"Well, if you mean about joining church this year, Sylvia isn't ready to be baptized. Since that's the case, I'm in favor of giving her more time."

Luke nodded slowly.

"We've talked quite seriously about it, but I'm not going to twist her arm," Earnest continued. "You wouldn't want a baptismal candidate who isn't ready, *jah?*"

"True, but what changed?" Luke asked. "She seemed so involved in the classes, even eager to move ahead with baptism."

"I can't say exactly, but she realized her heart wasn't in the right place. Sylvie's made her choice for now; let's see what she's thinking next year."

Luke seemed to understand but suggested that Earnest talk further about it with his daughter. "She's a fine young woman, and it's too bad 'bout the breakup with Titus Kauffman," he said. "I do believe it's God's will for her to make her vow to God and the church, however."

Earnest tried to cover his surprise that Luke knew so much about Sylvia's former ties to Titus. "All Amish parents want that for their children," he said, then thanked the deacon for seeking him out. "I know you care about Sylvie, and I appreciate it."

They exchanged a few more words before Luke wished him well and got in line to buy some kettle corn.

Earnest returned to his booth to discover that Ernie had sold a small table clock to Lois Peachey.

Do all the ministerial brethren know about Titus and Sylvia's breakup? he wondered.

The first two days in September, Sylvia helped make large quantities of applesauce, canning with Mamma, Mammi Riehl, and several aunts she always enjoyed being around. There was the typical banter, as well as a little gossip, and she wished Adeline could have been there to observe the process. *We have our own little assembly line!* she thought with a smile.

When the mail arrived that Thursday, Sylvia noticed two letters postmarked Atlanta, Georgia. One was addressed to her, and the other to her parents.

"Mamma! We have mail from Adeline!" Sylvia hurried into the house, waving both letters.

Mamma lit up like a moonbeam. "Go an' tell your Dat right quick."

Sylvia had just wondered when they might hear from her again. Rushing over to the shop, she called inside, "Dat?" Then, opening the screen door, she found her father clear in the back, scratching his head and apparently studying two varieties of wood. "I have a surprise, Dat," she said, holding up the letter addressed to him and Mamma.

For a brief second, he looked baffled; then a smile broke across his face. "From Adeline?"

She handed him the letter. "Now I'm going outside to read mine."

Dat chuckled. "She wrote you, too?"

"*Jah*, we must've made a strong impression." With that, Sylvia waved good-bye and made her way back through the shop and the small showroom before dashing out the screen door, letting it slap against the doorframe.

She spotted the tree where Dat had introduced Adeline to

Cousin Alma on the day Ernie was overcome with heat. For an instant, it seemed almost like yesterday, and she was eager to see what Adeline had written.

Earnest held the envelope, studying the unfamiliar handwriting addressed to him and to Rhoda, realizing that somewhere in the recesses of his mind he had sincerely yearned for this. Adeline's leaving had been too abrupt. Yet she had taken time to write, and as he opened the envelope and began to read, he recalled how she had been nearly overwhelmed at his gift of the pocket watch.

> *Dear Earnest and Rhoda,*
>
> *Thank you both once again for making me feel so at home there with the wonderful way you included me in your family! In spite of my being a stranger, your TLC made me feel like I truly belonged.*
>
> *And the gold timepiece . . . I can't tell you what this special gift means to me, Earnest. All during the long drive home, I kept reliving the moment when you presented it to me. Seeing Mom's words inscribed on the back touched my heart.*
>
> *But the main reason for this letter is to tell you that my time with you has stirred up something in me. You see, when she died, my mom left me her diary, which she started the year before her passing, soon after she received her diagnosis. She had given me a hint or two regarding what she was writing about, so I purposely shied away from opening it. Until you gave me the watch, I wasn't even close to being ready to read it. That was the nudge I needed.*

*Through meeting you, I learned certain new things about
my mom . . . and about you. I see the timepiece as a symbol
of the love that brought me into the world, and it awakened
the desire to read Mom's writings. I have you to thank for
this, Earnest.*

*As of now, I'm coming up on a quarter of the way through
the diary, and I see what my mother wanted me to learn
through its pages. She talks a lot about the relationship she
found with her "True North," her "loving Father in heaven"
. . . and as I read, more and more questions present themselves. If you're open to it, I would love to pick your brain about
the growing faith in Christ my mom embraced before she died.*

Earnest's neck muscles were tense when he looked up from
the letter. What sort of questions had Rosalind's diary brought
up for Adeline?

Taking a deep breath, he walked to the window and gazed
out, holding the letter. "Rhoda's the one who should answer
this," he mumbled, feeling as inadequate as when he'd first
come to Hickory Hollow. "I haven't learned anything."

Shaking his head and aware of a growing sense of frustration with himself, he could relate to Adeline's own desire to
purposely avoid her mother's diary, concerned about what she
might find there. For the moment, he was unable to bring
himself to read the rest of Adeline's letter.

*My own flesh and blood needs answers, and I'm incapable of
helping her.* It struck him as fascinating that Rosalind had gotten
a dose of religion in the months before her passing. *How ironic
that she's the one planting seeds of the Gospel in our daughter's life!*

Setting Adeline's letter aside, Earnest returned to deliberating over the choice of wood for his latest floor clock. Half

an hour had passed since Sylvia came dashing in to deliver the letter, yet he would not permit himself to ponder it any longer—not now, when he had no answers.

He looked around the small showroom at his attractive clocks, his workmanship on display all around him. *Every day, time slips through my fingers, no matter what I'm doing. The clocks just keep ticking, moving forward. There's no stopping time.*

He shook away the heavy thoughts and returned to sawing, filling up the minutes of this day with work, work, and more work, as he was accustomed to doing. Creating, building, polishing, selling . . .

"Time ran out for Mahlon, even though he was a man of strong faith in Christ," he whispered, startling himself. Earnest could only imagine what his encouraging friend and Amish father figure would think of all the chaos Earnest's secret had caused. But what had Adeline's coming meant? Earnest had witnessed firsthand her joy at meeting him and her half siblings, and dear Rhoda, too. *But how do I really feel about meeting her?*

He recalled Adeline's asking if the Bible verses he read to the family ever jumped out at him. He now wished he'd thought to tell her of all the passages in the Bible the ministers had him reading daily during his six-week *Bann. Jah,* he thought, *many of those not only jumped out but were convicting.* Yet the minute he was reinstated as a church member in good standing, he had abandoned his personal daily reading of Scripture, something he hadn't even realized until now.

When time runs out for me, what will my life count for? he wondered, trying to focus on his work. Folded up over there on his workbench, Adeline's letter plagued him as much as the tinderbox had after its troublesome revelation, and he shuddered to think he had no solid answers for her.

Twenty-Four

*S*ylvia was happy to read about Adeline's college activities, but there was no mention of her fiancé. *Hopefully, she's not reluctant to talk about Brendon now that Titus and I aren't together,* she thought, sorry that Adeline lived so far away. *Georgia might as well be on the other side of the world!*

Getting up and heading for the house, Sylvia walked barefoot through the thick grass, almost compelled to write a prompt reply to assure Adeline that she could share anything she cared to in future letters.

The next day, Sylvia walked with her mother over to Mamie Zook's to deliver a dried beef and noodle casserole so that Mamie wouldn't have to bother cooking that weekend. As before Mahlon's passing, Mamma continued to be involved in the grieving widow's life.

Upon their arrival, Sylvia noticed Mamie's youngest son, Benuel, and her grandsons Andy and Michael weeding the

vegetable garden. *Such a devoted family,* Sylvia thought, glad
for the dear woman's sake.

Indoors, Mamie smiled as she accepted the casserole dish
and set it down on the counter. She mentioned all the extra
help she was getting with the farmwork and around the yard,
too. "No more push mowin' for me," she said with a little laugh.
"My family's adamant that I'm no longer a spring chicken. *Ach,*
I can see that by lookin' in the mirror!" Another chuckle. "But
if I just sit around the house, I'll give up the ghost."

"We all care 'bout ya, Mamie," said Mamma. "And if you
ever need anything, just ring your dinner bell four times, and
we'll come runnin'."

"Yous are the best neighbors." Mamie wiped her face with
a hankie she pulled from beneath her sleeve. "You know I'm
stayin' put here, don't ya? Just a simple move next door to the
Dawdi Haus. Andy's offered to supervise the move toward the
end of next month, once the menfolk help fill silo."

Feeling a little awkward at the gleam in Mamie's pretty
eyes when she mentioned Andy, Sylvia wondered if word had
already spread that she and Titus were no longer together.
Must have, she thought.

They stayed for a while to visit over cold lemonade and some
red grapes and pineapple chunks Mamie insisted on serving.
There were orange raisin bars, too. And it was noteworthy
to Sylvia how many more times Andy's name crept into the
conversation.

Later, on the way down the porch steps as she and Mamma
were leaving, Andy himself glanced up from his weeding to
wave to Sylvia, offering a charming smile.

She waved back and wondered why he felt at liberty to be
so friendly. *Doesn't he know about my flawed family?*

That evening after supper, while Earnest sat outdoors with Rhoda, they discussed Adeline's letter. "How would you like to respond?" he asked as they relaxed on the back porch.

Rhoda looked surprised. "Well, dear, as I recall, her questions are addressed to you."

He waved that off. "Oh, but you're much better at letter writing." He mentioned all the practice she had, writing circle letters to cousins and to four other Amishwomen also named Rhoda who happened to share the same autumn birthday.

Rhoda frowned a little, as though she sensed he was looking for an excuse. "Here's an idea . . . what if I simply write down what you'd like to tell her?"

The old feelings of inadequacy badgered him and, not knowing how to respond, he looked out at the pasture he so loved. The truth was, he had a lot of growing to do spiritually if he was ever going to help Adeline.

Rhoda reached for his hand, and he held on, gazing at her with all the love in his heart.

"You know how lacking I am, don't you, dear?"

She paused a moment, then said, "Are ya seein' yourself in Adeline, maybe? In her searching?"

"The fact is, I don't have a deep faith like yours." After all they'd endured together, it was easy now to admit this. "Though I've tried, I can't hide my shortcomings or fix them."

"That's not something you can do on your own, Earnest— the Lord is here for you, and I am, too," she said seriously. "But Adeline's reachin' out to *you*, Earnest, and I believe you can make a difference in her life."

He nodded. "If I can just get over the hurdles."

"It would be worth the effort for health and for peace of mind. And most of all, for the soul," she said, tears welling up.

He looked at her, his precious wife who'd somehow persisted through the immense pain he alone had caused her. He squeezed her hand and felt incredibly blessed.

Later, after family prayers, Earnest and Rhoda sat together in their room, where Rhoda began to pen his letter to Adeline, sharing about his own difficult journey. "*I'll be honest, Adeline,*" he dictated, "*I put on a 'flawless' exterior for twenty long years, living as an Amishman in name only. I didn't take God's purpose for my life to completion, truly embracing the faith that went along with that. I hope you understand what I'm trying to say here.*"

Rhoda nodded. "That's a *gut* start, love," she encouraged.

"It's strange, but I seem to have a natural connection with Adeline," he admitted. "Not that I don't have it with my other children. It was just a surprise to discover I had it with Adeline, too."

Rhoda listened, pen poised over the stationery.

"So, back to the letter," he said, "let's get to the point, in case this is the only one we write."

"Oh, I think there will be more letters from her."

"I hope so."

Rhoda nodded. "I saw how she began to warm up to us, even though it was hard for her the first few days."

They discussed the visit, reliving the way things started and ended, and Rhoda recommended that Earnest suggest to Adeline that she read the Gospel of John. "What do ya think?"

"Well then, I should probably read it, too."

She smiled. "And if you do, you'll be able to write the next letter to her yourself, maybe?"

Earnest saw the wisdom in Rhoda's remark. "Will you be reading it, as well? The three of us together?"

"*Jah*," she said, reaching for her Bible. "Why not start now?"

Earnest leaned back in his comfortable chair and listened closely as Rhoda began, her soft voice sweet to his ears. "'In the beginning was the Word, and the Word was with God, and the Word was God.'"

A week after Adeline had mailed her letters to the Millers, she received two back—one from Earnest, and another from Sylvia. Settling in for the evening, she sipped her can of lemon sparkling water, thankful for the very honest letter Rhoda had penned for Earnest. *Whatever works for him*, she thought, giving him that latitude. The fact that he and Sylvia had replied at all, and so quickly, did her heart good.

Adeline walked over to the sliding door and stood on the small balcony attached to her apartment, where she looked out on a sea of brick and mortar, apartment complexes in every direction. *I was spoiled by the views of Amish farmland,* she thought.

Thinking of Sylvia's letter, she was a little perplexed by it, because Sylvia seemed too cheerful and practically anesthetized, as if the reality of her breakup with Titus still hadn't sunk in. *Kind of like I was after Mom died,* Adeline thought. *It took weeks. . . .*

Standing there at the railing after a hectic day of classes and before Brendon was to arrive with takeout—spicy Korean pork tacos—Adeline considered writing back to Sylvia. It was hard to know what to say when she still felt responsible for the way things had gone downhill. But surely Sylvie and Titus would realize soon how much they missed each other. *If they're in love, they will,* she thought, unable to imagine splitting up with Brendon.

She decided to take Earnest up on his suggestion to read through the Gospel of John—if she could locate her mom's Bible.

CHAPTER

Twenty-Five

September nineteenth, one day before baptism Sunday, Sylvia took stock of herself. One thing was sure: She was thankful Titus hadn't tried to contact her.

Time for us both to move on, she thought as she and Mamma prepared spaghetti and meatballs for the noon meal. Sylvia couldn't help recalling how disappointed Dat and the deacon had been when she dropped out of baptismal instruction. Yet despite the hastiness of that decision, she had not second-guessed it, though she did wonder how she would feel when she saw the other candidates bow their knees and promise to follow God and the church all the days of their lives.

"What are you thinkin' about, Sylvie?"

She looked across the counter at her mother. "Stuff that makes me frown, apparently."

Mamma smiled. "I thought so."

Sylvia told her more, and Mamma said, "Well, it's not like you can't be baptized next year, if you're ready by then."

"True," Sylvia said softly.

"You're still hurting from the breakup, *jah?*"

She shook her head. "Not so much that as the reasons for it, I guess."

Mamma went to stir the big pot of spaghetti noodles. "I'm anxious for the day when you're truly happy again."

"It's not as though I'm crying my eyes out. The worst of it happened weeks ago now." She wondered if she ought to say what she was thinking about doing next.

Mamma gave an understanding nod. "With God's help, we each handle sadness in our own way."

Sylvia considered that. "You might be surprised, but I'm actually thinking of goin' to Singing tomorrow night. I'm worried 'bout how Titus might take it, though."

"Well, you're not obligated to stay home," Mamma said. "Do ya feel like you are?"

Sylvia shook her head. "I just don't want to run into him."

"Maybe plan to sit with Cousins Alma and Jessie . . . and take the family carriage. That way, ya won't send a message that you're already lookin' for a new beau."

"*Gut* idea, Mamma."

"Although if ya ask me, I think you could have a new beau . . . once you're ready."

Sylvia frowned. "Someone you have in mind?"

Mamma clucked like a mother hen. "You'd have to be blind not to see what I'm seein'."

"Andy Zook?"

Nodding, Mamma added, "Trust me, he's fond of you, even though it's been from afar."

"He's always been a cheerful fella, but he's like that with everyone."

"Think what ya want." Mamma was grinning now.

Sylvia recalled that she had wondered why Andy seemed not to view her father and family as somehow tarnished.

"You'll find out if ya go to Singing."

"*Ach*, Mamma."

"Seriously."

Sylvia pondered that while she mixed the lean ground beef for the meatballs with eggs, onions, a little garlic, and bread crumbs, mixing everything thoroughly with both hands. *I just want someone to love and accept me for who I am,* she thought. *A rather tall order.*

At a sushi restaurant, Adeline looked across their table, enjoying her dinner date with Brendon, handsome as always in khakis and a pale blue golf shirt. His light brown eyes and stunning blond hair were an unlikely combination that had always intrigued her. She'd never known anyone else so fair-haired to have brown eyes.

They had been tossing around ideas for their destination wedding, and Sylvia mentioned Mackinac Island. "Sylvia liked the idea of our riding down Main Street in a horse-drawn carriage," she told him, laughing. "Naturally, considering her Amish background."

Brendon nodded and smiled. "Is that what you want, Addy?"

"Well, it's not just *my* wedding." Adeline smiled at him. "Your input counts, too."

Brendon tilted his head. "I appreciate that."

"So, what do you think?" She reached for the spicy dipping sauce.

"Let's do a spreadsheet on the costs involved—the ferry ride over and back will add up fast for everyone. And have you priced the hotel accommodations on the island? Spendy would be an understatement, I'm certain. But we can check."

Leave it to my number cruncher, she thought.

"I doubt you want to use your entire inheritance on our wedding, do you?"

Brendon had a point, and she appreciated his insight. "No. It's a good thing it's all tied up in a trust or, well, you know me. . . ."

"My adorable spendthrift." He grinned as he picked up his napkin, eyes focused on her.

"So are we back to the drawing board on the location?" she asked.

They discussed a gamut of options, but neither of them wanted anything too eccentric or showy. Many of their engaged friends were going for more creative, nontraditional venues, but they wouldn't let that influence them.

"Bottom line, it's *our* day," Brendon said. "And it will be memorable because you'll be the one smiling at me, promising to spend the rest of your life with the wonderful guy who loves you."

She blew a kiss to him.

He reached across the table, took her hand, and gave her a playful wink. "Seriously, how did I get so lucky?"

Adeline smiled back at him. "Hmm . . . you must have done something good—you know, to deserve me."

He chuckled at her teasing. "That's some really bad theology."

"Theology?"

He shrugged it off. "You know—the notion that good things come to people who do good is ridiculous. It's bad theology."

He has a point, she thought. *And where is Mom's True North in that idea?*

Later, after Brendon drove them back to her apartment, they sat out on the balcony, the glimmer of hundreds of lit windows in the night sky around them. With all the lights of the city, it was impossible to see the stars. And oh, how Adeline missed seeing them!

Adeline remembered what Earnest had said about taking time to appreciate the world around her, and she leaned back on the chaise to try to do just that. As she relaxed, she thought of Sylvia, as good as gold, and yet for some reason, Titus hadn't seemed to value her. Sylvia had been kind and absolutely lovely, but life had thrown her a curve.

"You're awfully quiet, Addy." Brendon reached for her hand.

"Just thinking about my Amish family."

"I wish I could picture them," he said. "Are there any photos?"

She laughed. "They don't do photos."

He leaned back in his chair, obviously enjoying their banter. "Do you miss them?"

"Sometimes." She nodded and, after a few more minutes, she invited him inside to see the pocket watch. Initially upon returning home, she had thought of keeping it to herself as a private keepsake, actually more from her mother than from Earnest. But tonight seemed like a good time to share it with Brendon.

She went to her room and brought it out to the living room, where she sat next to him on the sectional. Brendon leaned forward to look. "My mom gave this to Earnest their first Christmas together," she said, placing the timepiece in his hand.

Studying it closely, Brendon whistled. "Meticulously crafted."

She reached to turn it over in his hand. "Check out the inscription."

Brendon mouthed the words silently, then, looking at her, he asked, "How does this make you feel?"

She shook her head. "I'm still coming to terms with everything. But I'm glad to have it."

He slipped his arm around her. "It's beautiful, Addy. Thanks for showing me."

"I haven't decided where to put it," she said as she leaned her head on his shoulder. "I doubt I'll carry it."

They laughed a little, then Brendon handed back the pocket watch.

"I wanted you to see it first," she said as he lifted her chin to kiss her.

The day set aside for church baptism dawned with a brilliant sunrise as shafts of light shot high into the sky. Since all of her brothers had to get cleaned up last night, Sylvia hurried downstairs to shower and wash her long hair, having gone to bed earlier than usual.

The minute she was dressed for church, she helped Mamma with breakfast, putting a work apron on over her newest blue dress. Ernie and Adam came in with Dat from doing barn chores, and Calvin and Tommy ran downstairs dressed for Preaching service in all but their black vests and coats.

There was an air of expectancy around the table as Dat bowed his head to ask the blessing, and while Sylvia prayed the silent rote prayer, she added one for all of the baptism candidates on this most holy day.

During the buggy ride to Bishop Beiler's farmhouse for the Preaching service, Sylvia thought of Adeline and wondered what she was doing today and how soon she might write back.

During the second sermon of the service, given by Preacher Amos Kauffman, Sylvia had trouble focusing even though she had always found his sermons to be practical and sincere. Today, however, it was hard to receive the words Titus's father spoke. Sitting on the long bench between Cousins Alma and Jessie, Sylvia did not hate him or his family, but the way they had seemingly set themselves above her own family made her very uncomfortable.

When it came time for the baptism candidates to rise from the front row and answer the four questions asked by the bishop, she wondered how she would have felt, going ahead with joining church. She knew it was better to be honest with herself and with God. And with everyone else, too. *I want to get back to where I used to be with the Lord,* she thought.

Sylvia stood with the rest of the congregation as Bishop John Beiler read from the prayer book, *Die Ernsthafte Christenpflict,* about forsaking the world, the flesh, and the devil, then uttered his desire for each candidate to live only for Jesus Christ. "May God's mighty power grant you the ability to reject temptation and overcome sin," he said.

The People sat down again while the deacon brought the baptismal water over in a pail. When it was Titus's turn to be baptized, he knelt, and the bishop placed his cupped hands, filled with water, over Titus's head, slowly releasing them until water dripped down Titus's face and onto his black frock coat. Then the bishop offered his hand, and Titus stood to receive the expected handshake and a holy kiss of peace. "No longer will you be considered guests and strangers, but laborers and members in this consecrated and holy fellowship," the bishop told him and the other candidates.

With a little sigh, Sylvia realized she was actually glad for Titus on this milestone day. *He will be one to wholly follow the Ordnung,* she thought.

When the service was over, the menfolk turned the benches into tables, raising them up for the shared meal. And when it was time for the youth to be seated, Sylvia sat with Alma and Jessie, who seemed interested in talking about everything *but* the upcoming wedding season. *So dear of them.*

"Are yous goin' to the Singing tonight?" she asked.

"*Jah,*" Alma said, glancing at Jessie, who nodded.

"I'm thinkin' of going, too."

Both girls brightened. "We'll sit together, then," Alma said, patting Sylvia's shoulder. "This is the best news!"

Sylvia had to smile at their response, glad to be so welcome.

"I'll stay close by," Alma whispered later. "And you can get a ride home with Danny and me. Unless someone asks ya to ride with him. . . ."

"Oh, I'll come on my own, in Dat's family carriage," she was quick to say as they made their way outside to the shelter of the shade trees in the side yard.

Alma stood with Sylvia outdoors, watching as Titus walked near the barnyard with his cousin, who had also joined church that morning. Sylvia's heart no longer fluttered at the sight of him. *I must not have loved him very much,* she thought, wishing she had acknowledged early on how troubled their relationship had been. *Nearly from the start.*

To think she could have forced him to choose her and

her family was naïve, she understood now. Of course, there was always going to be extra scrutiny of her family because of Dat's deception. *But at the first sign that Titus shared those doubts, I should've walked away,* she thought, disappointed in herself.

CHAPTER
Twenty-Six

At Singing that evening in the bishop's big basement, Sylvia spotted Cousins Alma and Jessie right away. There, next to them, was Andy's younger sister, too, sixteen-year-old Susie, as blond as Andy. "*Kumme* an' sit with us," Susie said, patting the spot on the bench between her and Alma.

"*Denki*," Sylvia said as Mary Beiler, the bishop's wife, stood up and welcomed everyone. Mary blew her little pitch pipe and led out in the birthday song for all the youth present celebrating a September birthday, and after that, the hymns and gospel songs began.

Sylvia enjoyed sitting next to Susie and hearing her pretty soprano voice. During the refreshment time upstairs in the kitchen, Mary provided huge bowls of freshly made popcorn, along with Chex mix, yogurt-covered pretzels, and chocolate cake with homemade vanilla ice cream. It was a particularly generous spread of snacks, at least as far as Sylvia recalled. Of course, she hadn't gone to the Singing that Onkel Josh and

Aendi Ruthann had hosted weeks ago, where Jessie told her there had been hot dogs and hamburgers hot off the grill. *I'm glad I stayed home for Adeline's last evening with us,* Sylvia thought, noticing that Titus wasn't present tonight.

As they nibbled on popcorn, Cousin Alma whispered that, according to the grapevine, Titus was visiting relatives in Smoketown. "Might be for the best," Alma added, looking at Sylvia sympathetically.

"For him or for me?" Sylvia smiled. "You really mustn't worry. I'm fine—I really am."

"All right, then." Alma went with her to get some cake and ice cream. "I care 'bout ya, that's all."

Sylvia nodded. "Thank you, cousin. I'm grateful for your company."

They talked about Danny Lapp, Alma's beau, and the fact that he and his father were planning to go into partnership to buy an apple orchard. Alma seemed pleased about it. "I have a feelin' there'll be plenty of apple dumplings and applesauce in my future . . . or so I hope."

Sylvia didn't ask if she and Danny had discussed marriage, but she knew Alma wouldn't be tying the knot this wedding season, since neither she nor Danny had been baptized.

"Don't look now, but Andy Zook's comin' this way," Alma whispered discreetly. "Be sure to give him your best smile."

Sylvia laughed softly. "Ain't hard to smile round someone like him."

Quickly, Cousin Alma stepped away, leaving Sylvia alone.

Andy strolled over to the long table and stood there with his hands in his pockets, grinning. "Bishop and his wife sure know how to put out the food, *jah?*" he said.

She nodded and couldn't help noticing again how very

blond he was. He was so tall and good-looking that he surely had a sweetheart-girl somewhere.

"Of all the treats on this table, which is your favorite?" he asked, his hands coming out of his pockets as he leaned to reach for an empty cup and dipped it into the Chex mix.

"To be honest, I like them all." She laughed. "How 'bout you?"

Andy shrugged. "I'm not big on sweets, but anything with salt is perfect."

"Well, there's plenty of salt here, that's for sure."

He munched on his Chex mix. "I was hopin' you might come to Singing tonight," he said, glancing around them.

Sylvia put her toe in the water. "Well, I had to think about it. . . . Titus and I aren't together anymore."

Andy blushed and admitted, "Actually, I've known that for a while . . . straight from the horse's mouth."

Sylvia was somewhat taken aback, though she knew Andy and Titus were friends. She appreciated Andy's honesty but wouldn't go into any of what went wrong with the relationship.

"I noticed you didn't join church," he said.

She nodded, wishing he hadn't brought this up. "It was for the best."

He looked more thoughtful than surprised. "You'll join in *gut* time, *jah?*"

"Oh, I expect to. It wasn't because I don't want to be a member."

He seemed to consider that. Then his face reddened as he said, "I've been wanting to get to know ya better." He paused a second before continuing. "And whenever you're ready, I'd like to take you out for supper . . . if ya like."

Now it was her turn to blush.

His blue eyes were hopeful and kind as he looked at her.

Sylvia felt a little dizzy. "*Denki* . . . I'll let ya know, all right?"

Despite feeling downright *ferhoodled* by the invitation, she was grateful for his honesty. Even so, she wanted to ask Andy if it would be a problem for him to date a girl whose father had been under the *Bann* for living a lie for twenty years . . . a father who had an *Englischer* daughter he'd never met until now.

When she returned home, Sylvia was thankful to see her mother sitting in the kitchen, reading *The Budget* by the gaslight overhead. "Do ya have time to talk?" she asked.

Mamma smiled. "Why else would I wait up in my bathrobe?"

"I've been thinking 'bout something." Sylvia sat on the bench across the table from her. "And I'm guessin' you won't be surprised to hear what I'm gonna say next." She fought a smile of her own.

"You certainly have my attention now." Mamma set the paper aside.

Sylvia took a breath. "I'm wondering how long I should wait to accept Andy's invitation. That is, *if* I decide to accept."

Mamma's eyes lit up. "Oh, so Andy asked ya out, did he?"

"*Jah*," Sylvia said, telling her about the moment when he had invited her for supper.

"Well, what's wrong with accepting a date from a nice young man? Maybe ya just need to have some fun for a change."

Sylvia shrugged. "I don't want Titus to be hurt when he

hears about it. And he will." She paused and frowned. "I'm also concerned how it might look so soon after our breakup."

"Well, I wouldn't worry 'bout Titus, but that's your kind heart talkin'. As for how long to wait, it's up to you. Just remember that if you and Andy get along well, what matters is how you feel about things, not what other people say."

"*Denki*, Mamma."

"You're a *gut* and tenderhearted young woman, Sylvie," Mamma said. "Any young man would be blessed to court you."

I'm not so sure, Sylvia thought, recalling the ups and downs of the last couple months, but she soaked up her mother's words, glad for her loving affirmation.

Earnest looked forward to his time together with Rhoda each evening, when Rhoda read aloud from the Gospel of John. He enjoyed watching her expression as she held the Word of God; her zeal touched him deeply.

After today's baptism service, Earnest was feeling convicted about Sylvia's decision not to join church. He knew from the years he'd spent in this community that his priority as a father was to be the spiritual leader, and he hadn't done well in that. Besides his concerns for Sylvia, he wanted to impart some wisdom to Adeline, too. Recently, she had written again, this time sharing that she was more than halfway through her mother's diary and had discovered that her mother had claimed to embrace Christ's teachings.

Unbelievable, Earnest thought, as amazed to learn this as Adeline must have been. *Rosalind never showed any interest in that when we were together.*

Apparently because of her mother's words—and Adeline's time in Hickory Hollow—she had begun to search for answers for herself.

I can't let any of my children flounder without my guidance, Earnest thought now as Rhoda closed the Bible and rose to take down her hair in front of the dresser.

There was a knock at the door, and Earnest figured it was Tommy, coming to recite *Das Loblied*, as he had been doing lately each evening before bed. "*Kumme* in, son," he called, and Tommy entered, all smiles, the thick *Ausbund* hymnal tucked under his little arm. "Have a seat," Earnest said, eager to hear how far Tommy could recite tonight.

Rhoda sat on her side of the bed, brushing her waist-length hair and listening intently as their youngest sat next to Earnest and began to say the first verse of the beloved praise hymn. Tommy pronounced each German word correctly all the way up to the fifteenth line, his blue eyes shining. *He's enjoying his father's attention,* she thought.

Tommy opened the *Ausbund*, turning to the hymn and saying the sixteenth line to Earnest. They did this for at least ten minutes, Earnest with his arm around Tommy's shoulders, encouraging him along as he repeated each line.

Rhoda's heart swelled with love, seeing them together like this. She was so moved by her husband's affection for their son that tears came to her eyes. *My darling Earnest,* she thought as she set her brush aside. She realized how much she'd missed being close to him these past months. And in that moment, she realized that God had answered her prayer and opened her heart to her husband once again.

Before Earnest sent Tommy off to bed, he placed both hands on his small shoulders, then gently tousled his hair.

And after Tommy said good-night to her, as well, and Rhoda and Earnest were alone again, she slipped silently to their door and pressed the lock. Turning, she walked over to Earnest and moved into his arms.

"How I love ya," she whispered, leaning up on tiptoes to kiss him tenderly.

Over the next weeks, prior to communion Sunday on October eighteenth, the church members would be setting aside time for self-reflection and confession, Sylvia knew. During this time, each member was expected to prayerfully consider which man might best fill Preacher Mahlon Zook's former position. Then the drawing of lots would take place on communion Sunday, following the midafternoon foot-washing service.

During this period of preparation, Sylvia had seen her father kneeling and praying at his work chair in the clock shop. And on at least one occasion when she'd brought him root beer or an apple or other snack sent by Mamma, she witnessed Dat drying his eyes.

Around that time, two more letters arrived from Adeline, who had started to write some about her fiancé, Brendon Burgess. *With his accounting background and my knack for overspending, he'll keep an eye on our finances once we're married,* Adeline had written, adding a smiley face. Adeline had also shared a bit of what she'd read in her mother's diary, which made Sylvia feel honored.

Sylvia knew that Dat was corresponding with Adeline, as well, writing the letters without Mamma's help now. Dat had told her that he was attempting to answer some of Adeline's questions about God's will and other issues related to faith. It surprised Sylvia that he wanted to keep her up-to-date on what he was writing.

Meanwhile, she decided to open up to her half sister about Andy Zook's friendliness toward her, and in one of Adeline's replies, she asked Sylvia if she was going to pray about possibly dating him. Astonished yet pleased, Sylvia planned to tell Adeline that she had begun to talk more to the Lord about her future dating life, as well as everything else. *At least she understands now that Titus and I are finished for good.*

"Adeline's letters seem much more focused on faith than I imagined they'd be. She's changed a lot since she was here," Sylvia told her father one afternoon close to their pre-communion fast day. Dat had just returned from helping Benuel Zook sell unwanted items from Mamie's big farmhouse as she downsized for her upcoming move.

"I assume it's the influence of her mother's diary," Dat said, slipping his work apron over his head. "She may be looking at things in ways she didn't before."

Sylvia pondered that. "Losing a mother would be earth-shaking."

Dat looked at her with kindness. "It's not always a *bad* thing when one's foundation is shaken," he said softly. "Though it's hard to see at the time, the passing of a loved one or close friend can sometimes change a person's life for the better."

Sylvia assumed he was referring to the losses he'd endured in his own family. But then again, he might have been thinking of Mahlon Zook.

"And while it's natural to fret over past blunders or any shocks that come our way, sometimes when we look back on them, we find that they've become the things we're most grateful for," Dat added.

Thinking of Adeline again, Sylvia nodded. "I believe Adeline needs us right now, don't you?"

Dat nodded. "We all need each other on this step-by-step journey to heaven."

CHAPTER
Twenty-Seven

*O*n *Faschtdaag*, the Sunday one week before communion
Sunday, Earnest and his family drank only apple juice
for breakfast, and they spent time reading the Good Book
quietly together or in their rooms praying silently.

Late that morning, Earnest slipped over to his shop and
closed the door, strongly aware of his need to be alone with
God. He sat and read from the thirteenth psalm, stopping at
verse five to read it again. "'But I have trusted in thy mercy; my
heart shall rejoice in thy salvation.'" Suddenly overwhelmed
with the need to surrender his life, Earnest turned in his chair
and knelt to pray. *Please, Lord, take my will and make it Thine
from this day forward. I'm in need of Thy mercy and ask that I
might be found faithful in Thy sight, the only eyes that matter. In
the name of Jesus Christ, my Lord. Amen.*

For a time, he remained there, and he felt as if the Holy
Spirit was nudging him to mend the rift with Amos Kauffman.
Earnest recognized that he still held resentment over the way
Amos had handled his shunning, not coming around to visit

much during those six long, miserable weeks. Such reconciliation between church members was a vital part of the People's coming together for communion. Besides, he yearned to have the kind of relationship with God that his wife had. *And dear Rhoda is the epitome of forgiving,* he thought.

After a simple noon meal to break the fast, Earnest and his family lingered around the table as he read aloud from *Rules of a Godly Life* to remind them of the importance of solely trusting the Lord each day for everything.

That afternoon, Earnest and Rhoda rested in their room, as did the children, everyone taking naps after caring for the livestock. *I'll visit Amos first thing in the morning,* Earnest decided, his heart lighter at just the thought. The burden of bitterness had weighed him down so. He could only hope that Amos might be receptive to a reconciliation.

When Sylvia awakened from her nap, she sat up in bed, unexpectedly glad for this fasting day, which she had often dreaded as a child. In part because of her father's example, her thoughts had become more tender toward the Lord lately, and the day was especially meaningful as she considered the animosity she'd held toward Titus for much too long now. Today, while praying, she felt impressed to let go of her anger and forgive Titus, just as Ella Mae had encouraged her to do.

Quietly, Sylvia knelt at her bedside, tears welling up at the sorrow she felt over how long she'd waited to do this. *O Lord in heaven, I ask Thee for Thy great peace . . . and forgiveness, too. I have disappointed Thee, and I'm sorry for that. I long for*

Thy cleansing. She stopped to wipe her eyes before continuing. *Please help me as I trust all of my doings to Thee. In the name of Jesus, I pray.*

When Sylvia rose, she looked ahead to next Sunday's communion service with as much joy as if she'd been baptized. Sadly, she would have to wait another year to experience that most holy day.

Even before Calvin and Tommy went out to milk Flossie at four-thirty that afternoon, Rhoda had washed some fresh fruit for the table, then began making supper with Sylvia's help. While doing so, she noticed her daughter's face looked like she might have been crying. But knowing her, Sylvia would want to work through whatever it was in her own way and time . . . or possibly talk it out with Earnest, as she had often done in the past.

I hope she isn't being hard on herself, not being baptized this year, Rhoda mused. She felt certain that her daughter would take the kneeling vow eventually. And it struck her just then that if Sylvia had joined church, she, too, would have been permitted to nominate someone to be their new preacher.

Glancing at the wall clock, she realized that by this time next Sunday, the Lord God would miraculously reach down from heaven through the drawing of lots and choose a new leader to share the preaching duties with Amos Kauffman, as well as to help him bear the burden for this church district. The newly ordained preacher and his family would be expected to become model church members, carefully following the *Ordnung* in all things and living a godly life. *A shining example to the flock,* she thought.

The back door swung open, and Earnest entered the kitchen through the utility room, interrupting her reverie. They sat down at the table to wait for Calvin and Tommy to wash up at the well pump and the other children to come downstairs. Rhoda recalled how her father had once told her that Earnest would be a fine choice for preacher. Of course, with his divorce from Rosalind and the *Bann* on his record, that was impossible.

In a few minutes, the older children took their places at the table. Then Calvin and Tommy came running inside and plopped down on the bench. When they were all settled, Earnest folded his hands and said, "The Lord's presence is among us on this day of reverence." He thanked them for honoring the fast day with him, then bowed his head for the table blessing.

After returning from walking the field lanes encircling his property to get some exercise, Earnest had just sat down on the back porch when Sylvia came out the door. She looked so bright and cheerful that he said, "Something special's on your mind, I can tell."

"I've been prayin' again," she revealed. "To tell the truth, I didn't like how I felt these past weeks, cuttin' myself off from God by not opening up to Him like I should . . . and now I wish I didn't have to wait a year to be baptized."

Her father nodded, a smile coming to his face. "That's so good to hear, Sylvie. I've been keeping you in my prayers."

"*Denki*, Dat," she said. "God's answered your prayers. And Mamma's, too." She nodded and took a seat in the chair where Rhoda usually sat.

"What would ya think if we invited Adeline for Thanksgiving?" Her eyebrows rose and she tilted her head, birdlike, waiting for his answer.

"It sounds like you'd really like that."

Sylvia agreed with a smile. "*Jah,* but would you and Mamma?"

Earnest contemplated it for a moment and realized that this would give all of them, but especially Sylvia, something joyful to anticipate, now that she and Titus wouldn't be marrying. "I'll talk it over with your Mamma."

Sylvia looked like she wanted to hug his neck. "I'd love to see Adeline again."

"Bear in mind she might already have plans," he cautioned.

"We won't know until we ask," she said happily.

Earnest nodded. "If it's the Lord's will, it'll all come together."

Rhoda opened the door and came out on the porch just then, and Sylvia scurried away, heading for the meadow, where the boys were rounding up the livestock for the night. A slight chill was in the air.

"Sylvia wants to invite Adeline for Thanksgiving," Earnest told his wife.

"A delightful idea." Rhoda was already smiling. "How do you think we should go about that?"

He pondered it for a minute. "I think it might be nice if Sylvia's the one to invite her."

Rhoda was quiet before saying, "Who would've thought the two of them would bond so."

"I wonder if they even realize it."

Laughing, Rhoda agreed. "It's like they're walkin' round the edges of it. Makes me wonder how long before they notice how close they've become."

"Something good seems to be coming out of the chaos I

caused." Earnest looked at Rhoda and reached for her hand. "I hope you're no longer worried about Sylvia."

Rhoda shook her head. "Honestly, I think God has some nice surprises ahead for her."

Earnest couldn't agree more. "And just around the bend, too, the Lord willing."

CHAPTER
Twenty-Eight

*E*arnest hitched up the next morning to head over to Amos Kauffman's, praying as he went. He glanced toward the house and saw Rhoda and Sylvia carrying wicker baskets of clothes across the yard. He went over and kissed Rhoda, then walked back to the carriage through grass slick with heavy dew. Autumn weather would be upon them in another week or so, but for now, Earnest was grateful for the mild morning, the clear azure sky as he turned onto Hickory Lane.

He passed the familiar farms, Bishop John's blacksmith shop, and farther down the road, the General Store, enjoying the fresh air and this time to reflect. Now that he actually looked forward to sharing his thoughts and concerns with the Lord, his prayers had become more frequent. *I'm a new man,* Earnest realized, thankful for the mercy he had been granted.

When he turned into Amos's lane, it was obvious that Eva had risen earlier than Rhoda and Sylvia—or had more help—because her washing was already hanging high on the pulley line. Earnest chuckled to himself, thinking he wouldn't mention this to Rhoda—some of the womenfolk took a fair amount of unspoken pride in getting their washing out first.

He found Amos in his big barn scooping feed into a bucket, and called to him so he wouldn't be startled. "Hullo, Amos . . . how's your morning?"

"So far, so *gut*." Amos finished his chore before waving Earnest over. "I was just thinkin' I could use another set of hands." He chuckled.

"Well, here I am. What do you need?"

Amos smiled as he handed him the bucket of feed. "I'll get the hose for watering the livestock."

Amused, Earnest headed for the feeding trough to scatter the feed.

"Titus took off for Big Valley a week ago," Amos informed him.

"Oh?"

"One of my cousins needed help fillin' silo, and Titus jumped at the chance."

"He's a hardworkin' young man," Earnest said, recalling working alongside him in Maryland on the restoration of several storm-damaged barns. *Undoubtedly, he needs to get away.*

"What brings ya?" Amos asked as he walked, dragging the dripping hose.

Earnest took a quick breath. "I came to talk with you. You and I, we've always had a *gut* friendship . . . I've hated to see that fizzle."

Amos nodded as he caught Earnest's gaze. "That we did. And there's no reason why it can't continue."

"I appreciate it." Earnest went back to scoop more feed into the bucket and carried it back for the mules.

"Over time, things'll work themselves out for my son . . . and your daughter."

Over time? Earnest was baffled. What did he mean?

"Time mends most wounds," Amos went on. "And sometimes young couples just need to drift apart and learn more 'bout who they are as people. Individually they'll end up all the better for it."

Not saying anything, Earnest realized Amos believed that Titus was ready to move on.

"Sylvia's a right perty girl," Amos added. "I daresay she won't be single for long."

"Well, that's in the Lord's hands." Earnest felt he had to speak up, surprised at Amos's casual comment. *The man got what he wanted,* he thought, trying not to go back on his apology.

They worked together a while longer. Then Amos mentioned an errand he had to run, so Earnest helped him hitch up. The two men shook hands, and Earnest departed.

On the ride back to the house, Earnest couldn't decide if he was glad to know of Amos's thoughts on Titus and Sylvia's split, or if he'd rather not have known. But the words *"She won't be single for long"* clanged in his ears.

Between college lectures, Adeline read from the book of John on her phone, not to kill time, but to keep up with Earnest and his reading, thinking this was a cool way to connect across the miles. And in so doing, she had discovered ideas and themes she didn't know existed, like how Jesus of Nazareth was the personification of God's Word. She had never realized how much food for thought the Bible had to offer.

I'll ask Earnest more about this in my next letter.

The following Saturday market day, Sylvia was happy to go with her father to help sell his beautiful clocks while Ernie and the younger boys helped Onkel Curtis fill silo. Sylvia noticed right away that, because of the popular fall tourist season, more customers than usual walked the aisles past Dat's display. People also crowded around the homemade cider stand several market booths down from Dat's clocks. Another stand featured candied apples of every imaginable kind—dipped in chocolate or in caramel and then rolled in crushed peanuts or M&Ms or sugar-coated cereal. When Sylvia took a break midmorning to stretch her legs, she walked toward the display of candied apples and was surprised to see Andy Zook standing in line. He waved to her.

"Thought ya didn't have a sweet tooth," she joked, smiling.

"Oh, these are for Michael and Susie—they much prefer sugar to salt. Unlike me, as you know." Looking handsome in his purple long-sleeved shirt and black vest and black trousers, Andy motioned for her to join him in line. "I assume you'd like to purchase one?"

"Not really, but now that I'm here . . ."

They laughed together.

"So I didn't expect to see ya here today," she said quietly. "But I've decided something."

He leaned in to hear amidst the hubbub. "I hope it's what I'm thinkin'."

She nodded. "I'm ready to accept your supper invitation."

"*Wunnerbaar.*" Andy's eyes twinkled. "Next Saturday evening?"

She had to smile. "Sounds nice . . . I'll look forward to it."

They discussed where to meet, and instead of mentioning where she had always met Titus, she suggested farther up the road.

Before Andy placed his order, he asked Sylvia which kind of apple she wanted, and she pointed to the plain caramel. "*Denki*," she whispered.

He reached for his wallet. "Anytime, Sylvie." He flashed her a smile that made her feel as if he truly meant it.

And for a split second, it almost felt to her like they were already dating.

For Adeline, Saturdays were always a catch-up day on sleep, especially when classes were in session. Today she had slept in until nearly noon, having been out late at Brendon's, where he had invited three other couples to play table games and eat takeout.

Adeline had done her laundry for the week this afternoon, remembering how predictable Rhoda Miller's weekly routine was with laundry always on Mondays, ironing on Tuesdays, mending on Wednesdays, and so on.

Waiting now for her last load to dry, Adeline walked to the living room just around the corner and sat on the floor next to the coffee table, where she had laid out her Nine Patch wall hanging. Over the past two months, she had stitched the squares together by hand a little each week, doing the whipstitch Rhoda had taught her. There wasn't much left to do before pressing the patches and then attaching the backing. *It'll be a nice reminder of my visit,* she thought, moving her hand across the squares.

She looked around at her living room, decorated to the hilt with unnecessary items—knickknacks, books, and candles, all dust collectors—wall art and too many throw pillows. "Life's better when it's simple," she murmured, recalling the Millers' sparsely furnished guest room. "Simple and homey, like home-made bread straight from the oven, fresh clothes drying on the line . . . and evening prayers."

Adeline knew that if she had the time and the know-how, she could find a pattern online for the quilting stitches and make a pretty recurring motif when she attached the back. She was eager to show Brendon the finished product. Momentarily, she thought of Sylvia's hope chest and almost wished she had one, too. *For the charm, if nothing else.*

Early the next morning, Sylvia waved good-bye to her parents as they headed off to the long day of Preaching, com-munion, foot washing, and the ordination at the home of the bishop's eldest son, Hickory John Beiler. All in all, the landmark occasion would last nearly eight hours.

Returning to the kitchen, Sylvia went to sit in the front room with her New Testament, reading aloud to her brothers. It had been Dat's suggestion as a way to occupy their time and thoughts while the members-only meeting took place. Sylvia also had a letter to write—a Thanksgiving invitation to Adeline, something Dat had given her the go-ahead to do.

After she read to the boys, she went to the kitchen to write the letter, while her brothers headed up the road to visit their male cousins at Onkel Josh and Aendi Ruthann's.

Sylvia let Adeline know that all of them would love to see her for Thanksgiving, but they would certainly understand if she already had plans. *You're always welcome here, and I would love to spend more time with you,* Sylvia wrote, going on to tell

Adeline that Andy Zook was taking her out for supper next Saturday.

It's funny, but all of a sudden, I'm ready to date again, although with Andy, I feel like I already know him well. It's odd, really, how the few times we've been alone together, I've just felt so comfortable with him. I don't remember it being quite like that when Titus and I first started dating, but maybe I've forgotten. It's not a part of my past I think back on anymore.

Sylvia shared that her parents were attending the fall communion service today.

Because I didn't join church as planned, I can't be involved in the nomination process for Preacher Zook's replacement, but I know Mamma and Dat will have some good ideas.

Since you were here, we've put up hundreds of quarts of many different fruits and vegetables, as well as chow chow, applesauce, apple butter, and jams. It's the busiest time of year, but soon things will quiet down so Mamma and I can let our breath out a bit. I'm most looking forward to knotting comforters with Aendi Hannah and quilting with other women around Mamie Zook's large quilt frame. I'm not sure where she'll set that up when she moves to her little Dawdi Haus soon, but knowing Mamie, she's got it all figured out.

But I'm rambling. I'll be watching for your letter. We haven't told the boys, but if you can make it, I know they'll be excited, too.

> *Till I hear from you again,*
> *Sylvia Miller*

Putting the pen down, Sylvia reread her letter to make sure she'd spelled each word correctly. She had to keep on her toes, writing to someone so well educated.

When she was satisfied with her proofreading, Sylvia folded the letter and slipped it into an envelope, sealed it, and placed a stamp on it. *Adeline should have this in a couple of days,* Sylvia thought, hoping she might write back quickly.

A stray thought crossed her mind. *I wonder who'll be selected by the lot.* Just as quickly, however, she dismissed it. *I'll know soon enough.*

CHAPTER

Twenty-Nine

E arnest felt especially receptive to the sermon given by
Bishop John this special day—the instruction from God's
Word. He thought again of how Rhoda read to him each night;
her influence during their marriage had surely brought him to
this place of peace. *That, and her many faithful prayers.*

When the congregation turned to kneel, Earnest prayed for
God's will to be done in the drawing of the lot, which would
occur following the communion service after the shared meal.
He also prayed for wisdom and comfort for the man who would
soon find the words from Proverbs sixteen on a slip of paper
tucked in his *Ausbund* hymnal: *The lot is cast into the lap; but
the whole disposing thereof is of the* LORD. Upon that discovery,
he would be declared the new preacher, without any theological
training or formal education. Instead, the ordained man would
take as his guide all that he had witnessed in his years as a member, trusting God for the sermons he would preach to the People.

At three o'clock that afternoon, Bishop John broke the loaf
of bread at the approximate hour Christ was crucified that
long-ago day, explaining how the life of a Christian must be

like a grain of wheat that falls to the ground and dies, then springs to life with rain and sun. "Our old nature must perish, and the new man—our new nature in Christ—must grow and flourish," Bishop John said, his voice strong and fervent.

Thankful for divine grace and redemption, Earnest thought, *I allowed my old nature to take over for too long.*

The man of God humbly moved through the congregation, first to the men's side, offering a piece of bread to each one, and then across the room to the women's side, where he did the same. Witnessing the bishop serve them in this way, Earnest couldn't help but think of the verse in Mark that he had learned from his papa Zimmerman. *For even the Son of man came not to be ministered unto, but to minister, and to give his life a ransom for many.*

Before passing the single cup of wine, Bishop John dutifully described the process of putting grapes into a winepress to remove all impurities and ensure the sweet juice that came forth was pure. "Just as the Lord's blood cleansed us from our sins when He gave His life for us on the cross."

The shared cup was then passed from one person to the next, and Earnest drank from it before giving it to Elam Lapp, Samuel's eldest, on his right.

The foot-washing ceremony followed, with one person washing another man's feet, and a woman washing a woman's, everyone doing so as an act of humility. Afterward, the partners exchanged a holy kiss and offered each other a spoken blessing. Last of all, the congregation gave their offerings to Deacon Luke, who held the alms box as the People filed out of the temporary House of Worship only to line up again at the separate doors for men and women. It was the moment for each to whisper a nomination.

The suspense was intense as Earnest waited with the other men, experiencing for the second time in his life the anticipation of the process of *making a preacher*, as the People called it.

Who will the Lord appoint? he wondered, staying in an attitude of prayer and reverence.

While waiting for Dat and Mamma's return, Sylvia read from *Rules of a Godly Life* in the front room and heard a bird singing his little heart out near the front porch. She smiled as she paged through to the section on patience, knowing she would surely need that virtue as she waited to be baptized into the fellowship of like-minded Amish. She recalled Dawdi Riehl once declaring at a family gathering that the word *obedience* was the most significant in the English language. *If only I had followed through with my original plan to join church,* she thought sadly.

Ach, I mustn't live in the past, she thought, keeping her finger in the book her Mamma had so loved to read, and now Dat seemingly did, too.

Earnest whispered the name of his nominee as he passed by the slightly open doorway. Inside, the minister would write down names and tally the number of votes each received. Some men would get only a handful of votes, and others many more.

When he'd had his turn, Earnest walked around the front of the house to sit and wait on the men's side again, having nominated his brother-in-law, Curtis Mast, from the next farm over. Curtis was a devout man with a generous spirit and a kind heart.

Once all the votes were counted, the top five candidates would be put into the lot. Five hymnals would be placed on a table in a private room—only one would contain the proverb written on a piece of paper. A man in good standing as a member would be chosen randomly to put a rubber band around each hymnal before all five were shuffled and carried into the large room where the congregation had re-gathered for the ordination service.

Presently, Bishop John stood before the membership and stated the names of the five candidates for the lot, inviting those men to come forward to the table where the hymnals were lined up.

The atmosphere was thick with expectation as the bishop asked each of the five to proclaim the cornerstone principles of the church. Earnest saw how pale in the face several of the men looked and remembered what Mahlon had told him years ago about carrying the heavy weight of the new responsibility. *"My cross to bear,"* he'd said. . . .

Bishop John then asked for all the members to kneel in surrender to the heavenly Father and to pray for God's will in the choice of their next preacher. When the silent prayer was finished, the congregation rose to take their seats, and the bishop requested the candidates to choose one of the five hymnals. The men did so in no specific order, then waited for the bishop to go to each one in turn and open the hymnal to search for the paper hidden inside.

Four of these farmers will walk out of this service free of this tremendous responsibility, thought Earnest, holding his breath. *But one will soon be ordained.*

The first three men looked altogether relieved when the bishop did not find the proverb in the hymnals they held. One man's shoulders noticeably sagged as he blew air out through his lips, his cheeks puffing out.

The bishop moved to the next candidate and opened his hymnal, and in that moment, the suspense was quickly over as the slip of paper was found. Bishop John announced that God had chosen Benuel Zook to be a shepherd overseeing and nurturing this flock. "I beseech you to be steadfast and true to this holy calling," the bishop instructed Benuel before shaking his hand and welcoming him into the ministry with a holy kiss.

Benuel stood there, looking rather shocked at the responsibility that so swiftly had been placed upon his shoulders—a responsibility he had promised to accept back when he was baptized as a youth, many years ago.

Earnest felt for his friend and would keep Mahlon's youngest son in his daily prayers. *He'll soon be my neighbor.*

During the ride home after the service, Rhoda had a little quiver in her voice as she asked, "How do ya think this will affect Andy's interest in our daughter?"

Her question hit Earnest like a rockslide. "*Ach,* I hadn't considered that." He groaned—this had the potential to repeat the grief Sylvia had experienced with Titus and his preacher father.

But Earnest knew he must take the lead in trusting God on this matter. "Fretting isn't what we're called to do, dear," he said. "We must look to the Lord for the outcome."

"So will *you* tell Sylvia that Andy's father was ordained today?"

"*Jah,* but let's not make too much of it." He meant it. Today was not a day to sow doubt but rather a high and holy day.

"The same all-knowing God who chose Andy's Dat to be a minister can also be trusted to choose Sylvie's future mate," said Earnest, patting Rhoda's hand.

CHAPTER
Thirty

*E*ver since her visit to Hickory Hollow, Adeline had become conscious of a desire for a slower pace, especially on Sundays, as if her short time in Amish country had reset her personal rhythms. And although she hadn't attended church since her visit with the Millers, she chose Sunday to write letters to Sylvia and Earnest and to touch base with her family and friends, along with doing some homework and even working on her pretty wall hanging.

This being such a lazy Sunday morning, she reclined on her sofa and opened her laptop to Google the customs of the Lancaster County Amish, noting again that they accepted the Bible as their guidebook, like other Christians do.

There were times that Adeline wished Sylvia was permitted to have email. Except, of course, that would require a laptop or a phone. *Not exactly in line with their cultural expectations,* she thought, smiling to herself. No, she understood and respected Sylvia's not having a phone to text or use FaceTime and social media, but for Adeline, writing snail mail was like being forced to live in the Dark Ages.

Recently, when sharing her opinion on this with Brendon, he had reminded her of how peaceful she'd said she felt being somewhat unhooked from social media during her time away, and that writing letters longhand to her Amish relatives was a great way to slow down and cultivate patience.

He knows me well. . . .

Adeline figured that Brendon must think the day's more relaxed pace did her good, considering her hectic college life and near-endless hours of study. *He knows I'm stressed with this heavy course load,* she thought, sipping a can of sparkling water.

Continuing her online browsing, Adeline read that, by not working on the Lord's Day, the Amish believed they were honoring God's instructions to Moses in the Old Testament.

What would Brendon think of this? She knew she must talk with him at some point. *But how should I bring it up?*

Eventually, she closed her laptop and, still contemplating the way the Amish approached Sundays, she went to her bedroom and opened her bedside table to remove her mother's diary. Sitting on the bed, she plumped up her many pillows and got comfortable, then began to read.

This diary entry was a mere thirty pages from the end, so Adeline read very slowly, taking in every word her mother had written. Several times she had already gone back to reread entries she had bookmarked.

She looked up and gazed at the timepiece on her dresser, feeling a soothing warmth at the sight of it. If not for Earnest's unexpected gift, she might have put off reading her mother's diary, perhaps for years.

On this particular page, Mom had penned a few thoughts about the need for a wise mentor who could act as a guide and an encourager. *If you're reading this, Adeline, I pray that you will meet or have already met someone who can explain things about faith better than I can.*

"I love how she's writing directly to me in this entry," Adeline murmured, finding it endearing when, some months ago, she would not have taken too kindly to it. *I was in a different place then,* she thought, knowing that meeting up with Earnest and his family had made all the difference. *Spending time with them switched a light on in my head . . . and in my heart.*

She continued to read, surprised at what she was discovering. *To this day,* her mom had written, *I carry deep regrets for hurting Earnest so terribly. And while I cannot change the past, I know it was wrong to keep your birth from him, denying both of you that special relationship.*

"Amazing," whispered Adeline. And as she thought about it, she realized that God had somehow redeemed her past circumstances by leading her to Hickory Hollow.

Earnest might appreciate knowing this, she thought, turning back to the page where her mother had addressed her and staring for a long time at the precious handwriting, so familiar.

Choking up, she whispered, "I miss you, Mom. Every single day."

Getting up for a tissue, Adeline sat back down next to the diary. She caressed its cover, once again wondering what Brendon would think of all of the questions swirling in her mind. *He loves me,* she reminded herself. *Surely he'll accept my spiritual curiosity. Or is what I'm feeling more than that?*

Dismissing her worries, she directed her thoughts toward God. Adeline didn't pray in the traditional way, but she closed her eyes and simply breathed in the quiet moment, thankful for this time alone with her mother's diary . . . and her mother's love.

Sylvia followed her parents out to the back porch after they returned home and the horse was unhitched and stabled.

"The congregation prayed for God's will during the ordination service," Dat began. "And the lot fell on Benuel Zook to take his father's place."

Sylvia flinched. "Benuel, ya say?"

Mamma put her hand on Sylvia's. "I know what you must be thinkin', but it's our place to keep him and his family in our prayers."

"I will," Sylvia said, thinking how things were going to change for Andy's parents and his entire family. She looked at Mamma, then Dat. "I'm glad ya told me, instead of havin' to hear it from the grapevine." She glanced across the newly harvested cornfield, over to the Zooks' big farmhouse. "Guess we'll have us another preacher for a neighbor."

Dat smiled. "*Jah*, and it won't be long now."

Rather shaken by the news, Sylvia didn't feel like sitting there any longer. She needed to take a walk to settle her thoughts, so she politely excused herself.

"If you see your *Brieder* out strolling about the pasture, send them home," Dat called to her.

She turned and waved, nodding. It was apparent that Dat wanted to be the one to tell the news to the boys, and she would gladly honor that.

Heading for the pasture gate, she opened it and closed it securely behind her. It would never do for any of their livestock to get out.

As she walked away from the house, she could hear her brothers' voices in the distance, leisurely calling back and forth to one another. And for a moment, she longed to be a child again. *Oh, to be so carefree on a Sunday afternoon. . . .*

Thinking then of Andy and his family, she could only imagine how solemn it must be at their house right now. And she felt the same way, only for a completely different reason. She recalled that Titus had once shared how heavyhearted his whole family had been after his father's ordination. It had taken weeks, if not months, for the reality to settle in, Titus had said—that he and his siblings were suddenly expected to be examples of godliness for the rest of the community.

This thought made her shiver. *Will Andy still want to take me out for supper?* she wondered, not sure what on earth would happen now.

Thankfully, Ernie offered to take Sylvia to Singing that evening. Having missed going to church because of the members-only communion and ordination, she was glad for the opportunity to be around her girl cousins—she doubted that Andy Zook would be present. As for Titus, it sounded from her father as if she didn't have to worry about running into him, because he was in Big Valley working.

The longer he's gone, the better, she thought, guessing he needed a break from Hickory Hollow.

Adeline unlocked her mailbox in the cluster of mailboxes not far from the walkway to her apartment. Within the few pieces of Wednesday junk mail was a letter from Sylvia, and she nearly let out a *woo-hoo* but quickly caught herself, surprised at her own reaction.

Hurrying to her apartment, Adeline plopped down on the sectional, Sylvia's letter in hand. Then, laughing at herself, she murmured, "I don't get this excited about texts from Callie or Piper!"

She opened the letter and began to read, smiling at Sylvia's Dutchy way with words. *Ach, Adeline, I miss you ever so much and hope you'll think about coming for Thanksgiving here, just maybe.*

She gasped. The unexpected invitation to spend Thanksgiving in Hickory Hollow wasn't as much a surprise as it was possibly a subconscious wish come true. And Sylvia went on to make a case for Adeline to return for a visit, insisting that there was nothing to worry about now. *I'm truly over my breakup with Titus,* Sylvia had written. *Also, you might be happy to hear that Andy Zook asked me out for dinner on Saturday. It's funny, but all of a sudden, I feel ready to date again.*

Adeline grinned at the mention of Andy. *I always knew there was a reason to like that guy!*

I'll go for Thanksgiving if Brendon's okay with it, Adeline thought, since they hadn't made any plans. Brendon had tossed around the idea of driving to Missouri to spend some time with his parents on his own, because they had some family matters to discuss.

She would wait to contact Liam and her grandparents about the idea, giving Brendon first dibs. Since her mom's death, Adeline had begun to realize that life wasn't all about her choices and wishes. *The world doesn't revolve around me,* she thought with a little laugh. *What a shock!*

She got up to check on the slow cooker she'd purchased after returning from Hickory Hollow, her mouth watering as she lifted the lid on the chicken breasts and rice simmering inside. *Brendon would have enjoyed this.* She knew he was under a big deadline for a wealthy client and was holed up at his place to tie up loose ends. *I won't bother him with Sylvia's invitation tonight,* she decided, although it was all she could think about.

Sitting at the kitchen table, Adeline read the passage in the book of John about Jesus washing his closest followers' feet before their Passover meal. She wondered if the Amish patterned their foot-washing service after the one in these verses. But she was even more struck by the concept of water as a symbol of the cleansing Christ offered one's soul. All of this was still foreign to her, but the more she read, the more she felt drawn to this way of thinking . . . and living.

Later, when her dinner was ready, Adeline was happy to have made enough for a few meals. *Sylvie would be proud,* she thought, eager to write back ASAP.

Sylvia tore into cleaning the house on Thursday with every ounce of energy she had. She tried to imagine what Adeline might be thinking, fairly sure she had received the Thanksgiving invitation by now.

Outside on the back porch, a bushel basket of Rome Beauty apples waited to be processed for canning as Sylvia carried out the bedroom rag rugs to beat them on the clothesline. She could see Dat and Ernie out by the woodshed, assessing the amount of wood already stacked for the winter. Recently, Sylvia had spotted some fairly large mice out there and, come to think of it, the mares had sprouted an especially thick crop of horsehair. It was the time of year when farmers took into account the feed and bales of hay they'd stored for winter, while their wives added up the jars of canned goods and, if they were beekeepers, the gallons of honey.

Sylvia sometimes wished they kept bees, too, because she had once tasted a fresh honeycomb dripping with honey over at Annie Fisher Lapp's—sister-in-law to Katie Lapp Fisher. She still hadn't forgotten how delicious it was, or how smooth the honey was in her mouth.

Back outdoors after retrieving the broom from the kitchen closet, she pounded the broom against the oval-shaped rag rug on the line, relieved she hadn't received a letter from Andy canceling their Saturday supper date. *I shouldn't borrow trouble,* she thought, removing the rug from the line.

Adeline brought up Sylvia's Thanksgiving invite when she served leftover chicken and rice to Brendon Thursday evening. "What do you think, Bren?" she asked.

"It's fine with me if you want to go," he said quickly. "I have a few things to do around here." He paused, looking as if he had more to say. "You'll return that Saturday night . . . or when?"

She nodded. "That's what I was thinking. But wait—you're not going out to see your folks, after all?"

"I talked with them at length by phone, and . . ." He paused. "Something has come up here recently, so I'm fine keeping things quiet and having a low-key day here." He mentioned that some of his colleagues had invited him for Thanksgiving dinner. "Of course, that sounds far less fun than being with my family or you." He paused. "I'll definitely take you with me to Missouri at Christmas. How's that?"

"If we can fly," she said, mentioning how iffy it might be driving halfway across the country in winter.

"That's a possibility, sure," he said, adding, "My parents love seeing you, Addy."

She smiled at that. This man of hers was always so thoughtful. "Well, only if you're sure you don't mind my going solo to Hickory Hollow. I hate to abandon you."

"Hey, from what you've told me about the first visit, I think you'll have a great time, especially with all your half siblings."

Adeline knew he meant it. "I'll let Sylvia know I'll arrive Wednesday evening, before the big day." For a fleeting moment, she thought of telling him about how she was reading the book of John along with her father back in Hickory Hollow, but then she noticed Brendon's frown, as though he was deliberating something.

"Have you given any thought to inviting your newfound family to our wedding?" he asked unexpectedly.

Surprised, she said, "Well, I doubt they would even come, as private as they are." She paused. "I don't want to embarrass them or expose them to public scrutiny. And don't you think it would be awkward for Earnest and my mom's parents to be thrown together?"

"Fair enough." Brendon shrugged. "But someday I'd like to meet your father and his family."

"I'd love that!" She smiled.

Their conversation transitioned into a discussion about a garden wedding, and Adeline mentioned that she had nailed down a possible location, a beautiful place just south of Atlanta. "I checked, and it's available Saturday, May twenty-first." She planned to call for a tour this coming weekend. "You're still on board with an outdoor wedding, right? It's not the destination sort of wedding we discussed, though."

He agreed and reached for her hand. "If you're happy, I'm

happy. I know how special saying our vows in a garden would be for you. No second thoughts, not even a smidgen." He winked at her.

"Check." She smiled, loving this about him, too.

"So it sounds like things are good: We have a plan for Thanksgiving and for our wedding." Brendon picked up his coffee and took a sip. "Let's keep the latter as uncomplicated as possible."

He hasn't changed his mind about that, either, she thought. "Right. Skip the superfluous stuff." She grinned now, looking forward to that day and their life together.

Brendon stayed for another hour after dinner, and when he left, Adeline opened her mother's Bible, there on the coffee table, eager to look up a couple of verses her mom had referenced in the latest diary entry. *Did he notice it?* she wondered. She still didn't quite know how to approach him with her growing interest in all of this, but she hoped that Brendon would accept the news as graciously as he did everything else about her.

CHAPTER
Thirty-One

*S*ylvia walked up Hickory Lane to meet Andy Zook at the location they had agreed upon. Moving quickly along the roadside, she kept telling herself not to be surprised if Andy didn't show up.

Things can happen, she thought, recalling Titus's bold declaration last May: *"I'll always love ya . . . be right by your side. . . ."*

"Empty words," she murmured, pushing her hands into her coat pockets, aware of the changing temperature.

This evening she would guard her heart more carefully. *After all, Andy's interest in me came about before his father was made a preacher. . . .*

Adeline missed seeing Brendon that Saturday evening, but he'd told her earlier that he had a meeting to attend. So she enjoyed a quiet evening near the gas fireplace, studying for hours and then reading more of the Bible before soaking up every word of her mom's next diary entry. She had slowed down the pace of reading those now, wanting to savor what was left, prolonging this special time. She was curled up in the pretty quilt given to Mom and Earnest as a wedding gift so long ago, a mug of hot tea within reach on the lamp table. Every now and then, she found herself staring at the flames in the gas fireplace, wondering when to best share with Brendon what she was discovering spiritually. *How will he react?* she wondered, knowing he was preoccupied with work.

She shrugged it off, thinking the right time would present itself. *I'll know when to bring this up. . . .*

Later, she got her laptop to look at wedding trends, especially colors and styles of bridesmaids' dresses for her maid-of-honor and two attendants. *If I decide on even that many,* she thought, wanting to keep things simple, per Brendon's request.

Adeline's grandparents had offered to pay for a lavish wedding, but Adeline didn't want to take advantage of their generosity. After all, her mom's marriage to Earnest had taken place before a justice of the peace, and the marriage to Adeline's stepdad, William Pelham, had also been relatively modest. *It wouldn't be right to spend a bunch of Grandpa and Grandy's money on my wedding,* she thought. And she wouldn't ask the trustee her mom had appointed to shell out extra, either. *For once, I'll be frugal, like Brendon.*

Up Hickory Lane, Andy had already arrived and awaited Sylvia, much to her amazement. He stood outside his open courting carriage, dressed in black except for the white shirt collar that peeked out at the neck of his coat. His wide black felt hat made him look especially distinguished. She tried not to act surprised that he'd actually come, lest he not understand the reason.

"I thought of just pullin' up to your back door," Andy said as she met him. "No point hiding who you're out with tonight, *jah?*"

She smiled. "Well, there are still *some* couples who prefer to keep it a secret," she said, liking that he wouldn't have minded her family knowing. She appreciated that he seemed to like to have things out in the open. "I did tell my parents, though."

"I told mine, too," Andy confessed, helping her into the carriage.

Again, she was very surprised and would have loved to know what the new preacher thought about his son taking out Earnest Miller's daughter. But it wasn't polite to probe. *Besides,* she thought, feeling a subtle twinge in her heart, *maybe I don't want to know.*

"Are ya hungry?" Andy asked after getting into the driver's side.

"*Jah,* are you sure?"

"It's time to eat, for sure." He mentioned two restaurants. "Which would you like?"

"Dienner's is fine."

"My Dat's cousins run that one, so maybe we can get a family discount," he joked, spreading the lap blanket gently over her. "I hope you'll be warm enough. If not, I've got more blankets in the back."

She appreciated his attention to her and tried not to compare a single thing he said or did with Titus. It was only fair, but it wouldn't be easy.

Andy picked up the driving lines and signaled the horse to move forward.

Off to a good start, she thought happily.

Dienner's Country Restaurant was crowded mainly with tourists, but there were a few Amish couples eating in the secondary room off to the side of the buffet. The young Amish hostess, with a friendly smile on her rosy cheeks, directed Sylvia and Andy to their table amidst the background of dinner conversation and the clinking sound of utensils on plates. Sylvia didn't recognize the hostess, but Andy seemed to, and she assumed the young woman must be one of his many cousins or someone he knew from another church district.

When they were seated, Andy made a point of telling Sylvia that the hostess was Linda Esch, an in-law to his married sister. "Linda's also a storyteller at the little rural library out east, near Honey Brook."

Sylvia perked up at this. "She makes up stories?"

"Well, not exactly." Andy explained that Linda memorized stories and dramatized them for children. "To encourage them to learn to read."

"What a talent!"

Andy agreed. "She has a sharp memory."

"How many stories does she know by heart?"

"At last count, seven—everything from Dr. Seuss to *Aesop's Fables.* Do ya remember reading 'The Hare and the Tortoise' and 'The Fox and the Grapes'?"

Sylvia smiled as she recalled Mamma reading those to her when she was small.

Andy reached for the menu. "Well, I guess we should choose what to order before we forget, *jah?*" He winked at her.

Agreeing, Sylvia realized again how comfortable she felt with Andy. He was always so easy to talk to.

"Would ya like the buffet?" he asked with a glance at her. "Don't be shy . . . you can have whatever you'd like."

She thanked him but didn't think she wanted something as substantial as the all-you-can-eat buffet. In the end, Andy chose that, and she ordered a cheesesteak on a potato roll with a side of coleslaw.

Effortlessly, they resumed their conversation, talking now about the upcoming youth fall festivities, including the fall supper party to be hosted at the home of Ella Mae's son-in-law.

"It'll be loads of fun, and I hear David Beiler will have his nine-hundred-pound pumpkin on display," Andy said, grinning like he couldn't wait to see it. "David fertilizes it with phosphorous once the blossoms start."

"That'll do it," Sylvia said. She told Andy that Dawdi Riehl had once grown a fifteen-hundred-pound pumpkin.

Andy chuckled. "That *is* big."

They talked easily throughout the evening, and it wasn't until much later, when they were alone again in his courting carriage and bundled up with several heavy blankets, that she realized she'd scarcely thought of Titus.

As they rode out along Route 30, Andy talked of all the fun they would have together this fall, as if he planned on asking her out again. At North Soudersburg Road, they turned north for a little way, then went east on Irishtown Road, wending their way back toward Hickory Hollow.

A mile from her house, Andy slowed the horse. "Sylvie, I don't want to take you for granted," he said. "Would ya like to spend time with me next Saturday after the Beilers' supper party?"

To think he was asking her this far ahead made her smile. "That'd be nice, but . . ."

He turned to look at her. "What is it?"

"I guess . . . well, I thought ya might not wanna spend time with me anymore, not after your father's ordination."

Andy was so quiet for a moment, she was aware of her heart beating. *Ach, I shouldn't have said anything.*

When he spoke again, it was rather softly. "Listen, Sylvie. I know why you and Titus aren't together. It's no secret."

"You know?"

"*Jah.*" He paused and signaled the mare to a walk. "But I'm not Titus . . . and my father isn't Preacher Kauffman."

She was surprised that he'd immediately touched on the heart of the matter.

Andy continued. "My *Daed* and Dawdi Mahlon have been close friends with your Dat for more than twenty years now. Your Dat has been like family to them, and my father knows he's serious now 'bout living as he should." Andy looked her way, then back at the road. "But it's not only about the connection between our families. It's about you, Sylvie. I've admired ya ever since our school days."

She'd wondered how long Andy had been observing her. "That's a lot to live up to."

"Well, you don't have to worry. All of us are sinners, saved only by the grace of God."

His words echoed in her heart, endearing him to her, and she felt ever so encouraged.

"So if it's all right with you, I'd like to see ya next Saturday after the fall supper party, and at Singing on Sunday, too," Andy said.

Two evenings in a row?

"That'll be fun," she said, trying to squelch a grin.

"Okay then. It's settled." Andy gave a nod before signaling the horse to trot again.

She felt truly at home with him, just as she had the other times they'd talked. And while she liked that they were becoming good friends first, before he showed any romantic affection, she couldn't help wondering how long before he might hold her hand.

CHAPTER
Thirty-Two

The following Tuesday afternoon was chillier than the last few days, yet Sylvia dashed outside without a coat, down to the mailbox to check for a letter from Adeline. She spotted one right away, on the top of the pile.

"What will she say?" she whispered as she ran back up the driveway toward the house.

Sylvia hurried into the kitchen and sat in the spot where she always ate her meals. Sunlight poured through the windows and warmed her up. Mamma appeared to have gone upstairs to the sewing room, so Sylvia decided to read the letter now before announcing its arrival.

Not till I know something . . .

She started at the beginning with *Dear Sylvie,* and before she reached the end, happiness had filled her heart.

Before Dat came in for supper that evening, Sylvia went over to the shop to tell him the exciting news. She opened the door to the showroom, then went to the interior door and peeked inside. "Guess who's comin' for Thanksgiving?" she called.

Her father spun around on his work chair. "Well, I'll be!"

She held up Adeline's letter. "She'll arrive the night before Thanksgiving and stay till early Saturday mornin'."

Dat smiled. "That's great."

"And . . . she's bringing along her Nine Patch project. It'll be fun to see how it's progressed."

"Won't Tommy be happy to see her again," Dat commented as he stood and stretched a bit.

"I think *all* the boys will be," she said, though she agreed that Tommy would be especially thrilled.

"Your Mamma will want to have Dawdi and Mammi Riehl over for the feast, too."

Sylvia could hardly wait to tell Adeline in person about her first date with Andy Zook. *By then, I'll have seen him at least three times,* she thought happily.

Then, just that quick, Sylvia wondered what Andy would think of Adeline's return. Would it complicate things between them when things were starting off so well?

She recalled his kind words about her and the reasons he'd wanted to take her out for supper last Saturday. *I mustn't fret,* she decided, wanting to trust God in this, as Dat had been encouraging all of them to do lately about everything. He had even asked them to read chapter seventeen, verse seven, of Jeremiah each morning when they first got up. *Blessed is the man that trusteth in the LORD, and whose hope the LORD is.*

"I'll be sure to ask Adeline her favorite dessert," she said, interrupting her own musing.

Dat nodded. "*Gut* idea. And do I get to tell you mine?"

She laughed. "Sure," she said, heading back to the house to share the good news with Mamma, too.

Dat told the boys even before they sat down at the table for supper. "We're having a special guest for Thanksgiving," he said, grinning at Sylvia, who carried a large platter of fried chicken.

"Is it the new preacher?" asked Adam, taking his seat next to Ernie.

"Dat said a *guest*, not guests," Ernie told him. "Preacher Zook's not gonna come for dinner without his family."

Adam frowned and looked at Dat.

"Do we get a hint?" Calvin said with a glance at Tommy, who was nodding his head.

Dat dramatically pressed a finger against his cheek. "Hmm, let's see. This is someone who makes delicious omelets."

"So the person is a *she*!" Calvin announced.

Dat chuckled, and the boys were still for a moment, like they were thinking hard.

Then Dat gave one more hint. "She promised Tommy a ride in her car."

Tommy raised his eyebrows. "Adeline?" he asked quietly, like he wasn't sure he ought to say it.

Dat laughed. "You guessed it."

Even Adam was nodding his head happily, and Sylvia could hardly wait to write to Adeline and tell her how very delighted they all were.

That evening, Adeline texted Brendon that she had booked their garden wedding, complete with a reception tent. *There*

will be a luncheon for one hundred guests and a three-tier cake of our choosing. We'll save loads of money, not having a four-course meal!

In less than a minute, he texted back: *Perfect!*

Adeline laughed under her breath, pleased they were in agreement. She went to the kitchen table and opened her laptop to sit down and do some research for a class as the full moon shone in through the sliding doors to the balcony.

Looking forward to seeing Andy again, Sylvia asked Ernie to drop her off at David and Mattie Beiler's farmhouse, where the supper party was set to begin that Saturday evening. It was Halloween night, though none of the People in Hickory Hollow celebrated it.

On the drive over, she told Ernie about the supposed nine-hundred-pound pumpkin Ella Mae's son-in-law had grown.

"By now it's probably another hundred fifty pounds on top of that, if he hasn't cut it off the vine yet," Ernie told her as the driving lines rested loosely in his hands.

"Honestly, that big?"

He nodded. "Pumpkins like that can grow more than twenty pounds in a day."

Sylvia gazed out at the waning moon, still bright. "Why don't we grow any of ours that big?"

"Well, how're we gonna get them out to the vegetable stand to sell?"

"A forklift, maybe?" she suggested.

Ernie burst out laughing.

When they arrived, she thanked him for dropping her off and said she planned to get a ride home.

"With our new preacher's son?" Ernie gave her a knowing grin.

"So I guess the word's out."

"Can't keep somethin' like *that* a secret." He waved and clicked his cheek to signal the horse forward.

Sylvia didn't know what to think. Could it be all of Hickory Hollow knew already, after she and Andy had only had one date?

Sylvia thought it was awfully nice of Susie Zook and Cousin Alma to save her a seat at the table in Mattie Beiler's large front room, which was decorated with big paper leaves someone had taken a lot of time to cut out. Long tables and wooden benches crowded the space, and the lasagna supper was so tasty, more than a few fellows went back for seconds. Unfortunately, Cousin Jessie was under the weather tonight, so she was missing out on a wonderful meal and some good fellowship, as well.

"Tell her we missed her, won't ya?" Sylvia said to Alma, who sat to her left.

Alma nodded as she glanced over toward Jessie's beau, Yonnie Zook. "She and Yonnie are getting serious," Alma whispered. "I wouldn't be surprised if they tie the knot next fall."

"A year's a long time away," Susie said softly, eyes serious.

Sylvia thought again of her plans to join church next September and agreed with what Susie had just said. *A very long wait.*

After the plates had been cleared away, Mattie and Ella Mae brought out clear plastic bins of cookies—five different kinds in all. The fudge meltaways, Sylvia knew for sure, were

Ella Mae's doing. The oodles of nuts, coconut, chocolate, and graham cracker crumbs made for an especially delicious treat.

She took only one, and the first bite was pure heaven as it melted in her mouth. Going over to say *hullo* to Ella Mae, Sylvia thanked her for making them. "I would've come an' helped ya, had I known what you were up to."

"So thoughtful of you, dearie." Ella Mae's eyes shone as Sylvia gave her a little hug, the Wise Woman's soft white hair brushing Sylvia's cheek.

"It's nice seein' ya here with *die Youngie*," Sylvie told her.

"*Jah*, but I best be gettin' back to the *Haus* before I frighten anyone." Ella Mae tittered and patted her heavily wrinkled cheeks.

Sylvia shook her head. "*Ach*, you'd never do that!" She clasped the dear woman's hand.

"*Kumme* see me again, Sylvie," Ella Mae said as she smiled at some of the other youth who'd come to greet her now, too.

"I will," promised Sylvia. *She must've heard I'm seeing Andy,* Sylvia thought, unable to hold back her smile. *She wants news!*

After table games and singing a few gospel songs, everyone helped redd up before going outside to see the enormous pumpkin, even larger than Sylvia had imagined. Some of the guys sat on it, acting silly. One of Titus's cousins commented that, if they had a phone, they could all take a photo while pretending to lift the pumpkin. That made Sylvia think of Adeline, and she wished she could begin to describe how huge this pumpkin was.

Andy came over to talk with her. Just then, she spotted Titus, whom she hadn't seen at the supper party earlier. Had he come just to see the pumpkin, maybe?

Their eyes caught, and he gave her a faint smile before looking away.

She gathered up her black coat and outer bonnet, feeling surprised because she hadn't felt sad or discouraged at seeing him. *A good sign*, she thought, walking out to Andy's carriage with him. "That supper Mattie made was *wunnerbaar-gut*, ain't so?" she said as they settled into his courting carriage.

"Delicious! There must've been five kinds of cheese in the lasagna," Andy remarked, picking up the driving lines after covering Sylvia and himself with the thick lap blankets. "And I liked each one."

She chuckled. "And did ya taste Ella Mae's fudge melt-aways?" she asked as they headed toward the road.

"The first cookie I reached for," Andy admitted. "I don't think my Mamm has that recipe."

"I can get it for her, if you'd like."

"Would you?"

She nodded. "Ella Mae loves to share."

Andy agreed. "My sister Susie is a big fan of Ella Mae, too." He also went on to mention how fond his sister was of Sylvia. "She wants to get better acquainted with you."

Sylvia had to smile. *Is that something every fellow says to his girlfriend?* she wondered, then caught herself. *Am I his girlfriend?*

At the end of the evening, Andy turned in to her father's driveway and came around to help her down. "I'll see ya tomorrow at Singing," he said as he walked her up the back-porch steps. "You haven't forgotten, I hope?"

"*Nee*," she said, smiling under the light of the moon, never having had dates on consecutive nights before.

"Okay, *gut*." He paused. "Sleep well, Sylvie."

"*Gut Nacht*, Andy," she said softly and let herself in the back door.

CHAPTER
Thirty-Three

*E*arnest sat attentively as Benuel Zook preached the second sermon the next morning. He asked God to give Benuel the courage and the wisdom to deliver the words the Lord had put on his heart, wondering how it felt to stand before this large congregation for the very first time.

Earnest noticed other men with their heads bowed and believed that they, too, were asking God's blessing on their newly ordained minister rather than dozing off on such an important day.

Benuel's message was inspiring and focused on divine guidance and lovingkindness. Earnest wished Adeline might have been in attendance. *She has so many questions,* he thought, looking forward to seeing her in a little over three weeks.

He had been praying for Adeline every day since she'd left. He had also been asking God that his clock business would continue to stabilize. He needed a steady income, especially with the usual lull of winter after Christmas. There still seemed to be some hesitation on some customers' part to frequent his actual shop, but he was grateful for the strong sales each Saturday at market. Because of that, he had been talking with a landlord about setting up a clock showroom near one of the tourist traps in Bird-in-Hand. As of right now, he was waiting for a final offer on the rent.

The Lord knows our every need, he thought, glad for Sylvia's and Ernie's enthusiasm to help at the small showroom beside the house so that Earnest could tend the shop in town. *If it all works out . . .*

Sylvia loved joining her voice in song with the other youth that Sunday evening, even as she happened to notice Titus sitting with his male cousins. Determined not to catch his eye, she paid close attention to the parent sponsors, who were starting to announce the upcoming youth activities for this month of November. There was to be another supper party the Wednesday before Thanksgiving, but Sylvia knew she wouldn't be going, since Adeline was coming that evening. *We'll scarcely have enough time together as it is,* she thought, hoping this second visit wouldn't cause waves amongst the People.

As before, Andy was very attentive to her during refreshments and after the Singing, as well, making his way over to talk with her and her cousins. His cousin Yonnie mentioned possibly double dating in the future, and Cousin Jessie, who fortunately was feeling well again, fairly glowed at the prospect.

Later, during their ride around Hickory Hollow, Andy asked Sylvia if it was all right if they doubled with Yonnie and Jessie sometime.

"That'd be nice, but I've heard they're getting serious, so maybe they would rather not."

"*Jah*, they're close to being engaged," Andy agreed.

Sylvia assumed that since Yonnie was related to Andy, perhaps this idea had come directly from him. "As long as they're comfortable with us hanging around, I'm fine with it," she added, recalling how Cousin Alma had seemed to prefer not to double-date once she and Danny Lapp became more serious.

Andy chuckled. "I guess we'll find out . . . that is, if you agree to let me court ya."

Rather shocked, she almost asked him to repeat his words. Wasn't it too soon?

As if sensing her hesitation, he said, "If you're not sure, Sylvie . . ."

She shook her head. "I guess I'm just tryin' to catch up."

Nodding, Andy said, "Well, I understand it may seem quick to you, but you're the girl I've been hopin' to court for a while now."

He seems to know his heart, she thought. "How will it look?" she managed to ask him.

"Well, how long has it been since you and Titus broke up?"

"Nearly three months."

"So it's entirely up to you, Sylvie. Please take your time. I don't want to rush you. Just give me your answer later."

She appreciated his taking her feelings into consideration. And, while Adeline's upcoming visit was fresh on her mind, she decided to ask him another question. "Adeline will be here for Thanksgiving," she said, saying it quickly so she wouldn't shy away from what could be a sticky subject. "What do ya think 'bout that?"

He was quiet for a moment. "Is she curious 'bout the Old Ways, do ya know?"

"*Nee*, she's not about to become Amish, but she has been

askin' a lot about God and the Good Book lately." She told about Adeline's mother's diary and how it had made her think more about her purpose in life.

"It's a *gut* thing she's reachin' out to you and your family, *jah?*"

He doesn't seem to be opposed, she realized, nodding and adding, "Dat's been answering her letters, sharing Scriptures with her."

Andy signaled the horse to trot faster. "Surely the Lord's hand was in her comin' to Hickory Hollow. Don't ya think so?"

"Honestly, *jah* . . . and I think Adeline visiting again will be a real blessing for her . . . and us."

Settling back in the seat, Sylvia was glad she'd had the courage to share with him instead of fretting to herself what he thought about it.

To think Andy's ready to court me, she thought. *Am I ready?*

While the clothes flapped on the line the next morning, Sylvia went down cellar to sort more of the laundry. After that chore was finished, she wrote a quick note to Adeline, asking about her favorite dessert. Sylvia also wanted to keep her promise to see Ella Mae and also to ask for the fudge meltaways recipe. *Andy might think I forgot, otherwise.*

On top of that, Sylvia really wanted someone else's opinion about entering into another courtship this soon. Usually, when an engagement was broken, the young man or woman casually dated several more people before settling into another serious courtship. Would Ella Mae have some advice that Mamma might not be willing to give? *Mamma likes Andy Zook*, she thought, *and so does Dat. So there's that to consider.*

"No pressure," she whispered, laughing a little.

After the noon meal, Sylvia went on foot to visit the Wise Woman, enjoying the autumn foliage, many of the gold and orange leaves still clinging to the branches, and the sumac vines along the roadside still red. The mulchy trace of tilled soil hung in the damp, nippy air as Amish folk from her church district rode past in buggies and spring wagons, waving and smiling.

When she had turned in to David Beiler's long driveway, she made her way around toward Ella Mae's back door and saw her outside on the little white porch deadheading several potted purple mums. "Hullo," Sylvia called, glad to see the woman in such good health.

"Well, how nice to see you again." Ella Mae pointed to the potted flowers. "These here late-bloomin' mums are called Barbara, and they just keep flowerin' till a hard frost. I baby them along, protecting them at night, putting them up close to the house."

"They're so perty," Sylvia said, eyeing them.

"*Ach,* listen to me rattle on." Ella Mae pushed her long white *Kapp* strings back over her shoulders. "*Kumme* inside for some hot peppermint tea, won't ya?"

"You always seem to have some ready."

Ella Mae smiled sweetly. "In case someone drops by. Ya just never know."

Sylvia should have expected such an answer, humble as Ella Mae was.

Ella Mae invited her to sit down and relax. "You had a lot on your shoulders this past summer." She looked at Sylvia thoughtfully, as though she knew exactly why she'd come. "Am I right?"

Sylvia nodded. "You have no idea." Then, realizing what she'd said, she corrected herself. "Well, maybe ya do."

They shared a little laugh.

"New love is exciting, but it can fog the brain," Ella Mae said, pouring her signature tea into Sylvia's cup, her hand as steady as if she were twenty.

"Well, this new fella's already become a *gut* friend," Sylvia admitted while reaching for the bowl of sugar cubes. "And in such a short time, too."

"Ah, and friendship's the best place to start a lasting romance, I daresay." Ella Mae's smile made her eyes twinkle.

They talked more of courtship, and of love . . . particularly of giving one's heart away and then wondering if there was any love left for another.

"That's where I am now," Sylvia said quietly.

"Then I'll be askin' my customary question," Ella Mae said, her teacup poised near her wrinkled lips.

Sylvia waited, knowing what was coming next.

"Have ya given this up to the Good Lord in prayer?"

Being honest, Sylvia replied, "I've scarcely had time to—it's all happened so fast."

"Well now, dearie, it takes only a moment to breathe a prayer to the One who made ya. He's ever listenin', ever wanting to lead ya."

Ella Mae always points a person in the right direction, Sylvia thought.

"Our heavenly Father has a plan for each of us," Ella Mae continued. "Do ya believe that?"

Sylvia sighed. "For a while I thought Titus Kauffman *was* God's plan for me. And we were both praying 'bout our relationship, too."

Ella Mae looked at her kindly over her dainty rosebud teacup. "Could be that neither of ya really stopped to listen for God's answer—sometimes our hearts try to go before our heads, 'specially when it comes to romance. But that doesn't mean that your time with Titus didn't teach ya a thing or two about what a *gut* relationship should look like. We learn from many experiences in life, ain't so?"

Sylvia mulled this over before saying, "I hadn't really thought of it that way."

Ella Mae smiled. "Delightful as you are, there will always be someone interested in you, Sylvie, till you're settled into marriage," she said. "But I don't say this to flatter ya. Outward beauty can be a disadvantage at your young age . . . it can cause confusion. And one can't be so sure if a fella's interest is based on appearance rather than the heart."

Sylvia wanted to tell Ella Mae that Andy Zook was the new fellow, but she didn't want to say anything quite yet.

Again, Ella Mae urged her to commit her future husband to the Lord. "Then on your wedding day, you can tell the young man 'bout our conversation here today."

"*Denki*," Sylvia said, encouraged.

"If I can be of any help, just drop by, all right?" Ella Mae offered her another cup of tea, and Sylvia accepted.

They began to talk less about relationships and more about recipes, and Sylvia asked if she might jot down Ella Mae's fudge meltaways recipe "for a friend."

"Well now, that's interesting. Rebecca Zook mentioned during yesterday's fellowship meal that her son Andy commented 'bout the recipe for those exact same goodies."

"She did?" Sylvia's eyes met Ella Mae's, and while Ella Mae kept a straight face, Sylvia had to grin.

CHAPTER
Thirty-Four

*E*arnest didn't want to overreact, but he had something important to tell Rhoda. Hurrying into the house the following Tuesday afternoon, he found his wife redding up the sewing room and tiptoed in behind her to slip his arms around her waist.

"*Ach!*" Rhoda whirled to face him.

He leaned in and planted a kiss on her lips. "I have some *wunnerbaar-gut* news, love."

Eyes shining with anticipation, she reached around his neck. "Did ya get the lease terms ya wanted?"

"Not only that, but the landlord also threw in the first three months of utilities as part of the deal. I think he's mighty happy to have an Amish client." Ernest picked Rhoda up and twirled her around like they were young again. "Just what we prayed for."

She smiled up at him, stepping back. "This'll give your business a shot in the arm."

"*Jah*, if all goes well. . . . If I move in right away, I can attract all the folks buying Christmas gifts." He mentioned having Ernie help him paint an attractive sign to put over the entrance to the new House of Time.

"Excellent idea. Ernie will do a right fine job," she said. "You'll have to let him and Sylvie know when to plan to be on hand to help in the showroom here." Rhoda went to close the door. "And speakin' of Sylvie, she was up early this morning, kneeling at her bedside."

"Oh?"

"Something's goin' on with her. I can feel it."

Earnest frowned. "Not with her and Titus, surely?"

"*Nee*, might be Andy Zook," Rhoda said. "I could be wrong, but mothers usually aren't."

He grinned. "I'd have to say that's true."

"Whatever it is, the Lord knows."

Earnest relished the fact that they were in one accord once more, and not just on the matter of their daughter's dating life. He reached for Rhoda and kissed her again, longer this time. "I love you so," he whispered.

"We'd best be gettin' back to work or . . ."

"Or what?"

"We'll talk 'bout this another time," she said, pressing her hands against his face.

"*Jah*," he said.

She threw him a kiss before he turned to leave.

Earnest smiled all the way down the stairs and through the kitchen, looking forward to finishing their conversation tonight.

Wednesday's mending and sewing took up much of the day, and when Thursday came, Sylvia found herself busy in

Mamma's kitchen, baking loaves of bread and some pumpkin pies and pumpkin cookies, too.

That afternoon, a light rain began to fall, and she took the umbrella to check on the mail for Mamma. All week long, Sylvia had wondered if Andy might follow up their dates with a note or letter, but so far, there'd been no word.

The air had the distinct smell of coming snow as she made her way down the driveway. The day was cold and dreary, and she expected the rain to soon turn to sleet. Opening the mailbox, she reached in and discovered a stack of mail. Wanting to keep the letters dry, she didn't pause to look through them, instead hurrying to the house.

On the back porch, she shook out the umbrella before taking it inside to the utility room. Then she headed through the narrow hallway into the warm kitchen, where she breathed in the homey smell of baking bread. "Plenty-a mail today," she told Mamma, who was already rolling out dough for noodles on the long counter. "But I haven't looked through it yet."

"Would you mind checking for me?" asked Mamma, holding up her hands, all caked with flour.

"All right." Sylvia flipped through the mail, reciting what letters were addressed to Mamma. To Sylvia's surprise, two were for her: one from Andy, and another from Titus.

What in the world?

"I'll be right back," Sylvia told Mamma as she headed for the sitting room.

"Take your time, dear," Mamma said, sounding cheerful.

Sitting in the chair nearest the window, Sylvia opened Titus's letter first, curious what he had on his mind and recalling how he had looked at her at the supper party last Saturday evening.

The letter was short and to the point. He apologized for hurting her and said he'd noticed how happy she appeared while talking with Andy Zook the other day. *It makes sense that you settle in with someone new, and I'm glad it's Andy,* he'd written. *You and I went through such a difficult stretch toward the end of our relationship. I wish you well, Sylvie.*

He had signed off *Sincerely, Titus Kauffman.*

She returned the letter to its envelope, floored to receive something like this. *He's happy for me?*

She wondered, too, if Titus's letter was the sign she had prayed for. Could it be?

She felt almost teary eyed at the thought of Titus taking time to write this. *After all we went through . . .*

Then, opening the letter from Andy, she found a slightly longer note. And she leaned into the chair to read.

Dear Sylvie,

I hope you're having a good week!

You've been on my mind since we talked on Sunday after Singing. I think I may have surprised you with my invitation to court, which wasn't my intention at all.

I know I've already said it, but please take as much time as you need to feel comfortable with a decision. I understand not wanting to move forward until you're completely ready—a wise thing to do. I can be as patient as you need me to be.

Meanwhile, I'm praying for God's will in this and hoping you are, too.

Your friend,
Andy Zook

Staring now at the letter, Sylvia contemplated what he'd written, her heart warmed by his kindness and sensitivity. *And to think Titus wishes us well!*

Quickly, she carried the letters upstairs and placed them in her dresser drawer, Andy's on top.

Saturday evening, Sylvia stayed put at home, reading and working on some embroidery, although Andy would undoubtedly have liked to take her out, since there was no Singing till a week from tomorrow. Even so, his letter made it clear he understood her reasons for waiting. All the same, she would still miss not seeing him for another eight days, assuming she decided to go to the next Singing. *There's no need to rush things.*

Meanwhile, she spent the evening with her family, playing table games with her brothers while the snow fell and the wind blew it all around.

Rhoda mentioned again to Earnest later that night that she felt sure Sylvia was mulling over something. "She didn't go out tonight," she observed.

In his chair across the bedroom, Earnest looked up from his reading. "Have you talked to her?"

Rhoda shook her head. "Just waitin' for her to come to one of us."

"She'll talk when she's ready."

Rhoda knew he was right. "So how soon will ya be movin' your clocks to the Bird-in-Hand showroom?" she asked.

"The lease starts Monday. I'll get Ernie and Adam to help me," Earnest said. "Benuel's offered to pitch in, too."

Bless the new preacher, thought Rhoda. "I know you're thankful for this new location, but I'll miss seein' ya during the day."

Earnest nodded. "I'll have to take a brown bag lunch." He looked a little glum about that prospect.

"You'll be closed for Thanksgiving Day, ain't so?"

Earnest nodded and got out of the chair to dress for bed. "*Jah,* for certain."

Thanksgiving, Rhoda thought, grateful for a day set aside to count their many blessings.

She mustn't be concerned over Sylvia but instead must trust that God held her in His loving care.

Preaching service took place at Preacher Kauffman's farm on November fifteenth, and the evening Singing, as well. With Titus's letter lingering in her mind, Sylvia felt at ease about going, so she asked her father to drive her over.

"You won't feel strange bein' at Kauffmans' tonight?" Dat asked, concern in his voice.

"I've considered it all week, and since I'll have *gut* fellowship with my girl cousins, I'll be fine."

Dat nodded. "Just go and have fun."

"I will," she said, hoping to feel comfortable with Andy, if he came over to talk with her.

When they pulled into Kauffmans' lane, she remembered the morning she had gone riding with Dat and Adeline and their stop there at the roadside stand. That moment when the minister first learned of Adeline's relationship to Dat wasn't the most pleasant memory, but Sylvia was thankful

273

for the place Adeline now had in her family . . . and in her heart.

Sylvia thanked Dat for the ride and hopped out of the family buggy, then hurried toward the house, bracing herself against the cold.

During the midpoint of the gathering, Eva Kauffman served spiced hot cider in the kitchen, and Sylvia saw two of Mahlon Zook's grandnieces go over and talk with Titus. Seeing the three of them in a close circle didn't cause her sadness nor envy.

As she'd guessed, Andy Zook did not approach her, and Sylvia was content to visit with his sister and her cousins Alma and Jessie, whose boyfriends were over talking with Andy.

"Your father makes the best clocks," Susie told Sylvia, asking where he got his ideas. "The one Andy bought me for my birthday looks real perty on my chest of drawers."

Sylvia remembered how she'd helped Andy with the purchase last May. "Were ya surprised about your birthday gift?" she asked Susie.

"Oh, was I ever! Andy kept it all hush-hush so I wouldn't even guess."

"I'll tell Dat how much you like it," Sylvia said, thinking how humble her father, master clockmaker, was about such things.

Later, when more refreshments were served as the evening wrapped up, Andy gave her a big smile from across the front room. Seeing this, she hoped he might come over and at least say hullo, so she smiled back to encourage him. She felt a flutter when he pushed his hands into his trouser pockets and strolled toward her.

"Big turnout tonight," Andy said, looking especially hand-some, his blond hair the color of honey in the gaslight.

"Maybe they all came for Eva's delicious hot apple cider," she replied. "Word gets around." She smiled up at him. "Oh, which reminds me." She pulled Ella Mae's recipe from her pocket. "I think you wanted your mother to have this recipe."

"Fudge meltaways!" Andy thanked her, smiling broadly.

They talked about how quickly Thanksgiving was coming, and Andy brought up a few fall-related youth activities, but he didn't suggest they go together this time. He was being considerate, letting her take her time, just as he'd written.

"By the way, I received your letter," she said. "*Denki.*"

He tipped his hat humorously. "There will be more," he said with a wink.

She smiled even as she noticed Titus leaving with Betsy Zook, one of the girls he had talked to earlier. Sylvia took stock of her feelings and realized she was glad for him. *I really am over him,* she thought. *I'm ready to move forward.*

So there was no need to wait. She looked at Andy. "I'd like to talk to you."

He stepped closer.

"Are ya still interested in courtin' me?" she asked. "Because if ya are . . ."

His eyes searched hers, expression serious. And then sud-denly, his face lit up. "You don't have to ask!"

And when they walked through the kitchen and outside to his courting carriage, Sylvia didn't care one bit who saw them together.

CHAPTER
Thirty-Five

At noon the day before Thanksgiving, Sylvia sprinkled grated cheese atop the saucy winter casserole and carried it over to the table. Then, going back for an even larger bowl of steaming hot macaroni, she took that to the table, as well.

Dat and the boys were already seated, and Tommy was talking excitedly about seeing Adeline again. "Last time, she was gonna take me for a ride in her perty red car," he said, his small voice rising. "But she left before I could."

Dat glanced at Mamma, who was smiling in apparent amusement as she took her seat. "Maybe *all* of you can go for a spin," he teased.

"I don't think we'll all fit." Calvin grinned.

Ernie was shaking his head in disgust. "*Puh!* I won't be goin'. A car like that is too tempting."

"Glad to hear you say that, son." Dat patted Ernie's shoulder.

"Aw, but just once won't hurt nothin'," Tommy said, looking over at Sylvia, who sat down across from them.

"That's what Eve said to Adam, too, remember?" Dat said with a snap of his suspenders.

"You can't blame me for that—I wasn't even born yet!" Tommy stated.

They all laughed.

Dat was still smiling when he said, "If you really want to ride with her once, that's okay."

Tommy's eyes lit up. "I promise."

Adam joined the conversation. "We'll remember this talk when you're a teenager in *Rumschpringe*."

"Like Sylvie is now?" Tommy asked.

She realized that Tommy was right, even though since last May, she'd largely had the mindset of a baptismal candidate. *Not that I've ever wanted to live on the edge of what's expected of me.*

Unlike most fellows who waited till right before they married, Andy Zook had been baptized for two years already. It was interesting that he had gone ahead with it before he had a courtship. *He's devout but doesn't broadcast it,* she thought, bowing her head for the table blessing when Dat signaled to do so.

Adeline was thankful for good traveling weather, and as she turned off Route 340 and made her way to West Cattail Road, the once familiar farming landmarks looked very different under the starlight and a dusting of snow.

She was eager to see the Millers again, especially Sylvia, after all the letters they had written, sharing their thoughts so freely these past few months. She also wanted to talk with them about the things she had read for the first time—about

Jesus's life and the remarkable miracles He'd performed, the betrayal by His friend Judas, and the hideous torture Jesus endured before He was hung on a cross. *Killed like a criminal though completely innocent,* she thought, tears springing to her eyes.

Turning into the Millers' driveway, Adeline recalled the first time she arrived there, last August. The memories rushed back . . . her hesitancy to ask Sylvia if she could talk to Earnest, then meeting him and Rhoda and their four lively sons.

This time will be different, she thought, turning off the ignition. *I'm no longer a stranger. . . .*

She remembered to go to the back door, and before she could knock, Rhoda opened it, her smile spreading across her rosy cheeks. "*Kumme* in out of the cold, dear." Then Earnest was right there, too, taking her bags and welcoming her with a joyful expression.

It didn't take long for Ernie and the younger boys to come running, and she was touched by the warm reunion.

When Sylvia came downstairs, the two of them embraced.

"I'm so glad to see ya," Sylvia said as she walked her to the spare room, where a lamp was lit and Earnest had already placed her luggage on the floor. "I can't believe you're here!" Sylvia's eyes were bright.

"I am, and look at you, all glowing!" Adeline exclaimed. "Do you have something to tell me?"

Sylvia's eyes danced. "Later."

"I can't wait!" Adeline laughed.

"I'm sure it's exactly what you're thinkin'."

"Really? Well then, come here!" Adeline hugged her happily again.

"I'd love to say more, but Mamma has the dessert ready."

They headed back to the kitchen, where the boys stood around, waiting to take their seats on their same long wooden bench.

"How was the trip?" Earnest asked as he took his chair at the head of the table.

"Thanks to cruise control, I made excellent time, until I came through York, where there were some snowy patches," she said. "I got up at four-thirty and was on the road before six. I only needed to stop occasionally since I packed a lunch and some healthy snacks."

"You must be hungry, then," Rhoda said, bringing a big pumpkin pie to the table. Adeline had written to Sylvia in one of her recent letters that it was her favorite dessert. There was also homemade vanilla ice cream and pumpkin-cinnamon muffins. "If you want something more substantial, I can easily warm up some leftovers."

Adeline took her up on the offer while the rest of the family enjoyed dessert.

Later, after the dishes were washed, Adeline invited Sylvia to her room, and she asked how things were coming along with Andy Zook. Sylvia revealed that they were seeing each other once a week now.

"This is so great!" Adeline said with a smile. "This guy's obviously fallen for you."

Sylvia's face turned pink. "I like him, too."

"A lot?" Adeline asked, dying to know.

Sylvia nodded. "But keep it mum for now, okay? Otherwise, Dat and Mamma will have us hitched before the day's over."

They both laughed heartily at that, then continued talking late into the night. Adeline was surprised how wide-awake she still was after the early morning and nearly twelve-hour drive. It was Sylvia who politely suggested she take a nice warm shower and get some rest.

"I'll see ya in the mornin'." Sylvia went to the bedroom door and turned to smile at her. "It'll be a *wunnerbaar-gut* Thanksgiving Day."

Adeline agreed and watched her tiptoe out.

The next morning, Adeline's phone beeped her into consciousness, and she smiled sleepily when she rolled over to reach for it and saw Brendon's text: *Happy Thanksgiving to the love of my life!*

Aw, you're sweet . . . thx, she texted back, yawning.

I'll catch you later, Addy.

OK. Have a good turkey day! She smiled as she slipped out of bed, glad he would be spending the afternoon with close friends.

Sylvia and Adeline worked alongside Mamma in the kitchen an hour before breakfast, cleaning the big turkey and preparing it for stuffing. Sylvia was thankful for the extra company as, after breakfast, they peeled oodles of potatoes and boiled them to make creamy mashed potatoes for the feast. There would also be savory gravy, homemade bread, buttered carrots, and lima beans, with everything timed to be done at the same moment. In the meantime, Sylvia and Adeline went down cellar to get some apple butter and sweet and sour pickles.

Adeline gasped at the sight of the more than eight hundred jars of canned goods perfectly lined up and alphabetized. "Looks like you were busy after I left!" she observed, and Sylvia smiled.

At noon, Dawdi and Mammi Riehl joined them, pleased to see Adeline again. They asked her about the drive from Georgia and made small talk about her studies, too.

When they were all seated around Mamma's table, Dat bowed his head and prayed longer than usual. To her delight, Sylvia noticed that Adeline folded her hands and bowed her head with them this time.

After everyone had stuffed themselves on the delicious meal and dessert, Dat read a psalm. An atmosphere of thankfulness and love filled the house, and Sylvia couldn't remember a more special Thanksgiving dinner.

That afternoon, Adeline showed Mamma and Sylvia the progress she'd made on her wall hanging. Mamma seemed impressed as she noted the careful stitching.

"What sort of pattern do ya want for your quilting stitches?" Sylvia asked.

"Well, hearts, but I was hoping you could help me with the stitching," replied Adeline.

"Sure, I'll help ya stitch it, if you'd like," Sylvia said, looking at her mother. "Mamma could pitch in occasionally, too."

"Let's do it!" Adeline agreed.

So Sylvia and Adeline set to work, two sets of hands coming together to create something of beauty.

Later, after a supper of turkey sandwiches and leftovers, Sylvia invited Adeline to her room again, where she let Adeline read Titus's final letter.

"So you're totally free." Adeline gave her a thumbs-up. "How does it feel?"

"It gave me the added confidence I needed to move forward with Andy," Sylvia said.

"I'm happy for you, Sylvie. You deserve someone who loves you for *you*."

She didn't know whether to say thank you or what. It was exactly what Sylvia had hoped and prayed for.

They talked about how surprising it was that Andy, now also a preacher's son, had no problem courting her when Titus had.

Then, after they'd discussed all of that, Adeline said rather hesitantly, "I've been giving a lot of thought to this, so please think over what I'm about to ask." She was sitting at the foot of the bed, leaning back against a large pillow.

"Okay," Sylvia said, uncertain what to expect.

"Guess I'll just put it out there." Adeline inhaled and raised her eyebrows as if she was a little nervous.

"It's okay—we can talk freely, ya know," Sylvia told her, wondering what on earth was giving her such a case of nerves.

"Would you be in my wedding next May?" Adeline looked like she was holding her breath. "I'm hoping that would be permitted . . . but only say yes if you want to."

"Want to? I'd love that, and *jah*, I can be in it, since I'm not baptized yet." Sylvia explained that since she was still in her *Rumschpringe*, she could do practically whatever she wanted. "But what would I wear?"

Adeline smiled, pulling her hair back and letting it go. "I've decided on long black taffeta dresses for Callie and Piper," Adeline said. "Black for the maid-of-honor and bridesmaids is quite fashionable now."

Sylvia was still as she pondered this.

"What's wrong?"

"Just thinkin'," Sylvia said. "I could sew up a new black dress and matching cape apron, if ya like. I wouldn't think of wearin' fancy clothes, I'm sure ya know."

Adeline immediately agreed. "That's perfect. I just want you in it, because . . . well, you're the only sister I have."

Sister? Sylvia caught her breath. "I'm honored," she said, a little stunned. "Now maybe I should ask where the wedding's gonna be."

"That's another thing we should talk about." Adeline described the garden location, then mentioned that she'd be happy to fly her to Atlanta.

"Oh my." Sylvia wasn't sure if she should throw a damper on Adeline's excitement. "We Amish don't ever travel by plane. But I could come by passenger van or train."

"Whatever's best. I'll pay your way, so don't worry about that," Adeline said, then added, "This is so great!"

When they had said good-night and Adeline had gone downstairs to the spare room, Sylvia fell back onto the bed, scarcely able to believe it.

She thinks of me as her sister! she thought. *And we truly are.*

Earnest agreed that, unusual for an Amish person though it was, it would be special for Sylvia to be in Adeline's wedding. He hadn't realized until just now how close the two girls had become.

"Are ya sure you want to do this?" Rhoda asked their daughter as she sat with them in their bedroom.

"I am." Sylvia beamed. "I know Georgia's a long way away, but I'll be gone for only a short time, and I'll be with Adeline, too. But Preacher Kauffman might look on it as more unwanted drama happening over here, ya know."

"I see what ya mean," Rhoda said, glancing at Earnest. "What do you think, love?"

"Well, since Sylvia isn't a church member yet, it should be all right, *jah*? Technically she's free to do this."

"I'll only go with your blessing and Mamma's," Sylvia was quick to say.

"What about the bishop's?" Rhoda suggested.

Sylvia looked at her father, concerned. "Should I go an' talk to him?"

"Or better yet, Preacher Benuel," Rhoda spoke up.

Earnest considered this. "Might not hurt, *jah*." He paused. "I'll go with you to ask him, if you'd like."

Sylvia nodded as if glad for his support.

Hoping this wouldn't open another can of worms, Earnest wondered how Benuel would instruct Sylvia. *The most devoted and serious Christians practice self-denial. Will he ask her not to expose herself further to the world by being in Adeline's wedding?*

Sylvia said good-night to them and left their room, and Earnest outened the light.

Amos Kauffman was right, he thought. *It's one thing after another over here.*

CHAPTER
Thirty-Six

The next day, Adeline asked Sylvia to walk with her out to the wooded meadow after the noon meal, up toward the clump of trees she had so enjoyed back in August. Presently, crusted snow covered the dormant wildflowers awaiting spring's return next year. In the distance, white smoke curled out of Sylvia's uncle and aunt's chimney to the east, and the sky was growing grayer by the minute.

"Looks like we might get snow later," Sylvia said, bundled up in a black coat and woolen scarf and the cutest black outer bonnet, which looked like an old-fashioned candle-snuffer.

While Adeline thought how much fun it would be to get snowed in with her Amish family, she needed to return home in time to unpack before her early Monday morning class.

"Tommy's hopin' you'll take him for a ride in your car while you're here," Sylvia was saying. "Dat already said he could go."

"I'll take him once we're back from our walk," Adeline agreed. "Do you want to come along?"

"I would, but I think Tommy might want you all to himself."

Adeline smiled. "He's such an expressive little guy, isn't he?"

"You should've seen his face when he found out you were comin' again."

"Well, the honor is all mine!"

They talked about how short the days were this time of year, and Adeline mentioned that she was glad Christmas was celebrated in December. "It brightens up the whole month and gives people a sense of hope, too."

Sylvia nodded. "Christ's birthday."

"Exactly. This year, Christmas will be exceptionally meaningful to me," Adeline revealed. "It won't be just about gifts and decorating." She paused, wanting to tell Sylvia first. "I get it now . . . I really do."

Sylvia turned, eyes wide. "Tell me more."

Adeline collected her thoughts. "Do you remember my telling you how Earnest challenged me to read the book of John while he was reading it with your mother? Well, that coincided with my reading Mom's diary. It was so strange . . . no, *amazing*, how well those two things dovetailed." She patted her chest and pressed her lips together. "It's totally changed my thinking and pointed me to God. And somehow, He's changed my heart." She turned to Sylvia. "Does that even make sense?"

"Oh, Adeline! Such *gut* news." Sylvia stopped walking, as if to give Adeline her undivided attention.

"I wanted to tell you in person." Adeline blinked repeatedly, holding back tears.

Sylvia touched her elbow. "So . . . I can't help wondering . . . have ya talked with Brendon about this?"

"Not yet. And I'm concerned it will affect our relationship."

Adeline paused. "He and I were always on the same page about religion. We didn't want anything to do with it."

"When will ya tell him?"

Adeline felt a small stirring of sadness. "I keep putting it off."

"The Lord sees Brendon's heart. I hope you aren't fretting 'bout it."

Adeline shook her head. "I love him and want to marry him, but I've found the Light and Truth that I've been missing my whole life." She hesitated, then said, "I need to have an honest conversation with him as soon as I return home. A couple of times, I almost told him about the research and seeking I've done, but I got cold feet."

"Honesty is essential." Sylvia studied her. "You wouldn't want to marry someone who doesn't want to follow the Lord's ways, would ya?"

Adeline sighed, recognizing the significance of her decision. "Divine grace has become very important to me, and I'm still learning what that means."

Sylvia nodded her head. "Don't put off talkin' to Brendon," she urged. "The sooner, the better."

Adeline agreed, then shared with her about some of the entries from her mom's diary. "I don't know how to describe it, Sylvie, but Mom must have known when she was writing those particular words that God's grace would start to make sense to me. I really believe that."

"Ella Mae says that God exists outside of space and time—He's not limited like we are. He exists in eternity. This might be hard to understand. . . ."

"No, that makes perfect sense."

"That means He knows what's going to happen to us next week, next year, and far into the future. He also knows how

Brendon will receive the news about your newfound faith."
Sylvia smiled at her, as if to encourage her. "And even though
sometimes it seems like we're walkin' blindfolded, we can trust
Him to lead the way ahead when we keep our eyes on Him."

Adeline laughed, her breath rising into the air as miniscule
ice crystals. "I like that analogy." She laughed again, picking
up the pace as they neared the meadow gate. "I'll definitely
remember that."

While Tommy went for a ride to the General Store in
Adeline's car, Sylvia helped Mamma at Dat's clock showroom—
this afternoon Dat and Ernie were manning the shop in Bird-
in-Hand. Sylvia was excited to hear that Mamma had sold a
large table clock while she and Adeline were out walking. *Dat
really needs this,* she thought. *We all do.*

"In spite of the cold, the tourists are out and about in force
today," her mother said. Then, looking at her curiously, she
asked, "How was your time with Adeline?"

"Ever so *gut,*" Sylvia said, without revealing anything further. That was for Adeline to share. "We're becoming a lot
closer."

"I'm not surprised. You're both considerate young women."
Mamma nodded, then went to greet a middle-aged woman,
inviting her into the showroom. "*Willkumm,*" she said. "How
can I help ya?"

The woman remained in the doorway, looking around. "Do
you sell pocket watches?"

Mamma exchanged a glance with Sylvia and shook her
head. "I'm sorry, we don't. But we do have clocks for bedrooms
and such if ya want something smaller."

The woman looked a bit disappointed as she walked into the showroom. "I had my heart set on a smaller timepiece for my father's Christmas present," she said. "Does your husband know anyone who makes pocket watches, or does he accept custom orders?"

Mamma reached for a small tablet and a pen. "Would ya like to jot down what you're interested in, and I'll let Earnest know? Maybe he knows someone who could create somethin' to your liking."

The woman smiled for the first time and wrote down her name and phone number.

Meanwhile, Sylvia wondered how her father would react to this request, considering all the difficulties his own heirloom timepiece had caused him this past year.

That evening, Earnest lingered with Rhoda and Adeline in the front room after family Bible reading and prayer. This was their last evening before Adeline left for home tomorrow.

Quietly, Adeline told of her mother's written regrets about the past. "Toward the end of her diary," Adeline said, "she mentioned how sorry she was for hurting you, Earnest, including not telling you about me."

Earnest was surprised and grateful to learn this. "From what you've already said, she must have made her peace with God before she passed."

Adeline nodded. "I believe she wanted me to learn about that peace, too, from the pages of her diary."

Rhoda smiled sweetly at Adeline. "You were greatly blessed by it. And now, so are we."

They talked further about the Gospel, as well as how to share it with those they loved.

"Reading John alongside you was one of the best suggestions you could have made," Adeline admitted. "I really mean that. It was like I was supposed to read that at the same time as I read Mom's diary." She smiled. "I'm convinced now that Jesus is the Son of God."

Earnest was pleased beyond words. "Rhoda and I were prayin' each day for you while we read those same passages," he told her.

"I do have a question, though," Adeline said, "about the difference between your Amish beliefs and those of a more typical Christian. It isn't like I was really raised in a church, you know."

Earnest nodded. "Like other Christians, we believe that salvation is an unearned gift from God. But we also believe we're called to live separately from the modern world and technology. We believe we demonstrate our loyalty to Christ through our simple approach to life, one that follows the church ordinance and the Old Ways put in place by the People's forefathers."

Adeline seemed to take this all in before thanking Earnest, then looking at Rhoda. "You've inspired me to be a more loving and patient person. And maybe someday a fantastic cook, too."

Rhoda chuckled at that. "We rely on the Lord's help to be those things, and you will, too. Folks can't manage it on their own."

Earnest glanced at his first daughter. "We couldn't be happier that you want to keep in touch. And we'd like to get to know Brendon, too," Earnest added, "whenever he can come with you to visit."

"He's surprisingly interested in Plain life," Adeline said just then. "So it might be sooner, rather than later."

They talked about arrangements for Sylvia's travel to Georgia for the wedding, and as Adeline explained her plan for that time, Earnest felt confident that Adeline would look after her. "She's never been away from Lancaster County," he explained.

"I can't wait to introduce her to Brendon and to my two best girlfriends, who will also be in my wedding party." Adeline smiled. "Sylvia will be the topping on the cake, so to speak. I'm blessed to have the sister I always wished for in my wedding."

Moved by her remarks, Earnest looked away to gather his emotions. Rhoda, too, appeared very touched, her eyes glistening. "You're a *wunnerbaar* addition to our family," Earnest said, and Rhoda beamed in apparent agreement.

"I have no doubt in my mind that God brought me here . . . to you and to your family," Adeline said.

Rhoda wiped her eyes and nodded. "Our Lord surely works in mysterious ways."

"Amen to that," Earnest said heartily.

Sunday afternoon, Adeline and Brendon were sitting by the fireplace in her apartment, talking about her visit to Hickory Hollow. He was peppering her with more queries about Amish culture and spiritual beliefs. She, in turn, was slowly building up the courage to finally tell him about her recent change of heart when, suddenly, Brendon came out with the most unforeseen question. "What if we went to church together next weekend?"

Her eyes must have bugged out, because Brendon started to laugh.

At first, "Sure, Bren" was all she could muster. Then, "Wait— *you* want to go to church?"

He merely smiled and mentioned something about having met an outgoing young pastor, a friend of someone in the accounting firm. "I spent Thanksgiving dinner at his and his wife's house."

Adeline tuned in even more closely as she tried to understand what he was saying. Inquisitive, she wanted to ask questions but decided to let him do the revealing.

"So you're actually cool with going?" he asked.

Now's the time. Adeline took a deep breath. "Brendon, it's so strange that you should say that, because there's something I've been meaning to tell you."

His eyes lit up. "I think I know. I've noticed."

"Noticed what?"

He shrugged. "Well, it's a little obvious that things are different with you."

"It's *that* obvious?"

He nodded. "You know . . . leaving a Bible out with a bookmark in it, so you must be reading it. And you've been preoccupied learning about the Amish belief system. I mean *a lot*." He hesitated for a moment. "Actually, lately I've been curious about what it means to commit to Christ."

She listened, her heart beating hard.

He turned to her, took her hands, his eyes meeting hers. "So here's another thought. . . ." She smiled as Brendon proposed the idea of also going to six weeks of premarital counseling with his pastor friend. "I think you'd like him, Addy. He's been answering a lot of my questions about faith."

"You have spiritual questions?"

292

He touched her arm. "I guess we've both been tiptoeing around each other on this."

She tried to contain her excitement. "I'm in for counseling if you are," she said.

"Okay, I'll make it happen."

Adeline kissed him soundly, thankful for this breakthrough. *I can't believe it!* she thought. *Sylvie will be grateful, too!*

CHAPTER
Thirty-Seven

*M*onday morning, once the clothes were pinned to the line, Sylvia and her father rode over to Preacher Benuel Zook's to talk with him together. Several inches of snow had fallen in the night, and the mare's hooves on the road made muted sounds as they went.

When they arrived, Rebecca welcomed them into her toasty warm kitchen and pulled a third chair over to the side nearest the coal stove. Then she left the room, although Sylvia wished she might stay, sweet as the woman was.

Dat and Preacher Zook made small talk about the wedding season getting off to a strong start with weddings having taken place each Tuesday and Thursday since the first week of November. Meanwhile, Sylvia sat quietly, wondering if Andy's father had any idea that she, too, once planned to get married this very month. *He surely wouldn't bring it up, even if he did. . . .*

After they had talked about the weather and the upcoming farm auctions, Dat said, "Sylvia's half sister has asked her to be a bridesmaid in her wedding next May."

Preacher Zook glanced at Sylvia. "Is it your desire to do this?" he asked, looking rather serious all of a sudden.

"*Jah*," she replied and held her breath for his answer.

"Do ya know anything about *Englischer* weddings, Sylvia?" he asked, his hands folded on his lap.

"Not a speck," she replied.

He continued to regard her. "You might encounter worldly temptations you never have before. Are ya prepared to make wise choices?"

"I am."

"And are ya still committed to bein' baptized next year?" Preacher Zook asked.

She nodded. "Honestly, I'd be ready now, if it were the right time," she told him, saying she was sorry now for not following through back in September. "I've repented in prayer for being impulsive and upset," she said. "And thoughtless, too."

The preacher's expression softened, and a small smile appeared over his straight brown beard. "I appreciate your honest heart, Sylvia."

Dat nodded his head in agreement.

She didn't smile outwardly, but inwardly she felt sure Preacher Zook would not discourage her from going to Adeline's wedding.

"So I expect you'll be followin' the *Ordnung*, even though you'll still be in *Rumschpringe?*" Preacher Zook asked.

"*Jah*, I'm followin' it even now," she said. "And content to be."

During their first counseling session, Adeline soon realized that Brendon wasn't kidding about his leaning in the direction of becoming a Christ-follower, as his engaging friend Pastor

Todd referred to Christians. *Allegiance to Christ,* she thought, paying close attention to how the pastor described it.

After the session, they arrived back at her apartment and discussed further what they had learned, comparing Scripture verses each of them had individually discovered in the book of John, which apparently they'd both been reading.

At one point, Brendon shook his head at the seeming coincidence of their both finding faith at this time in life.

She leaned close to kiss him. "All that matters now is that we're on the same page," she whispered.

"The same *path.*" He chuckled, and they talked about getting involved with Pastor Todd's church. "How would you feel about that?"

"Sure, and we could ask him to marry us," Adeline suggested.

Since they had earlier decided on a civil wedding, Brendon reiterated that he normally was not a second-guesser. "But, in this case, I'll gladly make an exception," he said.

She smiled, nestled in his arms, and admired her quilted wall hanging across from them, recalling the combined effort on the final stitching. *United as family,* she thought of Sylvia and Rhoda, knowing that she and Brendon were also united now in that same love of Christ.

Heavy snows fell that December. Sylvia was glad to receive frequent mail from Andy Zook, whom she saw every weekend, double dating with Cousin Jessie and her serious beau, Yonnie. On the coldest, most blustery Saturday evenings or Sunday Singings, Andy thoughtfully borrowed his father's enclosed carriage for their use, making sure there were hot bricks on the buggy floor and plenty of heavy lap blankets for all of them. Yonnie brought blankets, too, and Sylvia had seen him and Jessie snuggled close in the seat behind her and Andy.

Sylvia most enjoyed going sledding and skating with Andy as part of a larger group of youth. As Christmas approached, there were indoor activities, too—table games, including Dutch Blitz, and Ping-Pong tournaments, dessert gatherings, and the annual caroling.

She also made time to create practical gifts for everyone on her list and keep up with Adeline's letters, relieved to hear about her openhearted talk with Brendon some weeks ago. Sylvia wrote that she had already sewn the new black dress and matching apron for the wedding. She also confided that she hoped to have a proposal of her own someday, though because Andy was already baptized, he couldn't propose to her until she, too, had joined church. Adeline's letter in response to that had come more quickly than some of the others. *So you must think he's the man you want to spend your life with,* Adeline had written.

Sylvia definitely felt that way and told Adeline so in her very next letter.

On the evening of Christmas Day, Andy arrived as planned to take Sylvia in his father's carriage, and they rode the short distance to the farmhouse where Mahlon and Mamie Zook had lived for so many years. Mamie had since moved to the *Dawdi Haus*, and tonight it was Preacher Benuel Zook and his wife, Rebecca, who had invited Sylvia to supper.

Sylvia had heard of other couples sharing meals with each other's families during holidays, or even of the beau visiting his sweetheart-girl in her parents' home, but until now, she'd never done that. She wasn't expecting anything romantic but knew without question that she was falling in love with Andy.

He's considerate of my thoughts and feelings, she mused as they rode. And his endearing looks were enough to know that Andy also enjoyed her company very much.

"My family's lookin' forward to having you with us at Mamm's table tonight," he said as they pulled into the snowy lane.

"I'm happy to spend time with all of yous," she said, smiling with anticipation.

"Susie's already asked to sit next to you—Mammi Zook has claimed your other side. You'll find you're quite popular tonight," Andy said as he helped her remove the heavy lap blanket. "Wait right there." He got down and tied the mare to the hitching post and covered her with a horse blanket, then hurried around to stand below where Sylvia would step down, offering his hand. "I hope this is your best Christmas yet, Sylvie," he said as she got out of the carriage.

She thanked him, and he escorted her to the back porch, where Rebecca warmly welcomed her, showing her where to hang her coat and scarf and outer bonnet. "You'll be sitting across from Andy," she said, which Sylvia thought was nice. *So we can look at each other.*

The doorway that led out of the kitchen into the next room was decorated with garlands of Christmas cards, and two tall red candles with greenery at the base already lit the table.

After the silent blessing, Rebecca passed a platter of savory meat loaf to her husband, who then passed it to Andy's brother Michael, next to Andy. As Andy had indicated, Sylvia sat between Mamie and Susie, two of her favorite people. Sylvia had become well acquainted with Susie at the Singings in the past months.

"It's nice to have ya with us," Susie whispered.

With a nod, Sylvia agreed.

Mamie seemed to have a perpetual smile on her dear face, and it reminded Sylvia of Ella Mae's cheery disposition.

Rebecca's spread of food was as plentiful as if they hadn't already had their Christmas dinner at noon. A large bowl of Basque potatoes sprinkled with parsley was within reach, and Rebecca invited her to help herself, after which Sylvia passed the bowl to Susie. Another large dish of cut corn, some pickled green tomatoes, chow chow, and dinner rolls still warm from the oven rounded out the delicious meal.

"Mamm outdid herself again," Michael said from where he sat over near his father.

"Twice in one day," Mamie agreed.

"She had lots of help," Preacher Zook said, glancing at Mamie and Susie.

Andy nodded, lifting his gaze to Sylvia just then and grinning.

"Well, it's Christmas, after all." Rebecca leaned forward to smile at Sylvia. "And we have ourselves a special guest."

"*Denki*," Sylvia was quick to say, then smiled at Andy, who seemed to be looking at her each time she glanced his way.

During the course of the festive meal, Susie asked Sylvia if she was doing any quilting this winter. Sylvia first thought of the wall hanging she and Mamma had helped Adeline finish, but instead she mentioned the quilted potholders she had made as gifts for her aunts and many girl cousins.

"Sounds like you've been real busy," Susie said, reaching for her glass of water.

"What 'bout you?" Sylvia asked. "Any quilting?"

"Oh *jah*. Mamma, Mammi, and I are workin' on something," said Susie, turning to glance at Rebecca. "It's a surprise, though."

Andy winked at Sylvia, and she guessed she had better not ask anything more about that.

Michael mentioned her father's new clock shop in Bird-in-Hand. "Does he plan to have the same amount of inventory in town as at your shop over yonder?" He tilted his head in the direction of Sylvia's house.

"Actually, more in town now, because of all the tourist traffic," she said, wondering why he'd asked. "You could drop by sometime and see the place. It's small but just the right size, really."

Mamie was fairly quiet throughout the meal, although she did make a point of saying how blessed she had been by Sylvia's parents after Mahlon's passing. "They went far beyond the call of duty for me."

"Well, we think of you as family," Sylvia said, truly meaning it.

"Mahlon thought the world of your Dat." Mamie gave her hand a pat. "I'm sure ya knew."

Preacher Zook nodded his agreement, and his eyes grew misty. He didn't say how pleased he was that his son was dating Earnest's daughter, but there certainly seemed to be that undeclared understanding.

After the meal, Andy invited Sylvia into the front room, and they sat near the coal stove alone together while the other women cleaned up the kitchen.

"I think it's safe to say that my family is quite fond of you," Andy said.

"Well, I like them, too." She was so happy to have this special time with him on Christmas night.

Just then, Andy leaned over and picked up something from the floor on the opposite side of the sofa. "Here's a little somethin' for you," he said, giving her a wrapped present. "Merry Christmas, Sylvie."

What a surprise!

"Open it," he urged, leaning closer.

Carefully, she removed the pretty green and silver bow and the wrapping on the rectangular box. Opening the lid, she found a whittled piece of wood with these words carved into it: *Love believes all things . . . hopes all things.*

She looked at Andy. "*Denki. Es is schee . . . so perty.*"

He smiled. "Glad ya like it."

She was delighted by the craftsmanship. "I know just where I'll put it . . . on my dresser," she told him. *That way I can see it first thing in the morning.*

"I chose First Corinthians, chapter thirteen, because I know you've endured some hard things where love is concerned."

How well he understood her! "You know, whenever I might be tempted to wish I could change certain things in my life, I realize that the sadness and heartache eventually led me on the path to you."

Andy's eyes searched hers as he reached for her hand. "I love ya, Sylvie. I truly do."

The sweetest words, she thought. Tears of joy pricked her eyes as she leaned into him, knowing she would remember this night forever.

Thirty-Eight

*M*arch came in blustery, though not bitterly cold. Earnest occasionally spotted a few of the hardiest farmers out doing early plowing. *They're as competitive as womenfolk on washday.* Some sowed clover or alfalfa seed, and others improved their soil quality by liming in order to fine-tune the pH to the correct levels.

Earnest and his sons worked together in the field after he returned from his shop in town, working into the evening to plow and cultivate in anticipation of planting corn the last week of April or early May.

In the time since her visit, Adeline's letters to him had dropped off significantly, but Sylvia was still receiving frequent letters from her, which made both him and Rhoda happy.

After months of reciting and practicing with Earnest, Tommy was ready to walk in with the boys at Preaching service on May fifteenth and sing all twenty-eight lines of *Das Loblied* from memory. Earnest couldn't help but feel a healthy dose of pride about this, though he would miss having his youngest son sitting with him from now on.

The end of an era, thought Earnest. *My children are growing up.*

A bittersweet shadow fell over him, and he was sorry there were no more little feet pitter-pattering through the house.

The following Thursday, Earnest paid one of his favorite longtime Mennonite drivers to take Sylvia in his passenger van to Georgia. Several other Amish from Lancaster County were traveling south, as well, so there would be pleasant company and a few stops along the route. He and Rhoda felt sure Sylvia would do fine, since she knew the driver and two of the older couples.

"We'll look forward to hearing all 'bout Adeline's wedding once you're back home," Rhoda said before she kissed Sylvia good-bye on the cheek.

Earnest watched their daughter step into the van. "Have a great time, and let Adeline know we're thinking of her and Brendon."

Sylvia waved and nodded.

"She'll be all right, dear," Rhoda whispered as the van headed toward Hickory Lane and was soon out of sight.

"*Jah,*" he agreed as they walked back to the house together. *We raised her right.*

Sylvia was touched by Adeline's thoughtfulness in involving her in the activities planned for the other two wedding attendants. To her surprise, neither Callie nor Piper seemed at all startled by Sylvia's Plain attire. *Adeline must've prepared them ahead of time.*

The four young women had their nails done, even their toenails, something Sylvia had never experienced. Sylvia, however, opted for a clear polish on her fingernails but none on her toes, recalling her conversation with Preacher Zook.

They had facials, too, as well as a special luncheon the day before the wedding. "So we're all nice and relaxed," Adeline told them, smiling especially at Sylvia.

The wedding itself was nearly breathtaking in its beauty as a variety of fragrant, brilliant flowers surrounded the area where Adeline and her beloved Brendon stood before the minister to say their marriage vows. An archway of white roses sheltered them, and the single flower girl wore a gown so similar to Adeline's that she looked like her miniature.

Sylvia's black Amish dress and cape apron blended in nicely with the other girls' long black sleeveless dresses, which shimmered when the sunshine caught them.

Because she was unaccustomed to services with musical instruments, Sylvia hadn't been prepared for the lovely strains of the string quartet, and she wondered if there might be such pretty melodies in heaven. There would never be such music at her and Andy's wedding, but she reveled in it presently all the same.

Later, before Adeline left with Brendon for their honeymoon to Mackinac Island, Sylvia spent some time with her after the wedding luncheon.

Adeline thanked her for being willing to participate in this wonderful day. "You're amazing, Sylvie," she said. "Everyone thinks you're very sweet."

"Well, I wouldn't have missed it," she said as they stood beneath the white reception tent, similar to the ones some of her Amish neighbors rented these days to accommodate the many guests.

"You stepped way out of your comfort zone for me, and I'll never forget it," Adeline said, her hands holding both of Sylvia's in this semi-private moment.

Lest she tear up, Sylvia took a deep breath. "*Ach*, ya made it real easy."

They embraced, and Adeline whispered that she loved her.

"We'll meet again, and Dat and Mamma will be shipping something special to yous real soon," Sylvia said with a smile.

"Hmm . . . what could it be?" Adeline asked, looking like she might have already guessed.

"I promised not to tell."

"Not one little hint?"

Sylvia smiled, seeing Brendon coming this way. "Say, I think your husband's lookin' for ya."

"Classic deflection!" Adeline laughed and turned to welcome her handsome groom in his black tuxedo, which somewhat resembled the long frock coats Amishmen wore to Preaching services.

Brendon beamed as he thanked Sylvia for coming. "I'm looking forward to visiting Hickory Hollow sometime in the near future," he said.

"I hope ya do." Sylvia smiled in return. "And be sure to bring along Adeline, too, won't ya?"

Brendon grinned, reaching to shake Sylvia's hand. "You're my sister now, too, you know."

"*Denki* for everything you and Adeline did for me." Sylvia

also mentioned how pretty Georgia was. "I never knew just how beautiful."

"You're always welcome to visit us, remember." Brendon glanced lovingly at Adeline, who nodded her agreement.

"Be sure to greet your parents for me . . . well, for *us*." Adeline hugged her again.

"I'll have plenty to tell them," Sylvia said, feeling a little sad when Adeline linked her arm through Brendon's and walked over to the bride's table.

I'll miss them, she thought.

As she ate supper with Earnest and their sons that evening, Rhoda talked about the differences between their Plain weddings and what Adeline had planned.

"Is she married yet?" Ernie asked with a glance at the wall clock.

"*Jah,* surely by now," Rhoda said.

"Sylvie should already be on her way home, actually. She'll get here in the wee hours," Earnest said.

"She'll be awful tired, I s'pect," Rhoda said. "But I'm sure it's worth it to be with Adeline."

Adam glanced over at them. "Do ya think we'll ever meet Adeline's husband?"

Earnest nodded. "I wouldn't be surprised if they visit us sometime soon."

"I hope so!" Tommy said, grinning.

Rhoda had to smile, as well.

"She'll always be an *Englischer,*" Calvin said. "Don't ya think so, Dat?"

Earnest agreed. "Remember, even though she's not Amish, she's a Christian now."

"Well, you weren't Amish either when you were her age," Ernie piped up. "So maybe there's still hope for Adeline."

Rhoda didn't know what to say to that, and she waited for Earnest to respond.

"Adeline's content with her life as an *Englischer*," her husband insisted. "She won't be going Plain, I can assure you."

"Will we get to meet her kids someday?" Tommy asked, looking hopeful.

"Oh, wouldn't that be nice?" Rhoda said, smiling at her boys. "Just think, you'll be uncles to both your sisters' little ones when the time comes."

Tommy and Calvin exchanged curious looks.

Then Adam asked, "Do ya s'pect Sylvie will get hitched up soon?" He looked sheepish. "I prob'ly shouldn't say, but I think everyone knows Andy Zook is courtin' her."

"A little patience, son," Earnest cautioned. "In *gut* time, we'll all know for sure."

Rhoda was proud of the way he'd handled these questions and was anxious to see how he would react to the news she planned to tell him in private . . . tonight.

Rhoda missed Sylvia's help after supper as she washed and dried the dishes by herself. Earnest and the boys had ventured out to do some fieldwork while it was still light.

Once the dishes and pots and pans were put away, she removed her white work apron and went out to sit on the back porch, glad for the longer evenings now and warmer temperatures. She reveled in the sweet fragrance thick in the air this time of year. The lilac bushes and honeysuckle were in full bloom and mixed delightfully with the honey-like scent of the rhododendron leaves.

New life after a long, cold winter, she thought, breathing deeply and gazing toward the field where Earnest and their sons worked together. Thinking again of Adeline's wedding day, she looked forward to hearing about Sylvia's Georgia trip. *She'll be starting baptism instruction next Sunday once again,* Rhoda thought. *After that, Andy's free to propose marriage.*

Rhoda sighed happily, because as often as Sylvia and Andy saw each other, she was hopeful that she and Earnest would be hosting a wedding come November.

Hours later, Rhoda was relaxing in their room reading her Bible when Earnest returned from the shower, dressed for bed. She glanced over at him and asked, "What would you say if I was in the family way?"

His eyelids fluttered. "Are you serious, love?"

"*Jah,* absolutely."

"Then I'd say hallelujah!" He went straight to her, reaching for her hands as she rose and he held her near. "We'll be old by the time this new baby reaches courting age, though, ain't?" he whispered.

"Not *that* old," she said and returned his tender kisses.

"When is this little Miller expected?"

"Close to Christmas, if my calculations are correct."

"Well, isn't that something!" Earnest had never grinned quite so big.

"Just think, we might have a wedding for Sylvia and a new

baby for us all in the space of a month," she remarked. "I'll need to line up plenty-a help."

Earnest agreed as he led her over to the bed and sat there with her on the edge of it. "A midlife baby . . . and near Christmas, yet."

Now Rhoda was laughing. "An added blessing for the Lord's birthday, I say."

He nodded and kissed her cheek.

"God is ever so *gut*," she whispered. "Another baby is just what I'd been hopin' for. . . ."

Sylvia leaned her head against the van window, glad there were fewer people traveling with her this trip. From where she sat in the second row of seats, she could see the dashboard clock and assumed she would be home within another two hours.

The traffic was light, but the few car headlights coming toward them flickered brightly and made her all the sleepier as she relived her time with Adeline and Brendon and their family and friends. *They're so happy*, thought Sylvia, wondering how she would feel on her own wedding day.

In her drowsiness, she missed Andy like never before. She thought ahead to the coming months of baptismal instruction, largely a review of all she'd learned last year. This time, though, she would not waver in following the Lord in holy baptism.

The miles became a blur as the motion of the van and the sound of the engine lulled her into a deep sleep.

When they finally arrived in Hickory Hollow, Sylvia woke up as they drove past the Zooks' farmhouse. Noticing a single golden light upstairs, she groggily wondered if Andy was up praying for her. The thought made her smile sleepily, and she counted her blessings, Andy being high on her list.

Bless him, O Lord, for loving me in spite of my imperfect family, she prayed.

Then, seeing Dat's house come into view, she yawned and sat up straighter, ready to go in and head right to bed. She could hardly wait to stretch out and rest after the long drive, glad that tomorrow—well, *today*—was not a Preaching Sunday, so she could sleep in.

Andy had mentioned prior to her leaving that he wanted to drop by for a visit in the afternoon to maybe take a walk together, so she would see him again soon.

Sylvia slept till Mamma came into her room at nine o'clock that morning. "*Ach,* I'm sleepin' my life away," she said, rousing herself and sitting up in bed.

"Well, ya didn't get in till nearly four o'clock, so ya needed the rest." Mamma sat on the bed, all dressed for a day of visiting.

"You didn't wait up for me, I hope."

"*Nee,* I did my best not to." Mamma's smile was very telling. "Someday, when you're a mother, you'll understand all about half sleepin'."

Sylvia reached to hug her. "If I'm half as *gut* a wife and mother as you are, I'll be glad," she said, meaning it with all of her heart.

CHAPTER
Thirty-Nine

Summertime for Sylvia and Mamma meant hours and hours of gardening, weeding, mowing, cooking, canning, and cleaning. On weekends, Sylvia happily attended Singings and other youth activities with Andy, as well as dates alone with him. She enjoyed sharing what she learned in baptism classes during their Saturday evening dates, sometimes over meals at Andy's parents' farmhouse. Her parents had also invited Andy for supper quite a few times, too, where Dat read aloud from the Good Book after dessert. It was heartening to see Andy interact with Dat over passages of Scripture. He never failed to treat him with respect and kindness.

When the longed-for third Sunday in September finally arrived, Sylvia bowed her knee and became a full-fledged member of the Hickory Hollow Amish church. She felt so tenderhearted and happy that she had at last followed the Lord in holy baptism.

It was a warm and bright Saturday afternoon one week later when Andy dropped by to see Sylvia. He asked if she'd like to take a leisurely walk out to the small wildflower meadow near the cluster of trees that Adeline so admired.

Glad to have finished her chores early, Sylvia agreed and left the house with her beloved, enjoying the warm September air. While the road horses wandered through the tall meadow grass, heads low as they wove back and forth, meandering along, the sky to the east was filled with large bands of birds flying in vast spirals.

After they had walked a ways, Andy stopped to pick several late-blooming columbines, their leaves maroon from the cooler nights. He handed the bouquet to her and then, smiling, he reached for her right hand. "Will ya marry me, Sylvie, and be my bride forever?"

Surrounded by wild ferns and the dappled sunlight, she had suspected Andy had a special reason for bringing her here. She fought back tears of joy as she nodded her head. "*Jah*," she whispered, looking up at him. "I'd be honored to."

With the dearest smile on his handsome face, Andy leaned down and kissed her for the first time, sweet and gentle.

"I love ya, Andy," she whispered, never having felt quite like this.

He kissed her again, holding her near. Then, stepping back, he reached for her hands and asked, "When would ya want to wed?"

All of this felt so sudden, even though she had been yearning for this moment. "We could talk with our families and see when it suits, *jah*?"

Andy agreed as they stood beneath the largest tree in the grazing land. "If it were up to only me, I'd say the first Tuesday in November . . . as soon as possible." He winked.

"Ain't so far away."

His eyes searched her eyes, her lips, like he wanted to kiss her again. "I love you so much."

Sylvia felt almost guilty, she was so happy. A rush of love and exhilaration made her think they'd better start walking again.

And as they began to stroll along, Andy told her of the rental house he'd picked out not far from Hickory Lane, since he would be working alongside his father, farming his Dawdi Mahlon's cropland. "That way I can walk to work, if need be," Andy said. "And you'll be within walkin' distance of *your* family, too."

She leaned her head against his arm as they slowly walked toward the horse paddock. "This is the best day ever," she said softly.

"For now, *jah*," Andy agreed.

Sylvia guessed what he meant and smiled. "I'll ask Dat and Mamma 'bout that first Tuesday in November, then."

Andy removed his straw hat and tossed it high into the air.

There was something else on her mind, but she held her breath at first, not sure she should ask. Then, gathering the courage, she did. "Is it all right with you if we stay the first few weeks at my father's house?"

He looked a bit surprised. "'Course. That's what the bride and groom always do."

"Okay, just checkin'," she said, breathing more easily.

They walked a bit farther, and two of the mules wandered across the meadow toward them. "Do ya think your sister and her husband would wanna come to our wedding?" he asked.

Again, she was pleasantly surprised. "Would ya mind?"

"Well, they're your family. They should be there."

Smiling, Sylvia loved that Andy was so accepting and kind. The minute her parents and Andy agreed on a date, Sylvia would write to Adeline to share her joyous news.

That evening, while drying dishes for her mother, Sylvia asked if she could talk with her and Dat soon. "I have somethin' *wunnerbaar-gut* to share."

Mamma looked at her quizzically. "My dear girl, it must surely be what we've been waitin' to hear since your baptism." She paused. "I can tell by your beaming face."

Sylvia wasn't the type to be coy, but she did want to tell both of her parents at once. "When's a *gut* time?"

"Well, how 'bout as soon as we finish redding up the kitchen?"

Agreeing, Sylvia reached for the next plate and dried it quickly.

Mamma wiped off the far counter, then returned to dunk the dishrag in the sudsy water and wring it out. "I have some nice news of my own," she said more quietly.

"Oh?"

"I'll just tell you, daughter, since ya might've wondered why I've been putting on some added pounds . . . and expanding the seams in my dresses here lately."

Sylvia smiled, acknowledging what she had come to suspect. "Mamma? You're expectin' a baby, aren't ya?"

Nodding, her mother smiled, as well. "Close to Christmas."

She reached to hug Mamma, whose hands were deep in the dishwater. "I couldn't be happier for you and Dat . . . and, oh goodness, for all of us!"

Three consecutive days late in October signaled the beginning of wintry weather with goose gray skies and brisk temperatures. Yet Sylvia did not experience the usual feeling of sadness that normally accompanied the tail end of autumn. This year, she could hardly wait for winter to arrive, since that would mean she and Andy would be settled in as husband and wife. *Not so long now,* she thought, looking forward to starting their life together as she sorted through her hope chest.

On the morning of November first, Sylvia's wedding day, she and Mamma, now great with child, talked quietly upstairs in her room while Cousin Alma and Susie Zook got ready in the sewing room down the hall. In a little while, all of them would go down together to the service, where the People were already gathering.

"The Lord's lookin' kindly upon ya, dear," Mamma said as she reached for her hand. "Your Dat and I have prayed 'bout this day since you were a wee girl."

"And God in His mercy has answered." Sylvia paused, trying to memorize the radiant look on her mother's face in this moment. "*Denki* for bringin' me up in the ways of the Lord."

Mamma's eyes met hers. "Our heavenly Father has shown us mercy indeed, giving us 'beauty for ashes, the oil of joy for mourning,' just as it is written in the book of Isaiah."

Unable to speak but agreeing with every precious word, Sylvia nodded and gently embraced her mother. *The dear Lord knew what we needed. . . .*

A few minutes later, there was a gentle tap at the door, and

Sylvia went to open it. "Adeline!" she said when she saw her, delighted to welcome her inside.

Mamma greeted her, too, smiling. "It's so *gut* you're here for the wedding."

Adeline hugged them both and explained that she and Brendon had gotten in late last night and were staying at a nearby inn. "We wanted to be with you, Sylvie, to share your joy."

"I'm so glad. The day wouldn't have been quite right without ya," Sylvia said. "I hope you'll get to stay for the wedding feast."

Nodding, Adeline said they would be around for two full days. "There's no way I would miss my sister's wedding." She looked at Mamma. "Sylvia told me your news last time she wrote. I can't imagine how happy you must be, expecting a baby at Christmastime."

Mamma nodded. "He or she is certainly active here lately, so whenever the Lord wills, I'm ready."

Adeline's obvious excitement and Mamma's coming baby made the already wonderful day all the more special for Sylvia. "*Denki* so much for sharin' this time with us," Sylvia told her. "You don't know how much it means to me . . . and to Andy, too."

Adeline gave her another hug and left the room to head downstairs.

"My whole family is here," Sylvia whispered to Mamma, who nodded sweetly.

Earnest watched intently as Bishop Beiler asked Andy Zook and his two male attendants to stand before him. Sylvia and her two female attendants, all three of them in royal blue dresses and white organdy aprons, joined them.

Seeing Sylvia and Andy up there together, about to make their marriage vows to God and to each other, Earnest remembered holding her as a baby, right after she was born. Midwife Mattie Beiler had placed her first in Rhoda's arms, and after they had both admired her, Rhoda had given her to Earnest. *A precious little bundle,* he thought, the memory still crystal clear.

In silent awe, he realized, *After these next few weeks, we'll never share the same house again.*

Drawing a deep breath, he listened in rapt attention now as the bishop asked the bride and groom, "Do you solemnly promise each other that you will love and care for and show patience to one another, and will not separate from each other as husband and wife till our Lord in heaven shall part you through death?"

In unison, Andy and Sylvia answered, *"Jah,"* and, as was the People's way, the couple returned to their seats with no outward show of affection.

Immediately, the bishop spoke a prayer over them, and afterward he invited the other ministers in the district to offer a blessing for the newly married couple, as well.

Earnest was impressed that Amos Kauffman was the first of the two preachers to rise to do so. *It won't be long and Titus will marry Mahlon's grandniece Betsy,* thought Earnest. *Marrying into a fine and unblemished family. . . .*

In that moment, Earnest realized that Titus's upcoming union with Mahlon Zook's family tree would link Titus to Earnest's family, as well—Sylvia having just married Mahlon's grandson.

No family is faultless, Earnest thought, helping to flip the benches into tables for Sylvia and Andy's big feast. *Thank the Good Lord for His unfailing forgiveness and grace.*

Epilogue

*A*ch, how swiftly the year has passed since Andy's and my wedding! Honestly, I never could have imagined being this content each and every day. Often, I dashed out the back door and across the yard to meet Andy on his walk home from working with his father. *Jah*, spending time with Andy was a joy for me and for our newborn son, Andrew, who resembled his Dat in every little feature.

Since Andrew's birth three weeks ago, I'd fallen a little behind on housework—I would rather nurse and cuddle him. It was just plain hard for me to put him down to sleep, which was all right with me. Work could wait for now. The bliss of becoming a mother was impossible to describe, really. Sleepless nights or not, there were ever so many tender feelings of love and wonderment!

Since I'd been at home a lot lately, I decided this mid-November morning to attend a Sisters Day gathering at the home of Cousin Alma and her husband, Danny Lapp.

When I arrived with my baby all bundled up, I discovered that Cousin Jessie was there, too, as were Susie Zook and her cousin Betsy, Titus's bride of one year. Mamma and Aendis Hannah and Ruthann were also in attendance.

Each of us had a project to work on as we sat in a cozy circle in Cousin Alma's spacious front room, the coal stove keeping us toasty warm, including the several new babies present.

Aendi Hannah's adorable son, Curtis Jr., was only six weeks old but already looked as robust as a three-month-old with his headful of dark hair. Dat and Mamma's surprise baby boy, named for Preacher Mahlon Zook, was ten and a half months old now as he sat, drooling and babbling, on the floor with blocks. Both Alma and Betsy were expecting their first babies in a few months, as well.

To say the Hickory Hollow church district was undergoing a growth spurt was an understatement, and there was a definite need for the tied baby comforters Aendi Hannah had been making. But with her own long-awaited infant to nurse and care for, there really wasn't much spare time for those. *Oh, how well I know!*

Mamma sat next to me, knitting purple squares for an afghan, and I crocheted a soft baby blanket in variegated pastels of yellow and green for my baby, Andrew. I couldn't tell for sure what Betsy was working on, but it appeared to be a small Nine Patch quilt, perhaps a wall hanging similar to the one Adeline had made. Seeing it brought back such good memories of my half sister's visits. Although there hadn't been word in Adeline's recent letters of a pregnancy just yet, I wasn't surprised, knowing how caught up she was with her new career. The way she described their busy lives, I felt sure she and Brendon were happy and doing what they enjoyed.

Adeline had even mentioned that they regularly attended church social gatherings and hosted a small group in their home once a month, with Brendon assisting their pastor on weekends with campus evangelism.

In her latest letter, Adeline had sent a photo of the glassed-in shadow box she and Brendon had made to display Dat's gold pocket watch, hanging it on the wall near the tall floor clock my father had crafted for their wedding gift. Adeline said that, whenever they decided to start a family, she planned to give the timepiece to their first child as a special gift on the twenty-first birthday. *The Lord willing, of course,* Adeline had added, the words followed by her signature smiley face.

My sister-in-law Susie, near me in the work circle, mentioned that her brother Michael was tickled to be working with my father at the clock showroom in Bird-in-Hand. Just yesterday, Dat had offered him a job as an assistant.

"Might there be another clockmaker in the makin'," I suggested.

"Michael hopes so," Susie said quietly. "He's not much for farmin', ya know."

Cousin Jessie nodded. "He should do what he loves . . . what he's *called* to, like Ella Mae might say."

I smiled. Even though she was absent today, the Wise Woman was often quoted at such get-togethers, and I always appreciated her wisdom.

When we paused for refreshments, Hannah asked me to hold baby Curtis Jr. while she left the room. Looking into the infant's dimpled face, I remembered what Andy had said before our own baby was born—that if we had a girl, he hoped she would look just like me. Of course, the dear Lord had given us a son, so we'd just have to wait and see if we had a daughter, too, someday.

Betsy came over to admire Baby Curtis. "By the way, Titus and Andy are ridin' over together to pick us up," she reminded. "Then we'll go back to our place for a light supper."

"That's nice of you," I said, glad there were no hard feelings between Titus and me, and that Titus and Andy were still great friends.

My baby brother came toddling over, and seeing that I was holding little Curtis, Mahlon held up his chubby arms. "Mamma," he said, pleading with his pale blue eyes.

"He calls every woman Mamma," I explained to Betsy, handing Curtis back to my aunt when she returned. "That and Dada are his two favorite words so far."

"Well, he's sure a cutie," Betsy said as I reached down and picked up my little brother. Then she added, "Titus is hopin' for a boy for our first child. And so is his mother. I guess Eva thinks Titus will need plenty-a help on the farm." She paused. "She certainly seems to have her heart set on a boy first for us."

I didn't ask, *"What if you have a girl?"* Instead I smiled, but not for the reason Betsy might have assumed. Knowing how easygoing Betsy was, most likely it would take a lot to really annoy her. *She and Titus are a good match in that way,* I thought, still smiling.

The Good Lord knew that my first beau would not be my true love, I thought, carrying little Mahlon over to the table to get him a piece of goat cheese. "Here's somethin' to nibble on." I glanced at my own baby, sleeping through all the chatter in the cradle Danny had made for his and Cousin Alma's coming baby.

"Mamma," my cuddly brother said again, leaning his head against my cheek as my mother caught my eye and smiled.

"*Schweschder,*" I whispered in his little ear.

As I tried to teach my baby brother to say sister in *Deitsch*, I considered Adeline and the special way God had woven our far-flung paths to cross right here in Hickory Hollow.

A sister is truly a gift, I thought, knowing full well that our heavenly Father had worked all things together for our good.

Author's Note

To my surprise, it has been exactly two decades since I wrote a novel with a single sequel, a two-book set. In this novel, it was a thrill to return to Sylvia Miller and her family—including Adeline—for the planning, crafting, and writing of *The Timepiece*. I loved bringing their story of forgiveness full circle, as it were. I think most of us have struggled at one time or another with forgiving another family member. It's amazing how the Lord can work in us through that experience to change us for the better.

Besides forgiveness, this novel is about time—past, present, and future—and the timeless aspects of life: the joy of sisterhood, the discovery of divine mercy, the legacy of family, and true love.

The quaint, real-life Lancaster County locations found in the fabric of this story include Kauffman's Handcrafted Clocks and Dienner's Country Restaurant in Ronks, BB's Grocery Outlet in Quarryville, Bird-in-Hand Farmers Market, the village of Intercourse, and the charming back roads of West

Cattail Road, Hershey Church Road, and White Oak Road. Hickory Lane, however, is quite fictitious, though I could show you right where it is!

Special appreciation goes to my insightful editors, David Horton, Rochelle Glöege, and Elisa Tally, and to all who played an essential role in the production process of getting this manuscript ready for you, dear readers, including Hank and Ruth Hershberger. Thank you, as well, to my devoted partners in prayer—extended family and lifelong friends—and to my supportive and tireless research assistants in the Lancaster County Plain community. I am also blessed by my wonderful sister, Barbara, for her creative input, faithful prayers, and excellent proofreading up to the final edit.

Loving gratitude to my husband, Dave, who never tires of reading my first drafts, brainstorming with me, encouraging me to reach higher in my writing, and making breakfast and lunch whenever I'm engrossed in a new storyline.

And now to my best-ever readers, who have followed my heart from book to book these many years . . . thank you ever so much!

Soli Deo Gloria—to the glory of God alone!

Beverly Lewis, born in the heart of Pennsylvania Dutch country, is the *New York Times* bestselling author of more than one hundred books. Her stories have been published in twelve languages worldwide. A keen interest in her mother's Plain heritage has inspired Beverly to write many Amish-related novels, beginning with *The Shunning,* which has sold more than one million copies and is an Original Hallmark Channel movie. In 2007 *The Brethren* was honored with a Christy Award.

Beverly has been interviewed by both national and international media, including *Time* magazine, the Associated Press, and the BBC. She lives with her husband, David, in Colorado.

Visit her website at www.beverlylewis.com or www.facebook .com/officialbeverlylewis for more information.

The Stone Wall

The Next Novel
from Beverly Lewis

Anna Beachy is excited to begin a new
life as a Lancaster County tour guide
in the picturesque area where her Plain
grandmother once resided. While there,
Anna finds herself drawn to two very
different and equally wonderful young
men—and in potential conflict with the
expectations of her Beachy Amish parents.
Will Anna find true love? Or will she,
like her grandmother before her,
only discover heartbreak?

AVAILABLE FALL 2020

◊ BETHANYHOUSE

 Stay up to date on your favorite books and authors with our free e-newsletters.
Sign up today at bethanyhouse.com.

 facebook.com/bethanyhousepublishers   @bethanyhousefiction

 Free exclusive resources for your book group! bethanyhouse.com/anopenbook

anopenbook

Sign Up for Beverly's Newsletter!

Keep up to date with Beverly's news on book releases and events by signing up for her email list at beverlylewis.com.

More from Beverly Lewis!

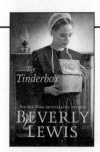

When Sylvia Miller finds her father's old tinderbox left unlocked, her curiosity is piqued. She opens the box and uncovers secrets best left alone. A confrontation with her father leads to a shocking revelation that will forever change not only her own life but also that of her family and her Amish community.

The Tinderbox

Also from Beverly Lewis

Visit beverlylewis.com for a full list of her books.

In the summer of 1951, Amishwoman Maggie Esh is struggling with a debilitating illness and few future prospects. When tent revival meetings come to the area, Maggie attends out of curiosity. She's been told to accept her lot in life as God's will, but the words of the evangelist begin to stir something deep inside her. Dare she hope for a brighter future?

The First Love

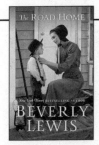

Sent from Michigan to Pennsylvania, Lena Rose Schwartz grieves the death of her Amish parents and the separation from her siblings as well as her beau, Hans Bontrager. She longs to return home to those she loves most. However, she soon discovers that Lancaster County holds charms of its own. Is she willing to open her heart to new possibilities?

The Road Home

When a young Amish woman takes a summer job as a nanny in beautiful Cape May, she forms an unexpected bond with a handsome Mennonite. Has she been too hasty with her promises, or will she only find what her heart is longing for back home?

The Ebb Tide

⬧ BETHANY HOUSE